Amulet Books
New York

THE RUNAWAY'S GOLD

A NOVEL BY

Emilie Christie Burack

Library of Congress Cataloging-in-Publication Data

Burack, Emilie Christie.
The runaway's gold : a novel / by Emilie Christie Burack.
pages cm
Summary: "The protagonist of this historical novel, which is set in the Shetland Islands and also New York City around 1840, is Christian Robertson, a crofter and son of a crofter (small, struggling tenant farmer). When Christian's brother frames him for the theft of a bag of coins, Christian must leave home and embark on a journey to return the coins and clear his name"— Provided by publisher.
Includes bibliographical references.
ISBN 978-1-4197-1369-9 (alk. paper)
1. Shetland (Scotland)—History—19th century—Juvenile fiction. [1. Shetland (Scotland)—History—19th century—Fiction. 2. Scotland—History—19th century—Fiction. 3. New York (N.Y.)—History—1775–1865—Fiction. 4. Emigration and immigration—Fiction. 5. Coins—Fiction. 6. Scottish Americans—Fiction.] I. Title.
PZ7.1.B87Ru 2015
[Fic]—dc23
2014029831

Text copyright © 2015 Emilie Christie Burack
Interior illustrations and maps copyright © 2015 Anna Bron
Book design by Maria T. Middleton

Printed and bound in U.S.A.
10 9 8 7 6 5 4 3 2 1

THE ART OF BOOKS SINCE 1949
115 West 18th Street
New York, NY 10011
www.abramsbooks.com

To George Robert Christie,
my grandfather, grandson of a Shetland crofter,
who took the time to record our family's stories

And to Tom, who never let me give up

*Adversity tries men,
and 'tis good to bear the yoke in youth.*

—DIARY OF THE REVEREND JOHN MILL,
DUNROSSNESS, SHETLAND, 1740

Contents

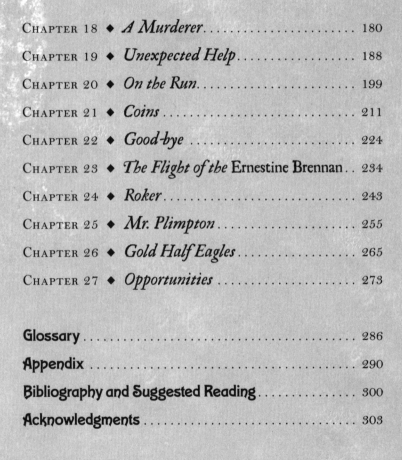

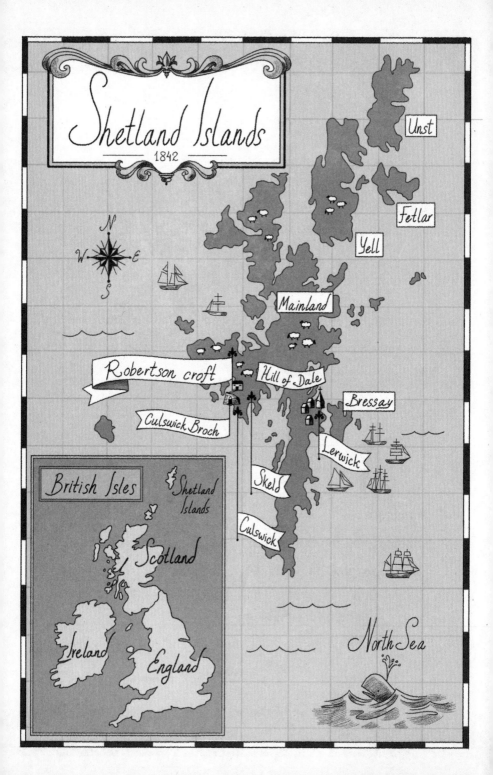

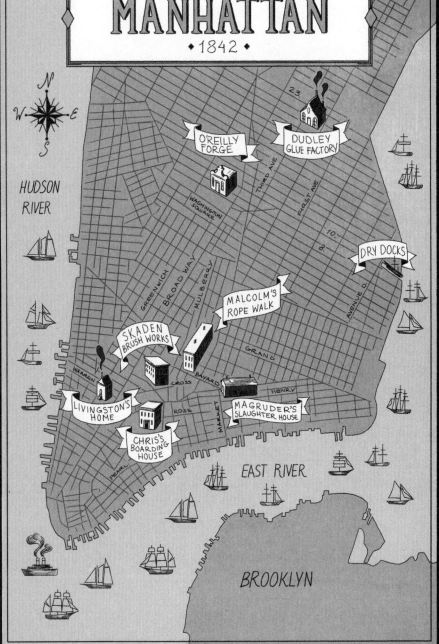

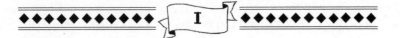

The Forge

New York City, September 29, 1842

I am apprentice to smithy Peter O'Reilly, first cousin of Billy Tweed, who happens to be the only person I know in the City of New York who was actually born here. Billy found me five months before, wandering lost and confused, when I first stumbled off the ship from Liverpool. The O'Reilly Forge shoes horses for the city's high and mighty, and I wouldn't have the work if it wasn't for Billy. Its low ceiling and soot-coated walls on Eighth Street and Broad Way are near Washington Square, where I often wander at dusk, damp grass at me toes, trying not to forget the stark, windblown hills of me island home.

Back in me homeland I'm wanted for one crime I committed and one I did not, so having the chance to learn the blacksmith trade is beyond me wildest dreams. I'm fourteen now, but still remember the day years ago when Andrew Johnson first noticed me eyeing his forge back home. I was too small to reach the anvil, so he gave me a stool. Then he handed me the smooth iron hammer.

"Give 'er a good swing now, lad!" He chuckled, cradling me wee hand in his massive, calloused paw. Together we struck the glowing rod, still soft from the orange coals of the forge. And when he dropped the newly flattened piece into a bucket of water, I screamed with delight as warm steam hissed wildly into the air.

The steam was still rising when me Daa walked in.

"Robertsons are no smithies!" he said, grabbing me with both hands. His fingernails digging deep into the pits of me arms. And then he dragged me, red-faced, out the door.

Here in New York, me Daa couldn't be farther away. And instead of fishing for cod in wee boats on treacherous seas, beholden to merchant Wallace Marwick, who owns our croft, I spend me days on firm ground. Make a fair wage. Answer to no one.

Or so I thought.

"Ah, Chris Roberts," Billy Tweed said, using the name I gave meself when I first arrived in America. Billy thinks I'm from Ireland, near Belfast, and I haven't said otherwise.

Billy likes to surprise you, coming up from behind. And

whenever he appears at the forge, everyone stops talking. Even Peter O'Reilly himself.

"My cousin tells me you're a hard worker," he said, peering over me shoulder. He can't be more than twenty himself, but he speaks like he's forty.

"Thank you." I smiled, pleased at the recognition, striking extra hard a strip of red-hot iron on the anvil.

"And you're enjoying your room on Pearl Street?"

I hesitated, thinking of the endless shouting through the thin walls. The rats on the floor, the gunshots from the street. "Aye, Billy. I'm grateful for a place to rest me head."

"Well," he continued, circling round me as he spoke, glancing at the other men busying themselves to our left and right, taking in every detail, like a schoolmaster surveying his pupils. "It's clear you've added some meat to your bones since the day we met. Earning wages enough to feed you, I see?"

"Aye, it's true, Billy," I said. "It's the first time in years I've had the chance for more than one meal a day. They say I've grown three inches in the last month!"

He was standing beside me when I felt the cool metal of the coin slip down the leg of me breeks and clink to the floor. In fact, had I repaired the tear in me pocket when I'd meant to, it might never have happened. But when I stooped to pick it up, Billy's spry fingers got there first.

When he saw the coin, it was as if everything ended and everything began, all at the same time.

"What's this?" he asked.

I tried to grab the coin from his open palm, but his fingers clamped down like a vise.

"I know Peter's been paying you," he said with a smirk. "But not in Pine Tree Shillings."

Peter whistled from across the forge. "Haven't seen one of those in years. Where'd you get that, boy?"

I glanced at Peter and then back at Billy. "A friend."

"Did you hear that, Peter O'Reilly?" Billy laughed. His brawny, six-foot frame towered above me. "He says he got it from a friend!"

Peter chuckled and me face grew hot. For a moment I thought of grabbing Billy around the neck till he let it drop, but even I knew his reputation for a mean left jab.

"So, in other words," Billy said, loud enough for all the men of the forge to hear over the pounding hammers and wheezing gush of bellows, "you stole it!" And as he spoke everyone, as if on command, roared with laughter.

"No!" I shouted. I'd been called a thief before, and it wasn't going to happen again.

"Ah, come now," Billy said, nearly knocking me over with a slap on the back. "Why do you think I like you so much? Peter O'Reilly or any of these boys can tell you fast fingers lead to great things here in the City of New York."

"Aye," I said, looking nervously about me, "a badge of honor to the rest of you, perhaps. Now, may I please have me coin back?"

The piece was worthless—Reverend Sill had said as much—so it couldn't mean anything to him.

As I pleaded, Billy held it above me in his palm, just out of reach.

"The man I got it from," I explained, careful with me words, "the man who had it before me—he was from New York."

"Was he now?" Billy murmured. He rubbed his finger over the coin's surface—a surface I had examined so closely for so many months I could have etched its twin in the dark. "And did this coin-owning man have a name? Or was it perhaps a buxom young lass from the backstreets of Belfast?"

The men roared with laughter once again, and Billy beckoned them closer so they could have a look.

"Livingston," I blurted. "Sam Livingston."

And the moment I said the name, Billy's eyes flashed.

"You know him!" I gasped, me heart beginning to race. Could it be, he was still alive?

"Hmm," Billy said, a smile tugging at his lips. "Now there's a name I haven't heard in years."

I wondered how a lad as young as Billy knew a man as old as Sam, who, should he even still be alive, would be well into his eighties. "Could you tell me where I'd find him, then?" I asked, lowering me voice. "I've been asking for weeks. No one seems to know the name."

He paused a moment. His broad chest filled his vest and jacket, and he looked me up and down with those deep-set eyes.

And then a smile stretched across his well-fed cheeks. They say Billy Tweed studied bookkeeping and I know it's true. As he speaks, it's as if he's adding, subtracting, and balancing all that surrounds him.

"Perhaps."

He dangled his words before me, brushing his calloused knuckles across his chin. "'Course, I'm a busy man. And this sort of information is hard to come by . . ."

Man? Hah! He was as tall as anyone I'd met in America, but even me brother, John, looked older.

"I'll do whatever it takes," I said, without hesitation. Like a fool. "You've done so much for me. I'd be happy for the chance to repay you." As I spoke I thought I heard Peter O'Reilly gasp. But I could tell Billy was pleased.

"Is that so?" Billy asked.

Then me throat suddenly tightened as his shrewd eyes locked onto mine. "'Course, I'd need to know why you're interested," he said, pocketing me coin as he turned to the door. "And then, of course, what you'd be prepared to do for an introduction."

I swallowed hard, me leather apron hot to the touch from the blood-orange coals beside me. Everyone in New York, it seemed, was escaping his past, and I was no exception. Me real name is Christopher Robertson. I am a Shetlander. And the true story of Sam Livingston and that coin was something Billy Tweed, of all people, could never know.

2

Mr. Peterson's Ewe

I watched, stomach turning, as Billy strutted from the shadows of the O'Reilly Forge into the bright sunlight of Broad Way. And as he tossed Sam Livingston's coin in the air and caught it in his left hand, I drove me hand into me pocket—and felt the hole. Then the wily thief turned, shouting over the withers of a mare that was tied fast between us, waiting to be shoed. "You know where to find me, Chris Roberts. When you're ready."

For the rest of the day me head pounded as I thought of Sam Livingston and what I would say to Billy. But later that night, back in me boardinghouse, it was me brother, John, I saw again and again in me dreams. He was but a willowy silhouette at the far end of the forge, his half-starved body rippling in the vapors above the white-hot coals that lay between us. Our eyes met as I glanced up from driving a nail into a left hind hoof, cradling a fetlock over me knee in me blistered palm. And when I looked at him, I wondered if it's possible to love a brother who'd trade your life for his. And why, even after all that happened, I missed him to me very core.

When I awoke in a cold sweat to screams and gunshots from the street below, and the hacking and wheezing of the five other men who shared me room, I knew I'd sleep no more. And it was then that me mind crept back to that night some seven months before, when me life began to unravel. And to those darting mud-brown eyes of the ewe struggling to give birth at the foot of me grandfather's chair.

It was late March and she was carrying twins, something Daa knew when he dragged her in from the storm. Our home was Shetland—the cluster of islands in the northernmost reaches of Scotland. A land of wee ponies and treeless hills, where the winds blow strong and the peat-riddled ground is so soft the roads are impassable by horse and cart. The cod banks had failed, the harvest was rot, and all but our landlord, Wallace Marwick, were hungry.

Me Daa was Shetland born, with a stiff left leg broken hauling peat, and of the last families named in the island tradition of passing down one's first name to his offspring. His father was Robert Christopherson, so Daa was named William Robertson, not William Christopherson like they do in England

and America. His sister, who lived with us, was Alice Roberts-daughter. But that wasn't good enough for Daa.

"I'll not have me family line confused with the other haf-krakked Williamsons scattered across this parish," William Robertson announced when me oldest brother was born. "He'll do as the English and keep his grandfather's name instead."

And that is how William Jr., John, me troublesome sisters Catherine and Victoria, and I, as well as the many generations to follow, came to keep the Robertson name.

There were few signs of affection in our croft house, the result of seven miserable people living in two smoky rooms, me Midder having died in childbirth just four months earlier and me oldest brother, William Jr., already lost at sea. Oddly, only me brother John, who often wrapped an arm round me shoulder as we trudged home from planting, or scooped up Catherine and Victoria, flipping them upside down amid a torrent of giggles, seemed able to bring warmth into the damp chill of our lives. John, the one person who'd do anything to leave.

Daa was the kind of man who was only partially honest, just enough to spread across the surface like the shimmery lüm of oil on water thinly coating many dark layers beneath. That's why, when he rolled up his sleeves to help pull the lambs from the struggling ewe, we said nothing about the lug mark cut in her left ear that showed she was from the Peterson croft.

We were supposed to think he hadn't noticed.

Shetlanders keep careful count of everything, especially

their sheep, but that March afternoon the sudden arrival of the southwesterly gale caught most of us off guard.

"Gutcher," Daa said to me grandfather, pulling on his oiled sheepskin. "Let's see what bounty this storm has awaiting!"

The two of them battled the wind down the half-mile path along the cliffs to the stony beach, through flans of sea spray twenty feet high, searching for driftwood or anything blown ashore. Something those on a treeless island such as Shetland were bound to do. It was on his return, with three barrel staves tucked under his arm, that Daa stumbled upon the laboring ewe, separated from her flock, nibbling on a patch of rotting brown heather, her back to the storm.

"Ho, ho! What a prize she is!" he announced, herding her home through the biting blast of wind and sea spray.

By Shetland law, should a stray sheep be found and cared for, for a year and a day, and the owner not discovered, it is sold—half the share going to the finder and half to the poor. But I knew giving to the poor wasn't quite what Daa had in mind.

"See, lad," William Robertson said with a nod to the skittish ewe, "it's me Anglican line rewarded again! You don't see good fortune like this coming to those low-life Presbyterians, now, do you?"

Our queen's Anglican Church of England, with its powerful bishops, was considered too similar to the Roman Church for most islanders' independent spirit. In fact, it had been mostly driven from Scotland since the time me great-great-grandfather was born. But me Daa, he had to be different. His world was full of enemies—the fire-and-brimstone rule of the Presbyterian Church of Scotland, which we called "the Kirk," at the top of his list, and me Midder the only exception. William Robertson, I heard our neighbors mutter, was a troublemaker—and a nonconformist of the worst kind.

And he did *look* different, after all, with his high cheekbones and large jaw—features he claimed as royal, no matter how distantly they might be traced.

As Daa herded the ewe past the table and through the door to the adjoining byre, I knew he had already calculated, to the pence, how much he could get for the extra wool she and her offspring would provide. And if he could mark the lambs as his own and then quickly return her to the scattald—the grazing area we shared with our neighbors—who would know they weren't his own? It had always worked before.

The croft house we leased from Wallace Marwick was a two-room rectangle and attached byre made of stones from the beginning of time and rafters salvaged from the wreck of the *Alice May* in 1667. The front room was dim, the air heavy with the earthen smell of peat burning in the fire in its center. Three snarling pigs rooted under our table, and when you looked up, you saw a ceiling of neatly stacked turf across a network of battens and ropes. The other wee room was for sleeping.

On most nights we could easily listen to the sounds of the cows in the byre through a many-gapped wall of stone, but that night the wind roared and moaned.

"Canna hear her," Daa grumbled, eyeing the door.

We hadn't been seated at the table but a moment when he left to drag the ewe back inside.

She was a Shetland, an ancient breed with a mixture of brown and white fleece, all of it hanging low to the ground and matted with burrs, nettles, and mud. She paced in the glow of the fire, bleating, panting, and soiling the cleanly swept floor as we made fast work of our shrinking ration of dried fish and oatcakes. John and I sat perched at the edge of our chairs, bellies churning, eyeing the plate in the center of the table where one last shriveled piece of cod remained.

When it was clear the ewe was in trouble, Daa flipped her on her side by the fire, his stiff left leg awkwardly pointing straight ahead, his right bent beneath him. He smoothed his thick purple-and-red chapped hand over her belly as she thrashed and kicked, her stomach rising and falling in a violent rhythm.

"Soli Deo Gloria," I whispered as she wrenched her mud-caked neck and stared at me with the same wild-eyed look I remembered on me Midder's face the night she struggled to bring our wee brother Michael into the world.

Little light made it through the croft's two windows of stretched lamb's hide. Only the glow from two smoldering lamps of foul-smelling fish oil and the orange-red flames of peat made it possible to see what little remained of last season's ling and cod hung by their tails from the rafters like a string of ghosts.

"Ooooo! Handsome Christopher's eyes are so, so blue. Ann Peterson canna keep her eyes off him." Nosy Catherine giggled from across the table, ignoring what we all knew—that Daa was once again up to no good.

John's right brow arched, his glinting eyes taunting me from across the table as Catherine prattled on. He knew—we all knew—it was he who stole the hearts on our side of the island. He who could focus his gaze on a lass's face and make her feel like she and only she held the key to his heart.

Catherine was seven, with a mouth that never stopped. I had nearly reached me fourteenth year, and John his sixteenth. Victoria was five, she being named, at Daa's insistence, for Queen Victoria, who had been crowned queen of Great Britain the year me sister was born.

As I reached across to cuff Catherine's ear for what must have been the tenth time that day, the wind suddenly shifted, bringing a blast of damp, salty air down the hole in the roof above the fire and scattering red sparks of peat and ash over Daa and the ewe. We coughed and sputtered, waving the cloud of debris from our faces, but Daa—he never flinched. One bread-loaf-shaped hand steadied the now frantic ewe, the other was sunk up to his elbow in her warm, wet belly, searching for heads and hooves.

When the rain started to drip through the thatch onto Gutcher's oatcake, I began to wonder how much longer the thatch would hold. In a wind such as that, the stone weights hanging over the roof would surely need securing. For a moment I even forgot that it wouldn't be long before Mr. Peterson came searching for his ewe. That the punishment for stealing was a nice long stay in Lerwick Prison, and if the sheriff took Daa from us, we wouldn't have enough hands to take in the cod we needed to meet our rent.

"Are there more oatcakes?" Victoria asked, casting her sweet green eyes on Aunt Alice as she leaned down to lick her fingers. The rest of us knew the answer without asking.

"Tuts, missy," me aunt murmured, tucking a loose strand of grayish-blond hair back under her coarse-woven hap. "That's the last of it, I'm afraid. But I'll heat you some water and sprinkle it with a bit of the bere. That'll take away the hunger. At least till morning."

"Catherine! Over here!" Daa suddenly cried. "Steady her head!" And as Catherine knelt at his side, stroking the beast's warm nose, Daa's well-schooled hands managed to pull out the first lamb. The second followed quickly, the rush of red-and-yellow faa spilling on the floor.

"Now will you look at that—a ram and a ewe," he announced as John and I exchanged nervous glances. "Not a bad night, this."

Catherine and Victoria set to toweling the newborns' noses as they had so many times before. The wee creatures, curly fleece still wet to their skin, had just started softly bleating when there was a pounding on the door.

"Robertson, you thieving haf-krak!" Peter Peterson's voice boomed through the roar of wind. The weathered driftwood boards rattled on their iron hinges. "Open this blasted door!"

"Damn," Daa muttered, beckoning Catherine and Victoria with a bloody hand as me heart began to race. "To the byre with them!"

Aunt Alice handed the girls each a piece of homespun wadmal in which to wrap the lambs as they slipped out the connecting door.

Then Daa, struggling to hold down the frantic ewe, looked at John and motioned to the tattered quilt tucked about me grandfather's knees. Gutcher snapped his toothless gums as John whisked the quilt from his lap, mopped up the afterbirth, and then stuffed the soiled cloth behind the basket of peat.

The ewe continued to thrash and squirm under Daa's powerful arms, bleating louder and louder, desperate to get to her lambs, her chest rising and falling faster with each breath.

"Gibbie Tait saw you slipping across the scattald with that ewe!" Mr. Peterson's voice thundered. "And may the Devil follow ya straight to Hell if you try to slip her out the back door of your byre, 'cause I'm watching!"

"Lor', Sister!" Daa hissed. He raised his shaggy, reddish-gray brows as he eyed me aunt. "Get the lad a rag!"

Wisps of hair falling across her sallow, pinched face, Aunt Alice quickly grabbed another piece of wadmal from a hook by the fire. Then she handed it to John.

"Hah!" John scoffed, pushing the cloth back at her. "I'll be no further part of this!"

Aunt Alice looked fearfully to Daa, who cursed and spat

on the floor. But he knew not to fight John. When John made up his mind, there was no going back. "Christ, woman!" Daa shouted. "Then give it to Christopher!"

I looked up from me chair, too stunned to move as she shoved the cloth into me chest, let out a faint gasp, and quickly backed into the corner.

"Use it, lad," Daa ordered, his flat, even voice nearly drowned out by the ewe's bleating. "I canna hold her forever!"

At first I didn't understand. And then, as the bleating seemed to crescendo and Peter Peterson's pounding grew more powerful, Daa, while still pressing down on the ewe, somehow balanced on his squatted right leg and swung the other fiercely into me calf.

"Snuff her out, I say! Peterson's watching—we canna slip her from the byre!"

I grabbed the table to keep from toppling onto him, me flesh bruised by the blow. And then, suddenly, a deep chill began to creep up me back as it came to me what he wanted me to do.

Me throat tightened as I limped to the ewe's head, squatted on the icy floor, and gingerly transferred the rag into me right hand. Me shaking palm hovered inches over her soft, warm snout as I glanced back into Daa's wretched, eager eyes, praying for a sign that I had misunderstood.

Spit flew from his lips. "*Snuff her out, lad!* We haven't the time!"

At first the ewe's eyes bulged, darting left and then right, as I attempted to seal her nose. But try as I might, I couldn't bring meself to clamp down me palm. In moments she wrestled free of me and was bleating even louder than before.

"I hear that ewe, Robertson!" Mr. Peterson's pounding grew more powerful, the door's iron latch bending under the strain.

"I said snuff her!"

She was a beast of the highest value—the proven producer of twins, an unharvested fleece on her hide, her breath hot and vibrant in me palm.

"Are you sure?" I pleaded, Daa's eyes boring into me, an icy-cold silence willing me on.

I glanced quickly at John—surely he, always the guide amid me Daa's violent storms, would tell me to stop. But as our eyes met, he winced. And then he looked away.

And so I grabbed her snout once more, clamping me shaking fingers around her moist nostrils and delicate, bony jaw as Daa's powerful hands held her body and struggling legs in place. Again she thrashed and twisted, fighting to push her head free, but this time I tightened me grip.

At first I squeezed softly, and then harder and harder, me pink palm just wide enough to seal off her air and clamp her jaw closed. Her nose was wet, fast, desperate—and as she struggled against me, thrashing left and then right, her haunting brown eyes searched mine. Then, finally, her chest lay eerily still.

I released me hand and stood, me entire body trembling, the imprint of me palm still pressed into the cloth covering her snout. And then I slowly backed away, so stunned by what I had just done it was all I could do to take another breath.

Beside me Daa sprang to his feet, dragging the dense, lifeless body into the back room and hoisting her with his powerful, booming arms into the box bed Catherine shared with Vic. Then he covered her with their quilt, wiped his hands on his breeks, and rolled down the sleeves of his gansey.

"Peterson, is that you I hear?" he called in a slippery voice as he reached for the door. "What brings you by in this God-awful gale?"

3

Culswick Broch

I t wasn't the death of the ewe that seemed strange that night. Like all Shetland lads, I had slaughtered sheep, swine, fowl, and even whales stranded helpless on the shore. But those killings had been with a purpose, kept at arm's length by the quick stroke of a sharp blade. Fast, direct, deliberate.

I looked first to Gutcher, then Aunt Alice, and finally John, but none would meet me eyes. Gutcher settled in by the fire, fishing line gathered in his lap. Aunt Alice stood staring at the floor for a moment, her long, bluish fingers still covering her mouth. Then she let out a faint gasp, reached for her knitting from the basket in the corner, and sat down.

That was when I saw John snatch the remaining piece of cod from the table and slip out the door to the byre.

When Peter Peterson burst across the threshold, a rush of wind came with him, blowing out the lamps and causing a change in air pressure that sucked another blast of wind down the vent in the roof and across the fire.

"Aye!" he cried, slamming his forehead on one of the rafters as he made his way through the cloud of ash. As the debris settled, his hunched frame towered over Daa's. "Where is she?" he growled, searching the room with his eyes.

Daa scratched his head and shrugged. "If you're meanin' yer lass Ann, who's always moonin' over young Christopher here, we haven't seen her yet today."

Mr. Peterson's face turned a deep purple as he raised his fist in the air. "It's the ewe I'm after, you fool, not me Ann!" he roared, spit flying as he spoke.

Daa told me to, I reasoned, the warmth of the ewe's breath still in me palm. *He couldn't do it himself.* A rush of bile rose in me throat as I backed slowly into the shadows of the far wall. Snuffed her out, I had. All for him.

Quietly as I could, I kicked open the door to the byre and disappeared inside. It being March, there were at least two feet of straw bound with peat mold and muck on the floor, making headroom scarce, even for a boy me size. By locking the cows inside for the winter, we collected the muck we needed to mix with seaweed and spread on the fields come spring. It was wet and heavy, with a stench so powerful it made me eyes water.

Grabbing the box lantern hanging from the rafters, I made out Catherine and Victoria. They were hovering in the corner, the now orphaned lambs weak in their arms. The harnesses for the ponies we no longer had swayed in the wind from the hook by the door. They banged against the wall near the shadows of the three emaciated cows leaning against the driftwood slats that divided their stalls. Their fodder had run out weeks before, and the bones of their once grand frames pierced sharply through their coats. They had survived near starvation before, but this time I had me doubts. When they could no longer stand, we would hoist them by ropes to keep them up—a gruesome sight I had already witnessed three other winters of me short life.

"I hear Mr. Peterson's voice," Catherine whispered, cradling the wet ram lamb in her arms. "Come to collect his ewe, has he?"

"Aye," I said, spitting on the floor.

"What did Daa do?"

"Hid her—in the ben."

"Lor'—she must be frantic looking for her lambs. Seems strange we're not hearin' her through the wall."

I thought of her limp body lying in me sisters' bed. "Resting, she is," I said. "All worn out, I expect."

"What will we do if Mr. Peterson comes in the byre?" Victoria asked. "There's no place to hide."

I shrugged, looking quickly about me. "Where's John? He'll know."

"Slipped out the back door," Catherine said. "Throwing another linksten over the thatch, I suspect. We'll be lucky if any of the roof survives this storm."

I remember the wind being so strong, and I so thin, that it was all I could do to push the back door open with the lantern in me hand. I pushed wildly through the blinding sheets of sea spray lifted from the waves and dragged ashore, calling for me brother. Pools of water had formed around our croft house, and before I knew it me rivlins, the sealskin shoes we Shetlanders laced below our ankles, were soaked clear through.

Snuff her out! Daa's words turned over and over in me head. I paused by the wall of stones we called a planticrub, built to protect me late Midder's cabbages from the unforgiving summer wind. It was there, as I thought of her kind, warm hands I'd never touch again, that me tears began to mix with the rain dripping down me forehead. Then I retched on the mud. She, the one person who protected us from Daa's rages. Who, with but a light touch of her fingers to our cheeks, let us know we would survive another day.

I thought of her grave, a common mound next to William's behind the Kirk—our family, like most, too poor to pay for a proper gravestone.

"Midder, what have I done?" I cried into the storm.

I was hungry—so hungry. We all were. And now Daa had

gotten us into another one of his messes. In this of all years, when we hadn't even the smuggling to rely on.

Ah, yes. The smuggling. In the eyes of the Crown, Wallace Marwick was a merchant of the highest stature, known for his trade in dried fish, timber, and coal. But he hadn't become the wealthiest man in Shetland by following all the rules. With the high duties charged by Her Majesty on imported items such as gin and tobacco, he found ways to hide them in his trading ships. Then, after officially registering the legitimate goods with the Customs House in Lerwick, he'd cruise to our end of the island to bring ashore the rest. In fact, there wasn't a crofter—man, woman, child—who hadn't hauled at least a cask or two of smuggled Dutch gin in the dead of night from a Marwick packet, and me family was no exception. Even Reverend Sill, the annoyingly pious leader of the Kirk and Daa's greatest enemy, was known to chide his parishioners not for gulping a dram of smuggled gin, but rather for not blessing it before it was swallowed.

Trouble was, last September, while barrels were being unloaded in the middle of the night, one of Marwick's packets was seized by Her Majesty's Revenue Men—the officers whose job it is to see that the Crown's import duties are paid. And when the Revenue Men found the barrels loaded with tobacco, Marwick's captain was arrested and sent to Lerwick Prison.

"There'll be a dry spell ahead," Daa had warned, "while mighty Marwick defends his good name." And how right Daa had been. Already it had been months since any of us had caught sight of a Marwick packet hovering in the distance, the much-welcomed lights flashing twice from her bow at nightfall letting us know a shipment was coming ashore.

I dropped me face in me hands, knowing what was ahead. From May through September, John, Daa, and the other men of the parish were bound to Marwick, fishing cod with horse-hair lines and baited hooks in the deep seas west of the island. Day in and day out, recording their catch by slicing barbels from the end of each fish's chin and collecting them in a tin box, knowing all the while that half the catch was Marwick's as rent for our croft, and the rest sold to and cured by Marwick at the price of his choosing. The cod banks having failed three out of the last five years, any hope of paying down even part of our debt had long since disappeared.

"Thief, he is," John muttered each spring when Daa signed for the lines, hooks, and other provisions before heading to sea. "Makes enough to line his own pockets while bleedin' the rest of us dry! Marwick's store, Marwick's prices, even if you can find better in Scalloway."

It had been generations since any crofter on Marwick land had seen cash for his pay, but Wallace Marwick wasn't the only reason for John's hate of the sea. Our brother William was also to blame. Two years before, there had been talk of a growing herring market. "They sell it cheap in the West Indies—feed it to the slaves," John had told me, his freckled face beaming one day after returning from Skeld. "Last year the demand was so high they couldn't keep up, so Lerwick merchants are taking on new men. They say after a year you can earn enough to outfit your share of a sloop!"

But you had to be fourteen to sign on, and John was two months too young. So it was William who found a spot on a half-decker out of Lerwick, and the family rejoiced. Then the early fishing failed, and in September, there was the Great Gale. All hands were lost on more than twenty boats, and none of us speaks of the herring anymore.

From that day on, John's fear of the deep waters was like no other.

It was a crack of thunder that startled me back to the present, and when I looked up, a streak of lightning slashed the sky, showing a strip of thatch on our roof blowing like the flag atop a mast. Then I turned to the scattald and scanned the blackness until another flash caught what I thought could be the outline of John racing in the direction of Culswick Broch.

Culswick Broch—our broch—was a tumbled fortress from ancient times perched on the hill above our croft. There are loads like it in Shetland, built by a mysterious civilization that had long since disappeared. Once as tall as eight men standing one atop the other, it was a massive structure of pinkish-red stone with views for miles in every direction: Straight ahead, the looming rock island that is Foula. To the north, the neighboring parishes of Walls, Aithsting, and Sandness. To the southwest, far across the North Sea waters, the faint outline of Fair Isle.

For thousands of years Culswick Broch had towered atop our hill, its roof finally collapsing when Gutcher was but a lad. What was left was a crumbling, five-foot-high, circular wall I couldn't see over and an enormous triangular lintel stone still in place above its only entrance.

Through sheets of rain and sea spray I sprinted. I scaled the hill dike around the grazing land startling clusters of sheep hovering in the storm, then continued up the rough, drenched path I had traveled so many times I could have done so blind. At the broch's wee entrance I shoved the lantern ahead of me and scrambled on hands and knees through an icy puddle of scree.

There, just inside the wall and illuminated through the driving rain by the weak light of me lantern, stood John, pulling something from a crack between two of the stones.

He snapped his head around at the light and slipped a hand quickly behind him.

"Chris!" he said, his eyes darting left and then right. He was still breathing heavily from his sprint up the hill. "Are you alone?"

I laughed when I saw him, his head just inches from the mysterious carving of the tree on one of the stones of the wall, remembering a time not long before when I had surprised him in that very spot, his lips pressed flat against Maggie Moncrieff's.

"Don't be daft. Do you think anyone else would be out in a gale such as this?"

Rain pelted down me forehead as I glanced from his face to the arm that he held behind his back.

John stared for a moment and then shrugged. "Well, you might as well know." The dim light from the lantern caught a glint in his eyes as he brought his hand forward. "I finally found it."

I gasped, having seen the wee caramel-colored pouch only two other times in me life.

"Took me five years of waiting and watching to finally figure out where the Ol' Cod stashed it."

John shifted his weight from left to right as he ran his fingers through his dripping yellow hair.

It was the pouch that held something no other crofter had, as far as I knew—coins. I had no idea how many, only that the family was forbidden to ever speak of it, so fearful was Daa that it would be confiscated to cover his debts. I had seen it two years before when he, with a scowl, pulled it from his pocket to pay Andrew Johnson, the smithy in Skeld, for repairing the tuskhar we used to cut the peat. Then again, four months back, on the night Midder and our wee brother Michael died, when he silently paid the midwife who had failed to save them.

Daa never trusted a soul with where it was hidden, so it was only fitting John had taken it to the broch, the one place Daa's stiff leg kept him from venturing. John and I knew every stone of that place, every curve of every rock. And when William was still with us—dear, lovely William, who would laugh at the drop of a hat, and smile so deeply at the littlest of things that his elfin cheeks raised clear to his eyes—the three of us had pretended it was our fort and we were the last mighty warriors of Shetland. The wonderfully strange picture of a tree carved on a smooth stone next to where John stood we fancied the symbol of our kingdom. Or, perhaps, a secret crest of valor. Imagine—a tree on the treeless island of Shetland! No other broch could claim such a thing as that. Some of the branches on the bottom right had been mysteriously left off, as if, we secretly guessed, its maker had been captured before completing his work.

What I didn't know that night was how close to the truth we were.

Lifting the lantern as John fondled the pouch, I caught a glint in his lively hazel eyes. The eyes that locked onto yours, no matter who you were, and held you fast.

"Last Tuesday I saw the crafty miser creep down from the ladder by the harnesses in the byre when he thought no one was looking. Next chance I got I stood on that same ladder and prodded among the turf above those rafters. Hah!" he shouted through the wind, his smile growing dark. "I'll not risk me life another year at sea, belly aching with hunger, and *him* hiding a pouch of coins!"

He turned to the scattald below.

"All that talk about us Robertsons being better than the others. Boasting of his ties to the English just because he thinks that proves his ties to royalty. Chris—have you ever wondered why you and our sisters have no friends?"

I thought of how Jeremy Williamson had come by to see me. And Nicol Magnuson. "Not our kind," Daa had warned. "I'll not have the likes of those families on our croft."

The carving of the tree above his shoulder, John clenched his fists as he spoke, his words roaring above the moan of the gale.

I had never seen him in such a state.

"Look at us!" he said, rounding on me. "Clothes in tatters, no flesh to speak of on our bones, and him with *this!*" He shook the pouch in me face, then started to pace. "The man's not right in his mind. You must know that! How many a Shetlander risked his neck hauling casks of gin in the dead of night for him to skim off a cut of their share? Him and his years of side deals with Marwick—we know he never gave the others what they deserved. Here, in me hand, is proof that Daa, through years of cheating, lying, and scheming, has enough to get us out! He had it all along! Do you know, Chris, how much is in here?"

I shrugged. Not only had I never touched a coin, I hadn't any idea what a pound or even a shilling could buy.

"Enough to outfit our share of a sloop for an entire season!" John closed his fist tightly around the leather, steam coming from his mouth into the chill of the storm. "We could begin to escape the clutches of Marwick! But no—Daa thinks like all the dim-witted Shetlanders: *Better the known evil of the merchants than the unknown of breaking free.* They've been waiting for generations, but no one ever dares! Lor', Chris," he bellowed, "don't you ever dream of being free?"

I shuddered, watching his wild eyes and swallowing hard. Did I want to be free? Did I yearn for a life beyond the struggles of the croft? "Me belly aches, John," I said quietly. "I think, perhaps, I'm too hungry to think of freedom."

But so much in a fury was me brother that night that he went on as if I hadn't spoken.

"Now, if it was Knut Blackbeard's coins, or Gutcher's, or some other gullible soul's," he muttered, "well then, of course, he'd find plenty of ways to spend it. But Hell itself will freeze before he parts with his own shillings to feed his own family's bellies and save us from the talons of Marwick. The way I see it, with the smuggling dropped off and Daa starting all this trouble with that Peterson ewe, I either leave with the pouch or starve by May."

"Leave?" His words hit like a stone to me gut. "We're past due on the rent! And the fishing starts next month! You know I'm not strong enough to pull in those cod lines meself!"

As he started to turn away, I surprised us both by dropping the lantern and grabbing his shoulders. "Wallace Marwick owns us, John! We've so much debt we'll be fishing the deep waters our entire lives before we pay him back. He has no other use for us. We'll be tossed from the croft by summer—added to the list of paupers—*left to the charity of the Kirk!*"

I knew—we all knew—about our neighbor Jeemie Black, his five younger sisters, and seven cousins. Father and uncles lost at sea, the family split apart. The Kirk shuffling them from croft to croft to work for a place to sleep and a portion of what little food the families in our parish could spare.

A crack of thunder shook the hill as our eyes locked, wind pulling across the rain-drenched stones that surrounded us. Then John ripped me arms from his shoulders and shoved me aside, saying words I never wanted to hear: "You're just like the rest of 'em!"

And for the first time in me life I feared him. Until he did what he always did when anyone challenged him—he started to laugh. Long and hard, throwing back his freckled face and closing his eyes as if I had just told him the most wonderful tale he had heard in months.

"Chris," he said, eyes ablaze, "let's not forget what *you've* done tonight."

"I—what have I—"

"Ya just *murdered* Pete Peterson's prize ewe, me peerie brother!"

Then he grabbed firmly to me shoulder, brows furrowed, and leaned in.

"Stolen property, that was! Why, should Sheriff Nicolson find out, you'll be starting a very long stay in Lerwick Prison. I've seen the place—deep inside the mighty stone walls of Fort Charlotte, perched high above Lerwick Harbor. They say that those that get locked up are never seen again. No, instead of worrying about me, you best make a plan for yourself before Peterson finds that dead ewe in our sisters' bed."

It wasn't until that moment that the horror of what I had done began to sink in. I thought of the caaing whales we spotted on occasion in the voes near our croft. Sleek, powerful creatures, some more than twenty feet long, all foolishly wedded to only one leader; something clever islanders had long ago discovered. By setting out silently, ten or twelve boats at a time, crofters find the leader and then suddenly go at him, hooting and hollering, waving pitchforks and brooms—until, in utter panic, he charges for the shore, the rest of his school blindly following by the hundreds. And there the marvelously sleek creatures lie, helplessly stranded on the beach, only to be slaughtered—flinched and boiled—the head blubber especially prized for lamp oil, the carcasses left to rot.

I, too, had followed blindly. Followed me Daa. And I had followed him straight to the Devil himself.

I opened me right hand wide, still feeling deep in me flesh what, just a short while ago, I had done. "But Daa—he needed me to. You were there." And somehow, I thought to meself, I had needed to be needed. Needed by him.

Rain dripped into me eyes as I shifted weight from one foot to the other. In me head Daa's voice screamed, "*Snuff—her—out!*"

"Try and tell that to the Sheriff Court in Lerwick," John said, laughing. "Christopher Robertson, when will you learn? Daa has never cared for anyone above himself. Never."

"He loved our Midder." The words tumbled out before I could stop them. I thought of the way Daa had looked at her from across the room. How he had so often walked past her as she stood at the fire, letting his hand touch her cheek ever so lightly.

"Hah! Did you even see him shed a tear the night she and wee Michael took their last breath? Ever see him visit her grave?"

I thought of that endless night. Of him sitting before her, his eyes vacant as her chest lay still. How he had slowly risen to his feet and walked out the door, gone for days without so much as a word.

"The man wasn't about to commit a crime so dark himself!" John continued. "Not a tenth-generation 'Robertson,' all convinced the entire island owes him their firstborn. The same man who talked his best friend, Knut Blackbeard, into spendin' six months in prison for the crime *he* committed! Certainly not when he could get some other luckless soul—his youngest son no less—to do the deed."

It was then, as I stared into me beloved brother's darting hazel eyes—the eyes I had grown to trust above all others since the passing of William—that I remembered something me Midder had said when I was just a wee boy of six or seven, but had never forgotten.

"Christopher," she had said, in a hushed tone, while we were planting cabbages, "take care with your brother John."

She had looked down as she spoke, working the earth with red, chapped hands, never meeting me eyes with hers. "For I fear," she continued, and then hesitated, "there are times when his honor is not as it should be."

Midder wit we called it. Words of truth passed down by those women much wiser than we. I remembered looking at the soft skin of her cheeks and the wisps of reddish-blond hair blowing across her eyes, puzzled by what had prompted her to say such a thing about the older brother I idolized. Not long afterward some of our butter and oat stores had gone missing, and I wondered if perhaps John had been responsible. But when, a few days later, I found a time when me Midder and I were alone and asked what she had meant, she quickly shook her head.

She looked first left and then right, her cheeks turning ashen. "Never would I have said such a thing about me own sweet bairn!"

From that day on she took great pains never to be alone with me, as if fearful I'd ask again. As if fearful of betraying the son she adored. And in the last moments before her heart stopped beating the night she failed in giving birth to wee Michael, it was John's hand she clutched, not mine, pressing it close to her heaving chest while I stood stiffly at her side. As I hovered silently, frozen in place, blackness and despair seeping into me heart when we knew all hope of saving her was gone, I listened in agony as John told her he loved her and tenderly stroked her fevered brow.

The rain on John's face shimmered as another wretched branch of lightning ripped through the sky. I glanced suddenly at the pouch. "And what's to keep *you* from Lerwick Prison?" I asked.

He laughed, playfully pressing the wee sack of coins to his cheek. "Oh, dunna worry about me. I haven't stolen anything. Only borrowing for a spell. The Ol' Cod doesn't even know it's missing."

"He'll find out, soon enough."

"Aye. But by then I'll be long gone. From what I hear, an English schooner was blown off course last night near Skeld Voe. On its way back from Bergen. Loaded with timber. Angus told me of it this morning."

I wasn't sure who I feared more: John's friend Angus Moncrieff or Daa. Angus was bigger than any lad in Culswick, and mostly because he had so effective a right jab, even his Daa couldn't keep him from stealing the food from his own plate. He was a tall, sullen brute of a boy, distinguishable from quite a distance by cheeks pocked with red pimples and a line of thick black eyebrows, which extended, uninterrupted, across his forehead. And though the rest of our family had no friends that met with Daa's approval, Angus and John had been nearly inseparable since the Moncrieffs settled in Culswick from Bressay Isle five years before.

I knew there was little doubt the report of a wreck was true. With its treacherous winds and jagged shoreline, the west coast of Shetland had always been a graveyard for ships. Most of us considered a wreck of good-quality cargo a gift, and though no one admitted to praying for a wreck, the island being treeless and of few resources led many to pray that, should such a wreck happen, the good Lord would direct it to a nearby shore.

John stepped back, continuing to toss the pouch from one hand to the other. "This gale will finish the schooner off for sure, even in a voe as protected as Skeld. They'll be desperate to unload the timber. I'll use the coins to buy what I can, and then resell to Marwick for a tidy profit. Then it's off to America I'll go. With enough in me pockets to start anew."

"America?" I gasped, the thought so preposterous—so utterly foreign to everything we knew—that I was sure he was joking.

"Aye! Where a crofter such as me can have a say in his future. And be free of the likes of Marwick and his kind forever!"

I was speechless, me mind drifting to William, sinking deeper and deeper with no line to grasp. Then, suddenly, I shouted through the wind what was clawing at me insides. "And when you've made your profit—before you leave—you'll return the coins? You'll come back for us?"

"Count on it," John mumbled, not meeting me eyes as he spoke.

Then he grabbed the lantern as casually as he had snatched the last piece of cod from the table earlier that evening and playfully slapped me on the back.

"For now, you and Daa have a ewe's body to get rid of and no time to waste. I'll sneak by the croft to see if Peterson's gone before I'm off. Keep a lookout—two flashes from below means it's safe to come down."

I nodded, rain dripping from me face. Then I suddenly grabbed his arm, me nails digging through his heavy, wet gansey. I tried not to sound desperate. "Please, John. You're our only hope."

"Aye, Brother," he said with a wink, breaking free of me grip and scrambling up and over the crumbled broch wall. "And there's nothing going to stand in me way tonight."

4

The Betrayal

In many ways, John and Billy Tweed were very much alike. A favor given, a favor returned. Everything in balance. Or so it seemed. For them, it was all about numbers.

"How do you do it?" I remember asking John years before, as we trudged home on the mossy path from the schoolhouse. "All that figurin' in your head?"

"Hah!" he laughed. "I've always had digits spinnin' round me brain. I guess all I needed was someone to show me what to do with 'em."

Me knack for reading and writing was nothing to his mastery of numbers. We all knew it, even back when he was no older than pesky Vic. Midder, being an educated woman, insisted we attend the school in Skeld run by the Society in Scotland for Propagating Christian Knowledge. "Nothin' but a plot by the Kirk to brainwash me bairns," Daa muttered, but at her insistence we went just the same.

Our master, George Henry, was a thin, crooked figure with a shadow over his lip that made him never seem clean-shaven. He had come up from Edinburgh the year before to replace Mr. Smith, who fled the island the day after Angus Moncrieff knocked him senseless.

From the day they met, John was overjoyed by Mr. Henry's vast knowledge of mathematics, bookkeeping, and navigation. I watched quietly from the other side of the room as he devoured addition, subtraction, multiplication, and division, and pored over maps and even spherical trigonometry. If anyone could break us free from Marwick, it was John. But that night in Culswick Broch I waited nearly an hour, straining me eyes in the storm for the promised flashes of the lantern that never came.

Had I missed them? What had gone wrong?

When me teeth began rattling, me gansey and underclothes soaked through to me skin, I knew I could wait no more.

The cows hardly stirred as I pulled open the weathered door to the byre and felt me way to the faint silhouettes of Catherine and Victoria. They were still holding the orphaned lambs in their arms.

"Chris?" Catherine whispered as I crouched between them. "You must be daft to come back here!"

I peered across the byre to the crack of light coming through the unevenly planed boards of driftwood in the door to the cottage. "Mr. Peterson still inside?"

"Och, no." Catherine drew her finger to her lips. "Daa sent him off ages ago. But he's threatened to be back after the storm. He's looking for you."

"Soli Deo Gloria," I muttered, rubbing me brow. "I best get with Daa."

"No!" She grabbed tightly to me sleeve. "He's in one of his states."

"There's no helpin' it, Cath. We've something to take care of."

She pulled harder as I started to stand. "That's not the worst of it!" she said. "He's raging about 'cause he canna find the pouch!"

"Already knows it's gone, does he?" I asked.

"Climbed up the ladder and started fishing round the rafters soon as we gave him John's note."

"Note?"

"The one he wrote when he came back here," Victoria said. "Told Catherine not to read it, but she did—every word—just like you taught her. Oh, you're in a mighty heap of trouble, Christopher Robertson!"

I looked away, wanting nothing more than to have kept them from the truth about what I'd done to that ewe. "It's over, at least," I muttered, me face hot with shame. "Daa and I'll have her body stashed far below the mossy earth before Peterson gets back."

"Look! Me tooth is loose!" Victoria said, pushing her face before mine and opening her mouth wide.

"Not now, Vic!" Catherine swatted her on the shoulder. "Chris, it's not just the ewe that's gotten you in trouble."

"Are you a thief, Chris?" Victoria asked, gripping her lamb tightly as it struggled in her arms.

"Me?" I looked at her sweet face peering from under her mop of curls. As pesky as she was, I found it hard not to smile.

"John's note said you took the pouch," she went on, her hand stroking the velvet curls of the newborn lamb.

"I'm no thief, ya peerie haf-krak!" I cuffed her gently on the head. "'Twas your brother John who took the coins."

"See, Vic," Catherine whispered, "I knew John wasn't telling the truth. He's the Devil, that one! It's just like when the cheese went missing and he told Daa it was me who took it. Me backside still smarts from the thrashing."

"Cath," I said, kneeling before her, "what, exactly, did this note say?"

"Let's see." She closed her eyes as she stroked the soft brown head of her lamb. "Something like *'Dear Daa,'* hmm, oh, yes—*'I saw Christopher take your pouch from above the rafters in the byre after he snuffed out the Peterson ewe. He confided in me he was bound for Lerwick to seek passage to America.'*"

I grabbed fast to her shoulders. "That's not funny, Cath! If you're playing with me now, you need to stop!"

"I'm n-n-not! Cross me heart," she stuttered—stunned, I

think, by the urgency in me voice. "Vic, do you remember what came next?"

"Oh, yes!" Victoria whispered proudly. "'*On my honor, I vow to catch him and bring back the coins if it is the last thing I do.*' That was it! Oh, and don't forget he signed it, '*Your faithful son, John.*'"

"You must have misread it!" I said, springing to me feet.

"You didn't do it, Chris, did you?" Catherine again grabbed the edge of me gansey. "You didn't take the pouch like John said?"

"'Course not!" I slammed me chapped fists on me thighs. "Would I be back here if I had?"

"Well, you better tell that to Daa," Victoria said, tucking her head behind her sister. "When he came down from that ladder he was smashing things this way and that!"

"Don't be daft, Vic," Catherine said. "Daa won't listen to him. Chris—we heard him tell Mr. Peterson you were the one who stole the ewe, and that you snuffed her out to cover yourself before he could stop you."

"Solus Christus!" I said, turning away from me sisters and pressing me face to me hands. Aye, me Daa could be cruel—but he'd never stooped to blaming me for his misdoings! And for John to write those words? It just couldn't be so.

Just then we heard the front door to the cottage burst open. "Well, there's no sign of him round the scattald," Daa's voice boomed through the wall. "By God, if John dunna bring that thieving dreep of a lad back here with that pouch by morning like he said he would, I'll send Knut Blackbeard to do the job!"

Catherine sprang to her feet, the squirming lamb baaing softly in her arms, and pushed me toward the door. "You've gotta leave! We heard Daa tell Gutcher that the note from John would be all the proof he would need to show your bad character to Sheriff Nicolson. If Mr. Peterson takes the matter to the court in Lerwick, Daa plans to use it to clear his name!"

"Run, Chris!" Victoria's wee voice quavered as she helped Catherine push me to the door.

I looked down at the two bony figures shivering in the shadows, the orphan lambs squirming in their arms. For all their bothering and teasing, it was all I could do to turn meself away. "Don't give yourself any trouble by tellin' Daa that you saw me tonight."

Then Catherine grabbed me hand, tears barely visible in the dark of the byre. "Will we see you again . . . ever?"

"Aye!" I said, suddenly wrapping me arms about their frail bodies. The lambs kicked wildly between us. They felt warm and soft. It was the first time I had ever hugged me sisters.

"But I've gotta get that pouch back." I slowly pulled away, remembering something Midder did the day she sent me off to school as I patted me heart. "While I'm gone, I'll keep you here."

And then, for the second time that night, I slipped out the door into the storm. This time, me life forever changed.

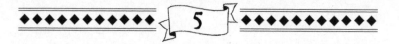

5

Unexpected Cargo

Just a wee bit closer!" John shouted, guiding me from above as I inched along a cracked, narrow ledge overhanging the jagged cliffs of Culswick. One hand clutched the precious rope of pig bristle and horsehair, the other reached into the nest. "There you go—that's it!"

It was the previous summer and we were fowling—gathering birds' eggs from nests along the sea cliffs for our dinner. Even the waves, crashing loud as thunder some fifty feet below, were drowned out by the cowlike moans of the swarming puffins, the raspy squawks of gannets, and the honks of razorbills. There were thousands of them nesting in cracks and burrows in the turf and rocks, none happy with our presence.

I didn't dare look down—me belly already so empty there was nothing going to keep me from those eggs.

It was as me fingers touched the cluster of brown speckled shells that the mother came at me, striking first me neck, then me arm, with her razor-sharp striped bill.

I cursed, swatting her back, as the precious eggs slipped from me fingers and smashed at me feet. And then, when I tried to regain me balance, I slid on the slippery yolk.

It was as I desperately tried to right meself that me foot somehow became wedged deep in a narrow fissure at the end of the ledge.

I grabbed the rope with one hand, the side of the cliff with the other, then looked up at John. "I'm caught!" I twisted one way, then the next, trying to pull meself free.

And then the angry mother struck again, this time at me face. And when I ducked I lost me footing.

"Chris!" John screamed from his perch ten feet above, but the rope had slipped from me hand. Before I knew it I was headfirst over the cliff, me pinned foot the only thing keeping me from plunging into the icy surf.

"Grab hold!" John shouted, swinging his rope toward me, an army of hotheaded puffins circling us.

Blood pounded to me forehead and cheeks, the weight of me body tugging at me wrenched foot as I tried desperately, again and again, to grab the rope.

I don't know how he did it, but in what seemed like an instant John scrambled down the slick, guano-coated wall and secured a loop around me chest. Then he wrestled me foot from the crack and pulled me to the ledge.

"Lucky there's not much meat on your bones," John said with a laugh, "or I wouldna' had the strength to haul you up."

Puffins by the hundreds swarmed before us, me trembling head buried in his warm shoulder. Like so many times before, he had saved me. Me guardian angel, William Jr. had called him. The one who managed to grab me, when I was but three or four, when I leaned too far over the gunwale of Gutcher's boat. The one who had somehow found me, lost in the fog on me way to school, when the others had given up.

And yet, there I was, running from me home in a fierce March gale, no lantern to guide me. All because of John. "I'll get that pouch *and* an explanation before he has a prayer of spending those coins," I muttered, pounding me soaked rivlins hard into the spongy earth, sea spray drenching me down to me shivering skin.

There was no road, of course, only a narrow path through layers of Shetland moss so soft no proper roads had ever been constructed. Even on the clearest of days I was known to lose me way, somehow baffled by similar, stark contours of the vast island landscape. In the dark I was hopeless. Before I knew it I had nearly stumbled smack into—of all places—the Peterson cottage.

Ann lived there, Mr. Peterson's beautiful black-haired daughter who was a year younger than me. Despite Catherine's constant teasing that Ann fancied me, I had never even mustered the courage to speak when she was near. No doubt her Daa had already told her what was soon to be the talk of the parish—that I had snuffed out his ewe.

I raced quickly in the opposite direction, the wind at me back, once sinking clear to me shin in the rain-drenched heather. Then I tripped over rocks and shrubs at the edge of the burn through the scattald. It was dark—oh so dark—and I remember breathing a sigh of relief when I caught the smell of peat, signaling another croft ahead. But what I couldn't see before me until it was too late was a wall of stone no higher than me knee. I tumbled over it headfirst into a puddle of muck, and it wasn't until I wiped the mud from me eyes that I made out the dim light from the window of the croft house of Knut Blackbeard not ten feet before me. And then I remembered Daa's words—should John not return by morning, he'd send Knut to find me.

Knut was a great muckle of a man with a bulbous red nose, pocked skin, and a ferocious beard as dark as night that was often flecked with straw, nettles, or remnants of food from past meals. Daa called him "the Viking," as it was Knut's claim to be the last of an old Norse family that arrived on the island a thousand years back with King Harald Fairhair of Norway. Knut was taller than any man on the island, with a frame so frighteningly solid they say it took twice as much wool to make his breeks and gansey as it did any other Shetlander's.

I wasn't sure if it was his beady gray eyes that sent chills down me spine or the gait with which he thundered about, his beefy arms swinging powerfully at his sides. To me and every other lad on the island, Knut Blackbeard was as dangerous as red-hot iron newly plucked from the forge.

He lived alone, always had, tending to his own crops and only joining the other Culswick men to fish for the cod on the sloop they leased from Wallace Marwick. But it was on Knut whom the entire parish depended when Marwick's shipments came ashore in the dark of night.

"See to it," Daa would say when word came of a drop, and the giant of a man would stand watch as the barrels and casks were hefted silently up steep cliffs and into caves waiting for Marwick's men to see to their sale. So legendary was Knut in wielding a club that they said Her Majesty's Revenue Men ran at the mere sight of him.

We never knew for sure why he was so fiercely loyal to Daa, but there was talk that he had been a small, homely child teased and beaten by the others in the parish.

"Daa watched out for him," John guessed. "Now he's returning the favor."

And I remember being but seven or eight when two of the Queen's Revenue Men came by. A suspicious packet had been spotted circling Culswick shores the night before, they said as they started nosing about the croft.

"As God as me witness," Daa said when they found a cask of gin tucked behind some straw in our byre, "I've no notion how that got here!"

It was the first time I remember hearing a quavering in his voice.

The officers sailed the cask to the sheriff's office in Lerwick and said they'd be back.

"You know, Knut," I overheard Daa whisper, as the two discussed the matter later that day, "if word gets out that Mr. Marwick is behind that gin, you'll be putting your club away for good." Then he looked at his brute of a friend—bushy red eyebrows twitching—and raised his voice an octave or two. "And what will become of me wife and bairns if they lock me up?"

By the end of the day Knut had claimed the cask as his own and spent the next six months in Lerwick Prison.

I hadn't noticed the flock of sheep by Knut's stone wall, huddling against the storm. But when I realized where I was and sprang to me feet, they shot like lightning in all directions, baaing nervously in the night. And then a light suddenly flashed but a few yards away.

"Who's there?" a voice demanded. I knew it well.

I flattened me body back into the wet behind a shrub. The light moved closer, until two worn, mud-caked rivlins stood but inches from me face. When I finally dared peer up at Daa, he was searching wildly about.

I held me breath, willing the sheep not to give me away. They cried frantically to one another, skidding this way and that while Daa held his lantern high.

"I know what I heard," he bellowed into the wind. "Show yourself or I'm comin' to find you!"

He stood there for what seemed like an eternity, eyes searching through the storm until I was sure I could hold me breath not a second longer. Then, muttering to himself, he turned slowly down the path to Knut's cottage. The moment he rapped on the door, I was up and over that wall, and I didn't stop running until I found me way to Skeld.

IT WAS NEARLY DAWN WHEN I PASSED ANDREW Johnson's forge, where I had first lifted a hammer so many years before. And then, when I came to the water's edge, I made out the outline of Wallace Marwick's fishing station, and slipped into the wee stone lodge where I and the other lads of the parish slept each summer while we worked to cure the fish.

Harold Inkster, the foreman of the station, saw to it that we worked every light hour of those long summer days, splitting and gutting boatloads of ling and cod, first pulling the livers for oil and then carefully bathing the carcasses in fresh water to keep the flavor from being spoiled by the blood.

"None in the British Isles does it better," he would boast as we layered the catch with salt in tall wooden tubs, our chapped, puckered hands throbbing from the sharp cut of gills and stinging bite of salt. Four or five days later he gave the nod and we pulled them to be washed again before we carefully laid each piece on the stony beach to dry.

"The Spanish like 'em green," he'd say, and so orders to Bilbao were dried skin-side up. But the Germans liked them white, so shipments bound for Hamburg were dried skin-side to the beach, allowing the flesh to be bleached by the sun.

A mouse scurried across the damp straw scattered on a bunk by the door. All I had to do now was wait for light and then meet John at the stranded schooner. With any luck, Daa and Knut Blackbeard wouldn't find me first.

Let me find him, Lord, I prayed, wrapping me arms across me chest to keep me soaking wet body from shivering. I suspected God might not be much help after what I had done to that ewe. Then I curled up on the bunk, all the while me mind racing over what had happened that night and what I might have done differently.

I hadn't meant to sleep, but the lodge had no windows and I never saw the morning light. And it was like most restless nights, where you finally slip into a deep sleep only an hour or two before dawn. In fact, I might have slept past noon if it hadn't been for the nasty wafts of boiling whale blubber from the shack above town.

"Aye," I muttered, rubbing me nose as I pulled meself from the bunk. Me legs and shoulders felt stiff, and I was dizzy with hunger remembering the last piece of cod John had snatched the night before.

The sun was so high—too high—that when I opened the door I winced at the light. The sky was an intense blue, as it usually is after such storms, with only a dark cloud billowing in the distance from the shack on the hill. Several gray seals lounged on a large, jagged rock protruding from the water, with skuas and gannets floating on the now calm sea, petrels circling and squawking above.

I looked out at the magnificent three-masted schooner anchored among hundreds of other small sloops and half-deckers on the sparkling voe before me. Her main mast was snapped in half and her hull tipped to the starboard like an old, crippled lady. Water was seeping in below deck, slowly taking her down, a Union Jack fluttering in the breeze from her foremast. Waves lapped over the name "Fortitude," painted in large red letters on the white band around her hull.

I counted at least twenty bedraggled seamen, scarves curiously covering their faces, dragging large barrels across her tilted deck. Two others were busy lowering barrels into a sixareen, the Shetland name for a six-oared boat, tied off her transom. Three men were rowing another boat already loaded with barrels to a sandy spit offshore.

Not far from me stood a tiny, whiskered man with a long pointed nose looking out into the harbor. Not seeing John or any unloaded timber, I brushed the mud and nettles as best I could from me tattered gansey and breeks and started toward him.

He glanced at me, smiling, then turned back to the schooner.

"What's in the barrels?" I asked, hugging me arms tightly to me chest.

"You a Robertson?" the whiskered man asked, then sucked on his pipe. "Have the look, I'd say. Cheekbones of your Daa—

the eyes." He looked at me closely, as I shifted nervously from foot to foot. "A bit more handsome than the others with those light blue eyes. And the ginger hair, o' course. Is that what they say about you, lad?"

We had no glass to look into. How I looked compared to me family had never crossed me mind. But I held me words, knowing we Shetlanders' deep curiosity about the business of others. One thing I knew for sure—by day's end this man and everyone else in the parish would know I had killed Mr. Peterson's ewe.

When I didn't respond, the man continued to look me up and down. "Seems you've had a bit of a rough night."

"Was quite a gale," I said, pulling me fingers through me hair.

He nodded, the wicks of his smile twitching. "That's what that other Robertson said earlier. Over from Culswick. Said his name was John."

I turned to him. "When?"

The old man chuckled, pulling the clay pipe from his lips and inspecting the bowl. "Oh, 'bout when the sun came up. But he's long gone now."

"How did he get the timber unloaded so fast?" I was furious with meself for sleeping as long as I had.

"Timber?" the old man asked, exploding with laughter. "So that's what he thought the *Fortitude* was carryin'!"

I grimaced as the breeze picked up an odor even stronger than the boiling whale blubber.

"I'm not sure who is givin' you Robertsons your information, but there's no timber in the wrecked hull of Her Majesty's fine vessel—just barrels and barrels of guano on their way from Gothenburg to Hull." He thrust the pipe back between his yellowed teeth and pointed to the loaded boat nearing shore. "If you think *your* eyes are waterin', just think of those poor lads! Looks to me like they've got more than enough muck in that ship to cover the crops of both England and Wales!"

The man made a *click, click, click* sound with his tongue and grinned. "The mighty English are goin' to have a hard time findin' a market for that here in Skeld."

So Angus Moncrieff had been wrong, I thought with a twinge of satisfaction. Then a sense of relief flooded me chest. Now all I needed was to catch up with John before he returned home and convince him to put back the pouch! At least there'd be something for the rent and to pay Mr. Peterson for the ewe.

"Good day to you, then," I said, turning back toward Culswick. "I expect me brother's hoping I'll catch him."

But I hadn't taken more than a few steps when the small man let out a long hoot.

"Ya won't find him goin' that direction." He winked at me in the morning sun. "Went that way."

He pointed north, to the path leading up and around the voe.

"And by the fire in that lad's eyes, I'd bet a kishie of peat he had a more exciting plan in mind than headin' back for the morning chores."

"That leads to Reawick and Garderhouse," I said, puzzled. "There's nothing up there but a few scattered crofts."

"Aye." The man nodded slowly. Then he pulled the pipe from his mouth and banged the spent bowl of tobacco against his thigh. "But it's the only way to Lerwick if you dunna have a boat."

6

An Unlikely Companion

erwick! John was going to Lerwick! A full day's walk on the other side of the island, the busiest port in Shetland. Crowded with ships from around the world, thieves, pickpockets, and a maze of streets and shops me mind could hardly fathom. Being only a short journey across the North Sea from Rotterdam and Bergen, it had, for as long as anyone could remember, been a stopover on the way to the rich fishing grounds of Greenland and Iceland. It was the home of Sheriff Nicolson. And of the island's prison, with its high stone walls overlooking the harbor. And the home of Wallace Marwick, whose empire of shipbuilders, coopers, chandlers, and seamen was a sight to behold.

The sounds of Skeld faded quickly as I raced past several crofts on the outskirts of the village of Reawick and then north. As I anxiously glanced over me shoulder for signs of Knut Blackbeard, I didn't notice that nearly all the sloops and smacks were sitting empty in the waves. And as I walked, me mind drifted to last September.

It had been an entire month with no smuggling. "Knut and I are off to meet with Mr. Marwick," Daa had announced. "Private meetin'."

"Then you'll be needin' me to carry your kishie," John said hopefully. And since the hull of Gutcher's fourareen was leaking and there was no money to repair it, they set out on foot.

For years John had begged to see Lerwick for himself, which is why Daa and Knut agreed to take him along. It was from his stories of that journey that I first learned of the place.

"There are rows and rows of real houses—some two and three stories tall!" he explained when he returned several days later, his rivlins worn clear to his socks. "With corners so square you could cut yourself on the edge and slate roofs the color of the sky!"

He described beautifully carved doors, and streets where the homes were set so close together you could see your neighbor through the window next door.

"And the people! Some with skin as dark as night, and many so well fed they had belts as long as the reins on a harness. All speaking different languages—I couldna' understand a word!" He told of mariners filled with fire whiskey, carousing in the streets at night. Of people bustling from shop to shop during the day buying everything imaginable. "Cakes, cheese, bread, books—even ready-made jackets and breeks! Why, you could buy jars of *red* and *green* paint!" His description of the lasses were hardest to believe. "No sallow faces or rough, worn hands—all plump, rosy-cheeked, and full of laughter and smiles," he said, confessing that, when it was time for him to take a wife, it was there he would return.

But it was the tale of the shipwrecked American spy that most piqued me interest. How he'd been blown off course to an island just beyond the harbor during the war with the re- bellious American Colonists, a trunk of gold ducats aboard his ship.

"It's been nearly sixty years," I said. "Surely someone's found the treasure."

"Don't think they haven't tried," John said, eyes gleaming as he looked off into the distance. "Daa knows of a man who's been digging for it nearly all his life."

As I staggered along, me empty stomach churned and me head began to grow dizzy. *Fill up with water*, I remembered Midder urging in those dark times when there had been no more food. *It will ease the hunger.* But as I veered from the path in search of a spring, a familiar voice made me nearly jump out of me skin.

"Peace be with thee, Christopher Robertson."

There, slumped awkwardly on a rock by the path, was the

Reverend Frederick Sill, the minister of our parish and a man despised by me family more than nearly any other on the island.

"You're a long way from Culswick, are you not?" His crackling voice boomed so loudly I stood frozen in place.

He was Shetland born, the son of a powerful Lerwick minister, and had been educated in Edinburgh and had taken over our parish at the request of the Earl of Cummingsburgh himself. For nearly fifty years he had led with an iron fist, preaching sermons each week that droned on and on for three hours a sitting, sometimes even longer.

According to Gutcher, the reverend had at one time been a man of great stature, but for as long as I'd been alive his ancient body seemed as weathered and crooked as the driftwood stauf he grasped. His skin was gray and lifeless, as if it hadn't seen much sun of late, and the white around his green eyes was bloodshot with a yellow tinge and deeply set under lids of flaking, wrinkled skin. Wild strands of hair crawled from his nostrils and rough, scaly ears, and his hair and beard were pure white except for the yellow pipe stains above and below his lips.

He groaned as he stood and then steadied himself on his stauf. "Should you not be back with your Godless family tending to the destruction from the Lord Almighty's fierce gale?"

Panicked, I attempted to dart back to the path, only to feel his clawlike fingers grab fast to me arm. As leader of the Kirk,

Reverend Sill was also the person responsible for what he called "all matters of morality and discipline."

"It is no secret your father's views of the Kirk," he said, pulling me back toward a tall, woven reed basket we Shetlanders call a "kishie," which sat beside him. "Prefers the mighty bishops of the Church of England to any *lowly* gathering of the Presbytery, does he not? And yet he is regularly in attendance at services."

Me face grew hot as I tried to pull meself free.

"Aye—me Midder saw to it." And she had, knowing as we all did that in times of desperation the Kirk was the only source of charity.

"Hmmph," he grunted. "You would serve your Daa well to remind him that it is not Queen Victoria and her ways that we, the polluted worms of this earth, are to worship. Men are not as beasts! And when life as we know it comes to an end, it is the saints who will be taken from the sinners!"

I glared at him, unable to hold me tongue, remembering the shame and humiliation he had already cast upon me family.

"Me Midder was a Godly woman. Of that there is no doubt."

"She disgraced the parish!" His faced turned crimson as he slowly enunciated each word.

I clenched me teeth, recalling the anguish in her kind, beautiful face as she stood, doing penance, before the parish each Sunday for four months, our neighbors' unforgiving eyes tearing her reputation to shreds. An ancient punishment the likes of which no islander outside our parish had been asked to endure in decades. But so convinced was Reverend Sill that the Devil was lurking in our midst that he saw to it no curse went without the severest of punishments.

"Mrs. Peterson is a meddler and a gossip," I blurted, the memory of that day two years before flooding back to me.

Reverend Sill raised an eyebrow, cocking his head ever so slightly to the right. "Perhaps. Nevertheless, for your Midder to curse her was Satan's work. The charge of blasphemy could not—would not—go without punishment. On this I have always been clear."

I dropped me eyes, recalling how Midder lost her temper when Mrs. Peterson came nosing about, catching her planting on the Sabbath. How she knew she was late in sowing the cabbages, having spent the week weaving cloth to help cover the rent. Time was running out and she hadn't dared wait.

"I see what you're up to," Mrs. Peterson had shouted, strutting down the path.

Me Midder, she was a patient woman—as patient as any I'd known. But that day she didn't hold back.

"May the Devil take your meddlin' soul from our croft!" she cried.

And that was all Agnes Peterson needed to hear.

By sundown she'd reported Midder to Reverend Sill, with the punishment for blasphemy and breaking the Sabbath set by morning.

"She was protecting me family," I said, pulling free me arm and starting back to the path. "Seeing to it we had enough to eat! There's nothing un-Godly about that."

He stared at me and shook his head. "Your temper gets the better of you, Christopher Robertson. Now, before you take your leave, I'll need to know where it is you are going."

I hesitated, turning to catch his eye and wondering which would send me first to the land of Satan—lying to Reverend Sill or killing Mr. Peterson's ewe. "To Lerwick," I muttered, knowing full well I could outrun him if he came after me. "On an errand for the family."

The ancient man cocked his head, making a strange clicking noise with his tongue as he pondered me answer. "Most go by boat, round the heads," he said, referring to Fitful Head and Sumburgh Head, the southern points of the island. Then he rubbed his shoulders as he studied me through the thick white eyebrows that climbed wildly in all directions and snagged his eyelashes when he blinked. "They say it's fastest."

"Aye." I nodded, thinking quickly. "But me Gutcher's fourareen's in need of repair. So they've sent me by land."

He paused a moment, then cleared his throat again. "I, too, am headed to Lerwick."

"Surely *you* are not traveling all that way by land?"

"Ah, but the Lord leaves me no choice," he nearly shouted, face once again turning crimson. "Lad, have you not heard of my recent trip home from Edinburgh?"

"No, sir." I sighed, looking longingly back to the path

and knowing full well his habit for long-winded responses. I was running out of time if I was ever to catch John before he boarded a ship for America, and by now Knut Blackbeard was surely on me trail.

The old man hammered his driftwood stauf into the ground. Then he stretched his arms wide to either side of his frail, cloaked frame, as I had seen him do so many times from the pulpit. "Just before Advent I crossed back from the Mainland, having, at eighty-four years of age, fulfilled my duties to the General Assembly of the Kirk in Edinburgh. Alas, the journey was on a ship full of sinful mariners and a captain whose language was so blasphemous that the Lord set about to teach them a lesson. We were but one day at sea when we were caught in crosswinds so wicked we were tossed about for three days, nearly to Foula Isle! I alone kneeled and prayed for redemption below deck, while four of those foul-languaged men were washed overboard! As the others grew close to despair and turned to me for solace, I reminded them that a man has no true loss until he loses his soul, and for that alone there is no reparation. That night God's will shook a rod over their heads and showed them his might!"

"Aye," I said, impatiently tapping me foot. Then I glanced nervously back down the path for signs of Knut. "You made it home. Soli Deo Gloria. And now, if you'll excuse me, I'm a bit pressed for time." But as I turned back to the path, it was as if I hadn't spoken.

"Aye indeed!" Reverend Sill continued, his voice raised an

octave, as if to emphasize the importance of what was to follow. "We anchored safely in Lerwick the very next day, Sola Fide! And when I touched land and kissed the beloved ground, I vowed never to step foot on another ship." Then he paused to massage his lower back and left buttock and glanced at his kishie. "I am expected in Lerwick by tomorrow for the monthly meeting of the Kirk elders. While I'm there, I intend to give charges of theft and blasphemy against Murdoch Bairnstrom, my patron Lord Cummingsburgh's agent. Instead of paying me his agreed-upon stipend, he has been seen in Lerwick spending the rents of his Lordship, carousing in the streets, and speaking foul language! This at a time when you, the pathetic sheep of a barren pasture, wait hungry in the fold!"

I laughed to meself that Reverend Sill, too, was in search of coins. "Doesn't the law require that Lord Cummingsburgh sees your stipend is paid?"

"Aye!" His eyes narrowed. "And it has been two years now I've been owed! Even a man as mighty as Lord Cummingsburgh need be warned—for it is the vengeance of Heaven that will not be avoided as one prepares for his unchangeable state."

Then he stopped suddenly, as if recovering from a trance. "Tell me, lad, have you had anything to eat of late?"

I hesitated, belly growling, me breeks hanging loosely at me hips, held up only by a piece of twine. "No, sir."

"Then you'll join me in breaking your fast."

I watched in amazement as he reached inside his kishie and produced an oval bentwood box, from which he pulled a loaf of bread and pouch of dried herring. "The good Mrs. Sill packed provisions for the journey, and you'll do me a favor by lightening this load."

I stared, dumbfounded. With me Daa's outspoken criticism of the Kirk and me Midder's past transgression, surely we Robertsons were a disgrace in his eyes. And yet, so hungry was I that when he handed me a chunk of bread and piece of dried herring, no amount of pride could keep me from accepting them.

Don't gobble like the swine and sheep, I told meself—me Midder's words coming back to me, and thoughts of John, for a moment, disappearing. I didn't think I could chew fast enough to get the food into the dark, empty parts of me body. But when I finished and looked over, Reverend Sill's eyes were closed, face tilted to the morning sun, his hands clasped tightly in prayer. And his food lay untouched on a cloth before him.

"May the Good Lord cast a warm light on this journey," he prayed, a wide smile pulling at the edges of his loose, wrinkled face. "For only He knows the limits of this tired, worn body, and the sacrifice I am willing to make to set things right."

Then he slowly leaned back against the rock, carefully chewing his bread and fish before taking a long swig from a small clay jug. "You'll not be wanting any of this to quench your thirst, lad," he said, grimacing as he swallowed. "There's a spring just over there."

I knelt down to the trickle bubbling up from a stone and drank the cool, refreshing water. Then, seeing him packing the remaining food and jug back into the kishie, I dashed to the path before he could start another lecture. "Best wishes for a safe journey," I called over me shoulder. "I thank you!"

But I was only a few strides on me way when I heard a moan so deep and pitiful I was sure his heart had given way.

Don't look back! Keep moving, I told meself, determined to not allow this one act of kindness to wipe away the memory of shame and humiliation in me Midder's eyes. But as the reverend's moans grew louder, it was me Gutcher's face that came to me—how he struggled each day, so plagued with the rheumatism, that it took both me and Catherine to pull him out of bed.

Don't think about that! I told meself. *You've no time to help. Remember what he did to Midder!* But when I stupidly glanced over me shoulder, the pathetic sight of such a frail man struggling to pull the kishie onto his back was more than I could bear.

"Wait, Reverend. I'll carry it." The words slipped out before I could bring meself to me senses.

He looked up, stunned at first, eyeing me skeptically. "Thank ye, lad. But it's beyond your ability, I'm afraid."

"I may be small, but me Gutcher tells me I'm the best in the family for carrying the peats."

But as I hoisted the kishie over me shoulders, I immediately regretted me boasting. How could bread, fish, and a jug of water possibly weigh so much? I staggered to get me balance and knew instantly it would be nearly impossible to catch up with John carrying a load such as this.

The moment Reverend Sill was satisfied that I wouldn't collapse, he opened his arms wide to the sky and leaned back his head. "The Lord has condescended to take mercy on me!" he proclaimed, the morning sun bathing his wrinkled face. "Providence has brought us together, and I am forever in your debt!"

"Aye," I muttered. It was too late to retract me offer.

His eyes watered as we set off, the beginnings of a smile tugging at the wicks of his chapped lips, as he urged me up the path. "For these past few months I have been suffering from the sciatica—a wrenching pain shooting from me buttocks down the side of me left leg. When I bear the weight of me kishie, it seizes me in such a violent manner I think of the evil souls frying in Hell and wonder if their pain for eternity can match the aching throb I have come to endure!"

I sighed, thinking of the entire day's journey in his company, the endless drone of his voice. But for the moment, at least, it kept me from the agony of thinking of John. "Is there nothing you can do? No herb or tonic?"

"I have tried it all, as you can imagine." He went on and on as we walked. "Lignum's Anti-Scorbutic Drops, Brodum's Restorative Nervous Cordial. Alas, none have shown the desired results. When I heard of a man-o'-war docked at Lerwick in January, I sent for its surgeon, hoping he might know of some new remedy or tonic that might help me in this pathetic state, but, alas, he knew only of severing limbs and treating the scurvy. Only Miss Bonnie Goudie, a young lass from Gruting, who often assists Mrs. Sill, is able to give temporary relief by clapping a hot bath of earth in the place affected. But it seems to rid me, at least temporarily, of the pain. And so, here I am—knowing only that it must please God to circumcise my carnal heart of things past for which I must repent."

I puzzled at how God might need to purify a man who preached the gospel and spent his life battling the wicked, whom people called the most Godly of us all. But as we crested the first of Shetland's many hills, it was as if Reverend Sill suddenly found a burst of new life. He quickly overtook me, setting a surprisingly energetic pace that, at times, I admit, was hard to keep up with. He peppered me with lectures on his battles for redemption, the curses of blasphemy, and Satan's increasing stranglehold on the island, as me thoughts strayed back to Culswick. To me fingers clamping down on that ewe. To John, and how I had trusted him. To how his smile and simple arm around me shoulder had made me feel I wasn't alone. Especially after William was lost to us. Especially when Midder was no more.

By noon we had already conquered the long stretch of water that Reverend Sill explained was Effirth Voe and were through the wee village of Tresta. And then it was around Weisdale Voe, that thin finger of sea cutting nearly four miles inland, its waters sparkling like jewels below us. It was already late afternoon when we ascended the treeless Cliff Hills beyond Tingwall and caught the first view of Dales Voe glistening in the sun.

But, alas, Reverend Sill's energy wasn't to last. The vast,

steep terrain began to prove taxing, and as he slowed, what little hope I had had of catching John before nightfall quickly waned. When we ascended the massive Hill of Dale, where a herd of Shetland ponies grazed happily on the glorious heather with nary a cloud above, his steps grew careless and uneven. Then he stumbled to the ground several times, once cutting his chin, and another bruising his forearm. He looked over at me, relieved, when I finally suggested we rest.

I was leaning against a large outcropping of stone, massaging me chest, now rubbed raw from the kishie's braided rope straps, as he took another long swig from his jug. But when he tried to put the jug down he lost his grip, and a strange black liquid splattered on me rivlins.

"Solus Christus!" he cried, trying to right the jug before all was lost. "Only Satan would keep me from this tonic!"

I crinkled me nose. "What is it?" Then I dipped me finger into the foul-smelling stuff.

"Go ahead," he said, his voice breaking. "Taste it."

I hesitated at first, touching me finger to me tongue, and then spat violently. "You've been drinking *this*?"

"Every day since December 29."

"But why?"

"Tuts, lad! For the sciatica, of course! The late Bishop Barclay suggested such a potion in his remaining papers, which I am privileged to hold in my possession. Tar and water it is. And I ask you, lad, what else but Divine Providence could direct him to suggest such a mixture as this?"

"Tar?"

"Not just any tar! Norwegian tar!" He quickly cleared his throat. "And I must say, I *have* been feeling a slight improvement of late."

It was when I turned back to the path to hide me laughter that I nearly choked. There, in the distance, but no less than a half mile behind us, trudged the unmistakable hulking frame of Knut Blackbeard. And the moment I saw him, Reverend Sill saw him too.

7

Mary Canfield

I s that . . . ?" Reverend Sill started to ask.

"No idea," I lied, heart pounding. "We've lost track of time. The sun will soon be setting!" I flung the kishie over me shoulders, grabbed his frail hand, and beckoned him back to the path. "We best get moving or it will be nightfall before we see Lerwick."

"Why, that's Knut Blackbeard—your Daa's companion," he said, his eyes narrowing. "I'm sure of it. We must wait and ask him to join us on our journey."

"Wait? No!" I tried desperately to calm the panic in me voice. "We've no lantern. Only an hour at most before the path will be impossible to follow!"

"Mr. Blackbeard is of my flock," the old man scolded. He yanked his hand from me grip so fiercely I nearly toppled backward. "A wayward sheep, there is no doubt, but one of my flock nonetheless. I'll not avoid his company."

"But—your meeting! And your charges against that evil Murdoch Bairnstrom! And what of your missing stipend?"

As I prattled on, the old man lowered his forehead, his chin jutting forward like a ram making ready to charge. "Christopher Robertson," he bellowed, his voice dropping several octaves, "is Satan putting you between me and Mr. Blackbeard?"

"Satan? No, sir!"

"Then why, may I ask, are you shunning a neighbor on a journey such as this?"

Me heart banged into me chest as I stared down at me worn rivlins. "Please, sir, I can't say."

"Hoot, lad! We are nothing without the truth!" He snapped his hands to his hips. "The Lord cannot help you, and nor can I, if the truth is not shared!"

And, oh, how I wanted to tell him everything about the night before! Of the shameful thing I had done to Mr. Peterson's ewe and of the terrible wrongs that had been done to me. But I couldn't—I wouldn't. Not until I got that pouch of coins back from John. I knew it was Reverend Sill's duty, as head of the church, to keep in order the moral behavior of the parish. If I told him, he would have no choice but to turn me over to Sheriff Nicolson.

I glanced over me shoulder at the outline of Knut Black-beard, fast cresting the hill we had crested just half an hour before, and to this day I do not know why it is I didn't simply turn and run. Instead, I looked directly in the reverend's ancient, watery eyes—the eyes me family hated—and from somewhere deep inside me, found the courage to speak.

"I have been wronged, sir," I stammered. "Badly wronged. And I fear if Knut finds me before I find me brother, John, I will lose the chance to set things right."

For a moment the old man held me in his stare.

"Can you believe me?" I pleaded. "Please—I speak the truth!"

"And will you not tell me why it is you must catch up to your brother?"

"No," I said, slowly exhaling. "I cannot."

He continued to stare, his eyes searching mine.

"I do not see Satan in you, lad, but I feel his presence close at hand. Are you certain there is nothing more about this you can tell me?"

I glanced away, willing back me tears. "Only that if I can't get back what John has taken, me family will not be long for the quartering."

I thought again of the humiliation of Gutcher, Aunt Alice, Catherine, and wee Victoria being added to the church's list of paupers—passed from the quarters of one family to the next for their food and shelter.

"I see." He sighed, looking out at the horizon. "Alas, those in such a state are already so many, I fear the day we cannot manage them all." Then he took a deep breath, opening his arms to the sky before turning back to me. "I suppose it wouldn't hurt a man as strong as Mr. Blackbeard to finish the journey on his own."

I looked at him, stunned. "You mean—we're to move ahead? Without him?"

"Aye, lad," he replied, stumbling back to the path. And to this day I still do not know why he chose to believe me. "Hoist on the kishie. It's downhill from here. Together we shall repair to Lerwick with all convenient speed!"

IT WAS DUSK WHEN WE STOLE OUR FIRST glimpse of Lerwick. Unlike the narrow voes of the western island, the sparkling water of Bressay Sound was jammed with vessels of every size imaginable, all silhouettes in rapidly fading light. And along the water were clusters of houses—more than I had ever seen—with Bressay Isle across the harbor, peeking above a bank of clouds.

"I have many times dropped to my knees and prayed upon seeing what lies before you," Reverend Sill explained while continuing down the path at a brisk pace, thrusting his stauf hard into the ground in keeping with his stride. "In my many years of service to our Lord, I have traveled treacherous waters by sloop and schooner. Once a year to Edinburgh, for my duties at the Kirk, and every other year to Fair Isle to celebrate the Sacrament of the Lord's Supper—the poor heathen there, having no other man of the cloth to see to their salvation! Alas, none of these places grasps my heart as the beauty we now see before us. But it is many a poor soul who discovers this only after flinging himself so far afield that he can't seem to get himself back."

To me delight, the path gradually transformed into a proper road cut deep into the moss—the first I had ever seen—wide enough, even, for a pony and cart! And the croft houses we passed were set in clusters, so close together there seemed to be no shared scattald or space for arable land.

"Where do they grow their bere and corn?"

"Hoot, lad!" Reverend Sill clicked his tongue. "The men of Lerwick are men of the sea, not crofters! Coopers, chandlers, and fishmongers—all bound to Mr. Marwick's docks."

"Then where do they get their meal?"

"Why, they buy it, of course—at the market!"

It wasn't another half mile before the road became even wider, and we came upon the first proper house I had ever seen up close. No thatch! No rubble stone! Three stories high, with windows framed with real glass! In the fading light I was able to make out the faint outlines of similar houses we passed, each seeming grander than the last, many with additional structures for windows jutting from the roofline, which I learned were called dormers.

Finally, Reverend Sill stopped short and pointed with his

stauf to a street leading to the height of land above the harbor. "This is Hillhead. Canfield House is near the end. It's where I'll stay the night."

"Lor'!" I exclaimed when we at last approached the wide stone steps to a dark and intricately carved door. "Where did they get the wood?"

"Ah, but this is Lerwick, lad. Much comes into this port from wealthier lands. And what comes in is often, well, *missed* by the Revenue Man at Her Majesty's Customs House." He winked at me quickly as he rapped the brass knocker. "Shetlanders honor the Lord before the Queen, and rightly so. We needn't pay Her Majesty *every* duty she asks for."

I peeled the kishie from me back. "Thank you for your kindness, sir," I said softly—as the massive door swung open to show a beautifully plump woman in the most elegant dress I had ever seen.

"Ah, Reverend Sill," she said with a curtsy. "The parish of the west has allowed you once again to wander to our side of the island?"

She was tall. In fact, by the looks of her, I was fairly sure she wouldn't have been able to stand in our croft house without brushing her graying hair against the rafters. And her face—it was full, flesh puffing from each rosy cheek, something I hadn't seen in any person these last years of hunger.

Her dress was of a deep blue silk, the color you saw in the sky only after a gale, with white ruffles clear up to her chin. It was clean and completely free of tatters, not a single patch or sign of darning or repair.

As I stared at her, the aroma of roasting meat and baking bread wafted through the door, and it was all I could do to keep me knees from giving way.

"Yes, indeed, Mrs. Canfield," Reverend Sill replied with a bow. "And should you have a room and warm meal left this dark night, I would be most grateful."

"Certainly," she replied. Her accent betrayed the inflections of another land I couldn't place. Her eyes narrowed as she looked at his face. "I see you have injured your chin! Please, come in so I can see to it!" She stood aside and swept her hand toward what looked like a sitting room, with a fire and the finest couch I had ever seen. "Knowin' it was time for the monthly meetin' of the Presbytery, we were expectin' you."

The old man nodded, touching his chin. "Not a matter for concern, I assure you. I took a few spills along the way, I'm afraid." Then he turned to me. "Mrs. Canfield, may I present Christopher Robertson. It was an arduous journey, and I'd not have made it without his assistance. For this I am most grateful."

I flushed as the towering lady nodded in me direction.

"You were kind to share your fish and bread," I said, handing the reverend the kishie.

"And what, young man, are your plans from here?"

I looked down at me worn rivlins. "To find me brother is

all." I shivered in the March air, pulling me cold hands up into the sleeves of me gansey, knowing how easily I lose me sense of direction in the dark. "I'll start me search at the docks, I suppose. From there . . . I don't know."

Mrs. Canfield studied me tattered attire and sighed.

"It's not far, lad. But you'll not be wantin' to go there to-night. The mariners are so mad on gin on account of the news that I fear there'll be rioting."

As she spoke Reverend Sill's eyes narrowed. "And what is the cause of this great disturbance, Madam? Surely Sheriff Nicolson keeps better order than this?"

"Oh," she said with a gasp. "Has the word not yet spread to your end of the island?"

The reverend cocked his head.

"Why, it's Mr. Marwick. Hasn't paid his workers in weeks. We think he's near bankrupt."

"But that can't be!" I blurted. "Me Daa says Mr. Marwick owns nearly all the Lerwick docks: the coal yards, the sailmak-ers, and cooperages. And at our end of the island there's not a crofter doesn't pay him rent."

"Aye, Madam," Reverend Sill added. "Nothing comes into Lerwick or any other part of Shetland that that gentleman doesn't own a piece of. Even the bank."

"Well, not for long, I'm afraid," Mrs. Canfield said with a sigh. "The word is that the failed fishin' these past three years has finally caught up with him. He's in Edinburgh this very day tryin' to work something out with the Royal Bank of Scotland. People doubt he'll be extended the credit to get even a dozen boats out to the cod banks by Whitsunday. The entire harbor is in a state."

I suddenly remembered the sloops and half-deckers we'd passed waiting empty in Skeld and Weisdale Voes. Without credit from Marwick, there wasn't a crofter in our parish who'd find the coins to pay for the nets and supplies for even a week at sea.

"Aye," Reverend Sill said, touching his long, knurled fingers to his forehead. "It is just as I feared. The Lord has only so much patience with the blasphemous behavior of our mariners and greed of the merchants. They and they alone have brought this cruel, cruel fate on the people of this island." He shook his head and for a moment closed his eyes. "I ask you, how will our people, who are already near starvation, endure more suffering?"

"To that I have no answer," Mrs. Canfield replied. "But they say that without Mr. Marwick and his bank, the wharf will be deserted in a week's time. Coopers, smithies, chandlers—they all depend on him for their survival. Why, I wouldn't be a bit surprised if Lord Cummingsburgh himself was tightenin' his belt." She sighed and shook her head. "Please, come in before I lose the warmth from the fire. You too, lad. It won't do to have a lad walkin' alone on the wharf on a night like this."

Her gentle, warm hand lightly touched me shoulder as she ushered me into the most beautiful room I had ever laid eyes on. The walls were magnificently high, at least two times me height, and light glowed from three brass oil lamps, each with its own tall wick and fluted glass globe.

There were no fish hanging across the ceiling to dry, no spinning wheels, or swine rooting at the floor. Just an exquisite portrait of a stern-looking gentleman hanging on one of the wood-paneled walls, along with a landscape of many green hills and a loch that didn't look at all familiar.

A rug, woven in red, orange, and blue in a most intricate pattern, touched nearly all corners, and unlike the shallow fire that burned on the floor in the center of our croft house, an enormous fireplace framed in sleek gray stone jutted out from the wall—a mantel of golden beveled wood, and andirons the shape of owls, their jeweled eyes sparkling in the firelight.

Two wing chairs of deep green velvet faced the fire on either side of a matching couch, and what I guessed was a clock, though I'd never seen one before, stood in the corner. It was even taller than Reverend Sill, its pendulum clicking back and forth.

On the far wall was another thing I had never seen—a five-shelved glass case filled with books! The house might as well have been a palace in comparison to the handful of croft houses I had entered in me nearly fourteen years of life.

Unable to resist, I reached me hand out to one of the chairs, feeling for the first time the tickle of velvet on me fingertips, both soft and shiny.

"Your hands best be clean," a lass's voice chided from across the room. I drove me hands into me pockets before looking over.

She was at least a head taller than me, with ringlets of butter-blond hair pulled neatly from her face by a large emerald bow. Until I saw her it hadn't occurred to me that Catherine's and Victoria's hair hadn't seen the attention of a comb since the passing of our Midder.

Her face was long and somewhat angular but perfectly proportioned, except for a nose that seemed to have been formed slightly left of center between wonderfully full cheeks. Her skin was like cream compared to the freckled, ruddy-complexioned lasses of Culswick. She hardly seemed real.

"Mary, don't be rude. Come and greet our guests," Mrs. Canfield said. "You know, of course, Reverend Sill."

I could feel me ears growing hot as she strode across the room and curtsied. There was a flicker in her eyes betraying a sense of warmth and confidence I'd never before encountered. Ever.

"And this is," Mrs. Canfield began. "Forgive me, lad—I've forgotten your name."

"Christopher Robertson, ma'am," I muttered, quickly running me fingers through me own tangled mop of hair. I dared not meet her eyes, feeling her study me ill-fitting gansey and worn rivlins.

"Christopher who?" she asked.

"Robertson," Reverend Sill answered, to me great relief. For if I had tried to speak again I wasn't sure the words would come out. "He hails from a croft in Culswick—on my side of the island."

"Welcome, Christopher. This is my daughter, Mary," Mrs. Canfield explained. "She has just turned fourteen."

"And how many years have you?" the girl asked. "Eleven? Twelve?"

"I'll be fourteen come August," I blurted, surprising meself by looking at her directly. "I'm bound to grow taller this year. At least me brothers did when they were me age."

I felt me temples throb, and I wondered what had possessed me to say something so brash.

"I see," she said with a playful glance.

Mrs. Canfield walked over to the fire and added a fresh brick of peat to the flames.

"Please, Reverend Sill, have a seat and rest your weary bones." The brogue in her voice sounded even, yet unfamiliar. "We have some Madeira from Captain Canfield's last trip to Bilbao. I'll pour you a glass while you share your news of Mrs. Sill and of the parish. When you have rested, we will eat."

The elderly gentleman's shoulders slumped as she spoke, as if all of the energy he had mustered for the last leg of the journey evaporated at that very instant.

"Sola Gratia, Madam," he said, collapsing on the couch. "I am indeed tired and empty to my very soul."

Mrs. Canfield walked over and gently touched me shoulder. "Aye! You're nothin' but skin and bones! And such a handsome lad, with those stunnin' blue eyes! The color of starling's eggs, they are."

I felt me cheeks color as she turned me chin to the light.

"And the hair! Remarkable," she said, as if trying to remember something. "True ginger, it is. Like me brothers' and sister's back home." She turned to her daughter. "Mary will take you into the kitchen and get you somethin' to fill your belly. And should you choose to stay, there's a pallet in the shed."

In me heart I knew that if I was ever going to find John, I couldn't spare the time. But me words came spilling out before I could think. The idea of tasting the glorious things I had been smelling since I arrived was far too great. "Thank you, ma'am."

The kitchen was wider and longer than the entire two rooms of our croft house, with clean, limewashed walls and a deep fireplace in which two steaming black kettles hung above the flames. To the right was a cupboard reaching nearly to the ceiling, filled with plates and platters of blue-and-white china. At the center of the room by the fire was a table with two chairs where three loaves of sweet-smelling bread sat cooling on a rack.

"Do you fancy beef stew?" Mary asked. "If not, we have stap as well."

"I love them both, Miss!" I said, hardly believing me good fortune.

I sat, fidgeting in me chair, as she ladled a bowl from each of the black pots and brought them over. Then I watched, anxiously, unsure of what to say, as she sliced one of the loaves and slathered two pieces in butter.

I still remember every detail of that meal. The beef, tender and juicy, floating in a broth of cabbage and potatoes sweeter than I had ever tasted. And the stap, a steaming mash of boiled whitefish and livers heaped with a heavy topping of bread-crumbs. I scorched the roof of me mouth before stopping to take a breath, shoveling in spoonful after spoonful for fear she might take it away before I had me fill.

"Crofters don't wait for a lady to be served before they eat?" Mary asked, eyebrows arched.

I gasped, dropping me spoon into the bowl, me face suddenly as hot as the steaming stew. "Forgive me, Miss!"

She looked down as she served herself and took the seat across from me. "Sorry. Midder always says we have more to eat than many on the island."

"You eat like th-th-this?" I stammered. "Every day?"

Mary nodded, pulling the spoon delicately to her mouth and blowing on it, then met me with her sparkling eyes. "Strange, is it?"

I shrugged, hoping not to show me ignorance all at once.

"You don't speak . . . like a crofter."

I winced, the words hitting me like the sharp beak of the puffins on the cliffs of Culswick. "And how is it that crofters speak?" I was unable to hide the resentment in me voice.

She hesitated, looking about the room. "It's just—well, your speech. It seems a bit more learned than that of the other crofters I've met."

"Me Midder was an educated woman," I said. "Made sure that we were careful with our words. The neighbors hated her for it—thought she was putting on airs—but me Daa, he admired it greatly." I thought for a moment how Daa would admire Mary. How she, with her manners and speech, might actually meet with his approval.

For a while we ate in silence, me staring at me bowl as I tried desperately to think of something learned to say. "You've a grand house, Miss," I finally managed, eyeing her delicate white hand resting just inches from me own. I had never seen fingernails so clean.

"Grand?" she said, throwing back her head. "Oh, there're many homes grander than this in Lerwick."

"Your Daa's a captain?"

"Och, no. 'Twas me uncle that Midder was speaking of. Me Daa's been dead now five years."

"Sorry."

"Aye. A chandler, he was. From Ireland—near Belfast. Me Midder's Irish as well. You can still hear it in her words if you listen carefully. In fact, he had eyes—they were very much like . . ." But instead of finishing she looked away.

"They came to Shetland."

"Aye. Me Uncle James—the captain—convinced them. To work for Mr. Marwick."

She spoke directly and deliberately, something I hadn't heard in the voice of one so young before, and as I listened, the rich whitefish and livers felt like velvet in me once hollow belly. But there was something else—something so strange in her manner that it took me a moment to realize what it was:

Mary Canfield's green eyes seemed always to be smiling. What a very strange thing indeed.

"He sails out of Lerwick?" I asked, allowing meself only glimpses of her, as me eyes jumped from her face to me bowl.

"Aye," she nodded, jostling her ringlets as she spoke. The large green bow held them from her face. "He's captain of the *Ernestine Brennan*, Mr. Marwick's most prized vessel."

I looked up with surprise.

"You know her?" Mary asked.

"I've seen her! Two years ago in Skeld. Then another time in the distance off the Cliffs of Culswick. Me brother, John, pointed her out."

"Uncle stays with us when he comes to Lerwick. Brings us wonderful things—books, dresses, pictures—from his journeys."

"The books in your parlor. I've never seen so many."

"You mean to tell me you read?"

Once again me face grew hot.

"I was taken to understand crofters did not—"

"Well, I do!" I said, abruptly cutting her off. "Whenever I can find a book, that is. And I write as well." Then, fearing meself rude, I softened me tone. "Your uncle—he sails far?"

"Aye. Wherever Mr. Marwick sends him. The West Indies, Belfast, Perth, Boston, Cape Town, Bergen, Rotterdam. He's been gone many months. This time with my brother, Charles, who's sixteen. We expect them back any day now. When I heard the knock at the door I worried it was they."

"Worried?"

She lowered her gaze. "I miss them terribly, especially Charles. But with the way things are with Mr. Marwick, I'm hoping they stay away . . . a bit longer." She delicately wiped her mouth with a napkin. "Word is, if Mr. Marwick can't get the loan in Scotland, his entire fleet—including the *Ernestine Brennan*—will be taken to cover his debt."

"Surely a man of Mr. Marwick's stature won't allow—"

"Perhaps." She bit off some bread and stopped to chew.

"Can't they signal him—turn him back to sea for a while until things get settled, so they won't get close enough to seize the ship?"

"Aye. Though it wouldn't be easy. The *Ernestine Brennan* is the most recognized ship in the harbor."

I raised me eyebrows. "Me Daa says she carries cargo to our end of the island from time to time."

Mary flashed a knowing smile. "Gin. Tobacco. Timber. No harm in the Revenue Men missing things on occasion, me uncle says."

When she refilled me bowl, I reached hungrily for me spoon, and then suddenly pulled back.

"Go on. Don't tell me a boy all skin and bones like yourself doesn't want a second helping?"

"But your Midder. And the reverend. Surely we must save the rest for them?"

"Oh, you mustn't worry about that," she said with a wave of her hand. Then she pushed the bowl closer. "There's plenty for us all."

"It's just," I started, me fingers creeping slowly toward the spoon. "Well, Miss, I—I can't remember a time when I was allowed."

"To eat before the aged?"

"No." I dropped me gaze. "To have a second helping."

She was quiet for a moment and shifted in her chair. "I see," she said, then picked up her spoon and nodded for me to do the same. "You don't need to call me 'Miss.' 'Mary' suits me just fine, don't you think?"

"Aye," I mumbled. A smile crept from me lips even as the roof of me mouth burned once again.

"You're far from home."

"Searching for me brother, John."

"Lost, is he?"

"Hoot, no." I scraped the edges of the bowl with me spoon to get the last drippings of stew. "Ran from the croft last night in the storm."

"Didn't he tell you where he was going?" Mary asked, dropping her elbows on the table and resting her chin in her hands. "How rude."

"I have a hunch he'll be down at the docks." I glared at the bowl, feeling her eyes on me as I spoke. "Has something that dunna belong to him. Something I intend to get back before—"

The door flung open and Reverend Sill burst into the kitchen. "Young Robertson," he said, "Mrs. Canfield has shared with me more details about the situation here in Lerwick. The streets are not safe for a lad from the croft. You're to rest here the night and continue your search come daylight."

"But, sir," I said, springing to me feet, "I canna wait!"

"Bah! There's nothing so important it can't keep till the morn."

"I—"

But before I could continue, he raised his weathered hand in the air, then glared at me with his sunken, yellowing eyes. "Satan lurks in the shadows this dark night, lad—don't you doubt it for a minute. I forbid you to leave until daybreak."

I started to protest, when Mrs. Canfield strode in and placed a firm hand on me shoulder. "That settles it, then," she said, then sashayed in her brilliant blue dress to the door by the cupboard. "Mary, show Christopher to the shed. And be sure to get him a blanket. It can be quite drafty back there, I am afraid."

But no sooner had Mrs. Canfield started back to the stove than there was a pounding at the door.

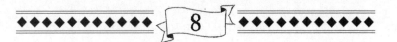

8

An Escape

Mary ushered me through the thin door separating the kitchen from the shed and closed it behind her. Then she lit the lantern hanging from the beam above us.

"Solus Christus!" I exclaimed as the light revealed all that was before me. "Me family could work ten years and not see the likes of this!"

In the corner I counted five sacks of flour. And above us on the rafters hung more pieces of drying meat and fish than I had ever seen in a home. There was a barrel of molasses, and several unmarked barrels that must have been coffee or tea. On the other side of the room, various tools leaned up against the back wall, and herbs and braided onions hung from a rope.

"Is your life so different?" Mary asked. "The past few years have been hard indeed, but surely there have been better times—when the fishing was good?"

I scoffed. "There's not a crofter in the parish gets a decent price for his cod."

"What of the markets in other villages? Surely they offer a fair price—"

"Burra or Scalloway? Hah! The last crofter who tried that was evicted by Mr. Marwick in three days' time. It's his price or we're gone."

"Mr. Marwick?"

I shrugged. "Without his credit we can't outfit our boats, much less buy our lines and supplies. Doesn't take but a few years of fishing the same failed banks till everyone's in so deep there's no way out."

Mary furrowed her brow. "There must be some way."

"You sound like me brother, John. He's full of ideas. And that's what's gotten me into this mess."

We heard voices in the kitchen and she beckoned me to a knothole in the door. "Shall we see who was pounding at the door?"

"Reverend Sill," we heard Mrs. Canfield say, walking back into the kitchen, "a rather large and insistent gentleman is here. He claims to be from your parish and insists on speaking with you about a matter of great urgency. I've tried to tell him of your exhaustion, and that he should return in the morning, but he refuses to leave—"

"Lor'," I gasped, me heart jumping to me throat. "He's found me already."

"Who?" Mary asked.

I put me finger to me lips as Reverend Sill settled into the chair I had been in just a few minutes before.

"If he's of my parish, I shall see him," the old man said. "As long as the Lord sees fit to keep me from that unchangeable state, I shall continue with my duties."

"Are ya sure?" Mrs. Canfield asked. "Mightn't you need your rest, having traveled those twenty miles all in one day?"

"Madam," he said with a sigh. "The Lord did not intend our journey through life to be one of leisure."

She stared at him for a moment, then snapped her hands to her hips. "As you wish. But I can't say I like the looks of this one. He's nettles in his beard and smells as though he hasn't bathed since Martinmas."

"I never shoulda' stayed," I whispered, springing to me feet. "Mary, is there a way out of here—where I won't be seen?"

"But Reverend Sill has forbidden it," Mary said. "Who is this person, anyway?"

"Knut Blackbeard."

"Such a peculiar name."

"Aye. He's a neighbor from Culswick. Thinks I've stolen me Daa's pouch of coins."

"Have you?" she asked, eyes widening.

"'Course not! But me brother, John, left Daa a note telling him was me who took it. And until I find John and get it back, it's his word against mine."

"Well, you best be sure it's him before you head out on the streets alone." She beckoned me back to the knothole as Mrs. Canfield returned, heavy footsteps thundering behind her.

"Ah, Mr. Blackbeard. Good evening," Reverend Sill said as Knut's forbidding form appeared in the doorframe. "Forgive me for not standing to greet you. My eighty-and-four years weigh heavy after a full day's travel."

"That's him all right," I whispered. "Mary—please. I've got to get out of here!"

"Why, he's positively frightening!" she said, taking her turn at the knothole. "And the stench—Midder was right about him needing a bath."

"I dunna think there's a tub big enough in all of Shetland," I muttered, looking about the shed for a way to escape.

"Look," she said. "Do you see those eyes? Midder hasn't the patience for this one. Not one bit."

I watched Mrs. Canfield glower at Knut as she ladled a large bowl of stew and brought it to the table for the reverend. "I'm sorry your meal is being interrupted, Reverend," she said, "but Mr. Blackbeard was most insistent."

"Look here, woman!" Knut barked, the flesh above his beard turning crimson. "This is a matter of the law!"

"Tuts, man," Reverend Sill chided. "You'll treat Mrs. Canfield with the utmost respect when in her home. Now tell me, how did you find me in Lerwick on a night such as this, when it has been months since you've found your way to the Kirk but a few miles from your home?"

Knut grunted. "They say you stay at Canfield House when you come to Lerwick. You weren't hard to find."

"And what can I do to assist you this evening?"

Knut turned sideways to fit his massive frame through the doorway, his dark eyes hungrily eyeing the pots of stew and stap at the fire.

"I'm in search a' the Robertson lad," he said, edging slowly to the table. "Sent by his Daa, I am."

Mrs. Canfield looked up.

"John or wee Christopher?" Reverend Sill asked.

"The wee un," he answered coldly. "With the bright ginger hair. Travelin' from the west, I glimpsed you in the distance. Thought sure you were walkin' with a lad that looked a lot like him."

I held me breath, too frightened to move, me fingers clutching the doorframe.

"Yes, indeed," Reverend Sill replied. "You are correct."

"You move spryly for a man a' so many years."

"The Lord provides me what is necessary."

"And the lad," Knut persisted. "Is he here?"

I froze, me eyes fixed on Reverend Sill, heart clanging in me chest. There was what seemed like a long silence as the aged man looked around the room.

"I don't see Christopher Robertson in here, do you, Mrs.

Canfield? Mr. Blackbeard, is there a problem with your eyes?"

"I'll not be made the fool!" Knut barked, leaning his face just inches from Reverend Sill's. "I know what I saw on that path today, Reverend!"

"Oh, there's no mistaking it, to be sure. He was kind enough to carry my kishie these twenty some miles."

"And now?"

"Come, man! Do you expect me to know the whereabouts of every lad I come across on the path from his parish to Lerwick?"

Rage flashed in Knut's eyes. "Well, then, you leave me no choice but to continue me search," he shouted, starting back to the parlor. "I'll show meself out!"

But just as I started to exhale, Reverend Sill pulled himself up from his chair. "What business, may I ask, do you have with the Robertson lad?"

Knut turned, a smile creeping around the wicks of his mouth.

"Stole William Robertson's coins, he did! And I aim to get 'em back."

"That's a harsh charge to lay on a lad as young as he."

Mary glanced at me as I shook me head.

"Aye. Well, it's the truth!" Knut said. "An' that's not all. Stole Pete Peterson's prize ewe the very same night. Carrying twins, she was."

I turned to Mary. "It was me Daa who stole her—not me!"

"An' that's not the worst of it," Knut continued, dropping

his face just inches from Reverend Sill's. I gasped, knowing what was coming next—the memory still strong in the very fingers of me right hand. To this day I don't know why, but at that moment, in every fiber of me body, I knew I couldn't let Mary, this lass I had just met, hear the truth about what I had done that night.

So before Knut uttered another word, I sprang to me feet and pulled her from the door. She looked at me, confused, as the sound of Knut's muffled voice droned on through the wall.

"I'm not a thief, Mary," I said, knowing in me heart that what I had done to that ewe was so much worse. And remembering me Midder's words that not telling the entire truth was nearly as bad as lying.

The silence weighed heavy between us. And then I looked down. "Just wanted you to know."

"Well, if it's any help, you don't look much like one to me."

I glanced at her, allowing me eyes to meet hers only for a moment. "How's that?"

"Running this boardinghouse, Midder and I have seen our share. Besides, I've never laid eyes on a lad as hungry as you. With a pouch full of coins, I suspect you'd be in a tavern by the wharf filling your belly rather than with me in my Midder's kitchen."

For a moment I almost managed a smile.

"So, tell me—why *aren't* you a thief?"

"Should I be?"

"Well, with your Daa and brother both taking a liking to it. Does it run in the family?"

I turned to the door to the kitchen and shuddered. "John, he's always had his brain filled with schemes and ideas to get off the croft. Sometimes I think he'd do anything to be free of Marwick—of this island. And Daa, he just thinks he's better than the rest." I took a deep breath. "All I know is that I have two wee sisters back at the croft, Catherine and Victoria, along with me Gutcher and aunt. Daa's lame, and now, with John gone, there's no one but me left to keep us going. If I don't get back with that pouch, the entire family'll be cast from the croft. What I want—all I truly want for me sisters and me—is to no longer be hungry."

I searched the room with me eyes, knowing that, with this new information from Knut, Reverend Sill would have no choice but to take me to Sheriff Nicolson.

"Mary, I've a hunch John'll be searching for smuggled goods at the docks—to buy and resell for a profit. Then he's off to America on the first boat he can find. I have to find him *before* he spends those coins, or I'll never have a chance to clear me name." I looked at her, knowing she had no reason in the world to help me. "Please—can you show me a way out of here?"

And to me surprise she nodded. Then she quickly rolled away the barrel of molasses at her side. Underneath was the outline of a door cut into the floor. "Through here. It leads through the cellar to the back of the house."

"Thank you!" I said, lifting it up as quietly as possible and swinging me legs onto the ladder down the opening. "Please—" I started, knowing I had no time to spare and yet, somehow, not wanting to leave. "If I can ever return the favor . . ."

"Perhaps you can. Tell me, Chris Robertson," she whispered, "can you keep a secret?"

"Aye. Though you have no reason to trust that I will."

"These past few nights—I myself have been sneaking down to the docks."

"Alone?"

"Aye."

"But is that not," I thought a moment, choosing me words carefully, "unseemly? For a young lass to be out alone, I mean. And at night?"

She looked away quickly. "Aye. Midder discovered me just last night and nearly tanned me backside. She made me promise I'd never try again. But, you see, should me uncle return unwarned—"

"They'll seize the *Ernestine Brennan*."

"Aye. And everything she's carrying. Ever since the fishing started failin', Mr. Marwick's increased his trips to Rotterdam. This is Uncle's fourth trip there this year."

"For gin?"

She bit her lip. "I suspect as much. And should the Revenue Men search the ship, Uncle will be sent to Lerwick Prison."

The sound of Knut Blackbeard's voice droned on through the door. "Mary, should I see the *Ernestine Brennan*, I'll do me best to warn your uncle. But I'm afraid I'm fairly hopeless finding me way in the dark, even on me end of the island."

Mary frowned. "The directions are a bit hard to explain."

I cringed, picturing the time I would waste turning up and down the narrow, dark lanes we had passed. "Aye. Well, I'll manage."

But as I started down the ladder, she suddenly grabbed me arm. "Wait—I'll show you the way."

"Lor', lass, you canna do that," I whispered, surprised by her touch. "You heard your Midder—the lanes are filled with drunken rioters. And for all you know, I could be the thief Knut Blackbeard says I am."

"Well, you're far too young to be a good one," she said, a smile sneaking from her lips.

"But you heard the reverend. It's not safe!"

"And if the *Ernestine Brennan* arrives tonight? Who's to warn Uncle and Charles?"

"Surely Mr. Marwick's thought of that."

"Hah!" she said, releasing her grip. "He's in Edinburgh trying to get the loan. No one expects him back till month's end."

Suddenly she grabbed a hap from a hook by a sack of flour. Then she sprang over to a high-domed kist against the wall and pulled out a canvas sack. "The choice is yours, Christopher Robertson," she said, thrusting the sack so forcefully into me chest that she nearly knocked me down the ladder. "Waste time lost in the dark streets of Lerwick or take someone who knows the way."

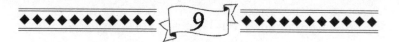

9

George

We climbed from the cellar through a narrow window into the courtyard behind Canfield House.

"That Blackbeard man'll be looking for a crofter." Mary wrapped the hap tightly around her head and shoulders as the unpredictable Shetland wind whipped about us. Then she stuck her hand into the sack and pulled out a thickly woven, dark blue coat. "Leave your gansey here and put on this."

Me eyes widened as I ran me calloused fingers along the soft wool.

"It's Charles's," she explained, "but he hasn't fit in it in years.

It's what I use to disguise myself when I sneak down to the wharf."

"Perhaps it's not me place," I said, hesitating before pulling me frayed gansey over me head.

"Don't be silly!" she replied, helping me into the coat and quickly fastening the four brilliant brass buttons. Then she reached back in the bag and laughed. "Here's the cap. I'm guessing they don't dress like this back in Culswick."

Me face hardened as I slipped the cap awkwardly on me head, though I had to admit she was right. "Aye. I'd be surprised if even John recognized me now."

"Now—the breeks. Go on! Quickly! It won't be long before they discover we're gone."

I jumped back, me face growing hot. "Well, I'll not be stripping to me underdraws in front of you, if that's what you're thinking!"

She laughed. "Behind the hedge with you, then, just by the rock wall." She searched the bag again and handed over a pair of boots. "Try these, but no dallying. They might be a bit large, but that's better than having them squeeze your toes."

Boots! There wasn't a single member of me family who had ever had a pair of boots, not even Daa. I was stunned by the stiff feeling around me ankles and calves and the firmness of the soles.

"Will they work?" Mary asked as I stepped from behind the hedge, trying not to look as pleased as I was to be wearing such fine clothes. "Because if they rub the wrong way, I guess

it wouldn't be the end of the world if you kept your rivlins on."
She must have seen me smiling in the moonlight. "Good, then.
Now, be sure to tuck your things behind a rock in the wall
where no one will see them."

I could hardly contain meself, tapping each heel to toe.
Imagine—after all that had happened, I was standing in Lerwick wearing a pair of boots!

"Must you clunk so?" Mary chided as we raced across the
cobblestones. Me steps seemed louder than thunder, the rhythmic *click, click, click* with every stride.

But we had hardly reached the end of the street when we
started hearing voices. And then we saw the shadows cast by
a group of staggering men. They were singing in a tongue I
didn't recognize.

"Mariners—stranded, no doubt. Waiting for Marwick's
pay," she whispered, pulling me quickly into the shadows of a
neighboring house. "They've been carousing every night this
week—filled with fire whiskey."

We crouched low, hardly daring to take a breath as they
meandered by. When they were at last out of sight, she led
me down a maze of narrow, high-walled lanes, each lined with
stone houses and buildings so close to one another that there
was only a few feet of space between them. If I had ever had
a sense of where Hillhead was and how to get back, it was instantly gone.

The air was chill, the smell of rotting fish and smoldering
peat wafting about us until, finally, Mary stopped at an inter-

section and pointed down a lane that curved sharply to the left. "Just one quick stop down here and we'll be on our way."

"Stop? What for?" And then it dawned on me how foolish I'd been. Not only did I hardly know this girl, I had no idea where exactly she was leading me.

"Chris Robertson, there are hundreds of docks in Lerwick Harbor! If we want to find what we're looking for, we need to know where to look."

"You said you *knew* where to look!"

"Told you I knew how to get to the docks. But in case no one's explained, Lerwick's got more than you can count. That's why we need George. If anyone knows of goods coming in, it's he."

"George, Mary—you've been kind, but I need to find me brother *tonight*. I've no time for meeting—"

"Shhh!" she chided, grabbing me arm and practically dragging me to the end of the lane, past two imposing stone pillars to an elegant, three-gabled house. "Do you want all of Lerwick to know we're here?" Then she unlatched the iron gate to the courtyard, and together we crept through the formal gardens in the back.

"What're you up to?" I asked as she motioned me into the shadows, picked up some pebbles, and then, with precise aim, lightly tossed one after another at a lit window on the second floor.

It wasn't but a few moments before the window shot open and the head of a plump-faced young man, not much older than John, popped out.

"Mary?" he called. "Is that you?"

"Well, of course it is!" she said, dropping her hap to her shoulders.

"What are you doing down here on a night such as this? Don't you know the streets aren't safe?"

"Aye!" she said. "It's important!"

The young man rubbed his hand across his brow and sighed. "All right, then."

A minute later the back door swung open.

He was taller than me by at least a foot, his curly hair wetted and combed over to the side in an attempt to calm its naturally unruly state. He was dressed as a gentleman, wearing a white shirt with a dark cravat tied at his neck, and his vast belly strained the buttons of his gold silk vest. He smiled warmly at Mary, but I couldn't help noticing that his eyes seemed filled with fatigue and worry.

"There's no one here but me tonight," he said, ushering her into a kitchen twice the size of the one in Canfield House, stopping short as Mary beckoned me from the shadows.

"George, meet Christopher Robertson of Culswick," she said. "He needs your help."

He glanced at me, eyes narrowed, and then back at Mary before tentatively extending his hand. "George Marwick," he said.

"M-M-Marwick?" I asked, looking at Mary, aghast.

"Come, now," he said, his thick pink jowls spilling over his collar. "I can't be that frightening."

"Wallace Marwick is George's Daa," Mary explained. "You can trust him."

I stared at him, mouth ajar. Until that moment it had never occurred to me that Wallace Marwick, the person who caused me family and so many others such anguish and suffering, had a son, much less a family. "*The* Wallace Marwick?" I asked, wondering how anyone could have so wide a girth in times such as these.

"The very same," Mary said. "George and my brother, Charles, have been close friends since they were bairns."

She looked quickly about the room as I stood frozen in place. "Where's Cook?"

George scowled. "Gone—since last Tuesday. The manservant gone as well. Daa thought it best."

"But they've been with the family all your life!"

"Aye, and until we get a shipment we can turn over quickly, we have nothing to pay their wages."

He waddled to the fire, adding several bricks of peat to the flames, then showed us to the chairs around a table in the corner. I shifted uncomfortably in me seat as Mary explained the story of John taking Daa's coins, while George stared down, stroking sunken eyes and arched eyebrows as if trying to rub away a nagging headache.

"We need to know," she continued, "where someone might go with a pouch full of shillings he hopes to invest. Where, perhaps, there could be some *unofficial* activities that he might be trying to get a part of."

"And I suppose you wouldn't mind finding out something about when the *Ernestine Brennan* is expected, am I right?" he asked.

She smiled, placing her hand on his plump arm. "I knew you would understand."

"Mary, lass," he said, smiling at her hand, "why on earth do you always get yourself wrapped up in trouble like this? For once in your life, can't you simply stay home and be content to help out your Midder?"

"Hah!" she laughed, jumping to her feet. "I wouldn't know what trouble was if I hadn't spent so much time all these years with the likes of you and Charles."

For a moment his eyes came to life, a mischievous smile cracking his sullen features. But when he finally spoke his expression darkened considerably. "Things have changed, Mary. I'm not at liberty to talk about any shipments, much less the whereabouts of the *Ernestine Brennan*. Daa's trusting me to keep our business affairs to myself. There's just too much at stake."

"But—with your Daa in Edinburgh—I thought surely you'd be free to—"

"Aye! And left me here to appease the coopers, carpenters, sail cutters, blacksmiths, mariners, and warehousemen who haven't been paid in a month. Or haven't you heard? Mary, you've no idea how dire the situation has become. They say there'll be rioting again tomorrow if I don't get them something!"

His story sounded so pitiful that, for a moment, I almost felt sorry for him.

"Imagine," she said, snapping her hands to her hips, "leaving a lad in charge. Whatever was Mr. Marwick thinking?"

"I'm not so much a lad!" he quipped. "I'm nearly eighteen! And don't you see, Mary, there's no one else. Daa let Mr. Burns go last week, and he's been keeping the Marwick books for over twenty years. Should Daa not be successful getting the loan from the Royal Bank of Scotland, we'll lose the ships, the store, the bank, this house even!"

"So it's as Midder feared. I didn't want to believe it. The moment the *Ernestine Brennan*'s discovered in the harbor, she'll be searched and seized for debts. Oh, George—we must warn Uncle! If they find what's on board he'll be sent to prison!"

"That's for me to worry about," he said, flashing her a stern look. "I'll be keeping watch at the docks tonight with that very purpose."

"Wonderful! We'll go with you!"

He jumped to his feet. "You'll do no such thing! This is no night to be out in the streets. Now come. I'll see you home and get on with my business."

"I'll see her home," I blurted, not knowing what I wanted more—for Mary to be safe or simply away from George Marwick. He who nearly burst the buttons of his vest while me wee sisters were nothing but skin and bones. "We've taken too much of your time already."

"Will you, then?" Mary asked, surprising me with a glare.

"And who put you in charge? Seems you have your own worries with that Blackbeard man looking for you."

I glanced away, face hot, wondering for the second time that night how I could have been so brash. What was it about Mary Canfield that made me say things I shouldn't say?

"Aye," I mumbled, turning to the door. "I'll be off, then. Sorry to have troubled you, Mr. Marwick."

"By yourself?" she asked, as me hand grabbed the latch. "Heavens, no! You'll be lost before you get four feet from here. Seeing how George won't give us even a hint of information, I'm coming with you."

But as she turned to me side, George quickly maneuvered his overstuffed frame between us. "All right, all right," he muttered. "If you must know, there's a ship due tonight with an important cargo from Rotterdam. Robertson's brother may have heard word of it among the men along the shore."

"Where will she be docking?" Mary asked.

He hesitated a moment. "The Marwick Lodberry. Our men are expecting her."

"Lodberry?" I asked.

"A building built out into the harbor," Mary explained. "The shore is lined with them. Makes it easy for the merchants to receive their cargo."

"From Rotterdam?" I asked. "Gin, is it?"

"Aye," George nodded. "And the only shipment expected for some time."

He walked back to the fire and added another brick of peat.

"Daa left me with strict orders to make sure everything goes without a hitch, there being a great urgency to move goods of high value as quickly and as secretly as possible."

"Then it's the *Ernestine Brennan* you're speaking of," Mary said.

"Aye, lass. I knew I shouldn't have told you! So don't go getting any ideas about going down there with him! We *absolutely cannot* risk drawing attention to her, or the Queen's Revenue Men will come aboard and make an inspection. The Crown already knows we're desperate. They'll be keeping watch."

"Wouldn't there be less risk unloading her cargo on me side of the island?" I asked.

"Naturally!" George said, eyeing me with a look of disdain. "But we haven't been able to get word to Captain Canfield. The man has no idea how badly things have turned while he has been away."

"But casks of gin—where can you hide them when they're unloaded?" I pressed. "You canna tell me Lerwick has hidden caves like we have in Culswick."

George glanced at Mary and then back at me. "Unloading within sight of the Revenue Men is far from ideal, but our lodberry is quite capable of taking the shipment."

"It has an underground passage," Mary explained. "Connects the warehouse to the store across the street. Me Daa helped build it."

"You unload under the nose of the Revenue Men and never pay the duty?"

"Of course," George said. "There must be ten other lodber-ries just like it along the Lerwick shore. After all, a Shetlander doesn't build a fortune such as ours on dried cod." He swallowed hard. "This time, of course, things are a bit more complicated. The gin we off-load in this shipment will only tide us over for a bit. So the *Ernestine Brennan*'ll be taking on a most special cargo from our lodberry when she gets in—from me Daa's own supply. We think there's a buyer in Belfast. Making *that* delivery is our only chance to survive."

"Even with the loan from the Bank of Scotland?" Mary asked.

"They've as much as told us there'll be no more loans. Daa's journey to Edinburgh is a formality."

"And if the Revenue Men discover the *Ernestine Brennan*?" I asked.

George looked up, expressionless. "The Marwick enterprise collapses and the entire island goes hungry."

Suddenly the peril of the situation hit me. No matter what I thought of Wallace Marwick, without him there would be no more loans for fishing lines and bait. No more credit for boats and lines. No more fish to sell, no matter the meager price. No more chandlers, sailmakers, or coopers. Should he go down, all of Shetland would go down with him.

"But they won't discover her!" Mary said, ushering me though the door. "We'll see to it!"

"What do you mean 'we'?" George asked, slamming his thick arm over the latch. "My Daa put me in charge of getting

Captain Canfield his instructions. I'm to trust no one in my place."

Suddenly there was loud chanting from the street at the front of the house.

"Marwick!" a voice shouted. "We know you're in there. Pay up or live to see the consequences!"

George's face turned ashen. "The workers from the docks!"

Mary and I followed him into the parlor facing the street. I gaped at its plush furniture, crystal chandeliers, and warm, colorful carpets as George quickly slid the thick brass bolt across the front door.

"Been coming round every night this week screaming and hollering with torches and clubs," he said.

"Are they daft?" Mary asked. "They must know you have nothing to give."

"Aye," I muttered. "But that doesn't stop them from being mad and hungry. It's his Daa owes them their wages."

George shot me an icy glare.

Then there was a wild cheer from the street and, to our horror, a rock the size of a small cat came smashing through the window, just missing Mary and showering her boots with glass.

"Lor', lass! Are you hurt?" George cried. He stumbled to her side and lifted her back to the kitchen, with me close at his heels. "If anything should happen to you . . . ," he said, kneeling before her and picking frantically at the shards of glass on her boots.

"I'm fine," she said. But her voice was trembling.

"Then out the back with you—quickly!" he commanded, taking her hand and pulling her to the door. "It's not safe!"

"We canna leave you to fend for yourself," I said. He might be Wallace Marwick's son, but I wasn't about to leave a lad alone with a drunken mob at his door.

George stared at me a moment, as if shocked by me offer, then puffed out his chest.

"I've held them off this long," he said. "Another night won't be the end of it. Besides, Sheriff Nicolson promised me Daa that his men would keep watch on the house. Lor' knows Nicolson owes him some favors after all these years."

"Are you sure?" Mary asked, grabbing his sleeve, hand trembling. "Promise me you'll be safe."

"Aye, lass! And I'll get to the lodberry—eventually! Now leave—quickly—before they catch a glimpse of you!"

But as I followed her out the door, George's thick fingers held fast to me arm. "Robertson, is it? From Culswick? A Marwick tenant, are you not?"

I nodded, me breath quickening as he spoke.

"I remember the name from my Daa's books, your rent being long past due. Do you deny it?"

"I cannot," I said, willing meself to stare defiantly into his deep-set eyes.

"Then it's in *my* hands that your Daa's pouch of coins belongs, is it not?"

I looked away, brow furrowed, his words slicing into me

like the shards of glass he had just brushed from Mary's boots. "You own me, sir," I breathed. "You own us all."

George nodded, eyes narrowing, and then leaned but inches from me ear.

"Then know this," he hissed, sweat forming on his pale, dimpled brow. "See to it Mary Canfield gets safely home and then bring me those coins. *By morning.* Or I'll have your family cast from their croft by week's end."

Spit flew through the gaps in his brilliant white teeth as he spoke.

"Do we understand each other, crofter?"

"Aye, we do." Hate flooded like venom into me veins as it never had before. "We understand each other perfectly."

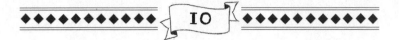

10

The Lodberry

Stop! Mary!" I raced after her down a dark alley, darting left and then right, until finally I reached her side. "Where are you going?"

"To the shore, of course. To warn me uncle. But we must take the back lanes to avoid being seen."

I grabbed fast to her arm and pulled her around. "Thought George was taking care of that," I said. "Besides, I gave him me word I'd get you home."

"Hah!" She pulled her arm free. "With townspeople rioting at his window? He'll never get away. Besides, you can't find your way in the dark. Why, I bet you couldn't find your way back to Hillhead even if you had a compass!"

"It's not safe," I said. "You can't walk the streets at night with rioting mariners round every corner!"

"Aye, but I can. Been doing it every night for the past week." She turned from me and marched ahead. "Someone has to warn me uncle."

"George said he'd—"

"Trust me, he won't."

"Then I'll do it. I'm headed there to find John. Just tell me how to get—"

"Chris Robertson," she said, turning abruptly down a narrow lane to her right, "you've no idea where you are. If you're not careful, it'll be that smelly Blackbeard man you'll find— not your brother."

As I opened me mouth to protest, she cut me off with a wave of her hand. "Either follow or let me be. I'll not be returning home just yet."

The moon was high when we finally came upon the marketplace along the water. Despite George Marwick's parting threats ringing in me ears, I couldn't keep me eyes from darting to the shop windows along the shore, all brimming with things I had never before laid eyes on. T. Shakman, Clockmaker, with all sizes of clocks, their pendulums swaying back and forth as if in a frenzy. Van der Kloot Chandlers, with its stacks of ropes and lines, barrels of tar and turpentine, mops and brooms. Beatrice Le'Hare Sweets and Confections, with its cakes, bowls of licorice, and platters of what Mary told me were called pralines. How was it possible, I wondered, that people had even a copper to spare to purchase such goods?

When we passed Larsen Brothers Map Makers, I could hardly break meself away.

"Have you never seen a map?" Mary asked.

"Aye, I have. Just one. Not nearly as fine as this."

I was looking at a map of the British Isles propped on a stand directly against the glass, beautifully colored with greens, reds, and blues.

"There," Mary said, pointing to the north of Ireland. "That's Belfast. Near where me Daa and Midder are from." Then she pointed to a cluster of islands to the north of Scotland. "Here's all of Shetland. And here's Lerwick."

I studied it a moment, running me finger from Lerwick to Skeld Voe, and then a bit farther to the west. "This is me home. In Culswick."

"Are there many crofts?"

"Och, no. Only five. All tenants on Marwick land. But the scattald is a sight in the summer—a deeper green you'll never see. And there's an ancient broch, just up here," I said, pointing to where I guessed it must be. "The view is grand. You can see as far as Fair Isle when the sky is clear."

Suddenly there were voices.

"Quick—back here!" Mary said.

We ducked into the shadows at the corner of the building

and watched in silence as a group of men, one carrying a jug and the others stumbling behind him, drew closer. When the fellow with the jug fell to his knees and began to retch, the others erupted in laughter.

"Ah, old Mick canna take the whiskey!" a balding man with a short-cropped beard taunted. He kicked the fallen man squarely in the gut. I winced as the other men laughed, thinking of Daa and Knut when they'd had too much of the gin.

"Hey! You dunna boot a mate when he's down," another said, charging the balding man and pulling him to the ground. They twisted and rolled on the sand, just feet from where we squatted, snarling and punching as the others cheered.

Then, suddenly, the balding man drew a knife.

It was when Mary gasped that I grabbed fast to her hand and pulled us back through an alley between the buildings, so narrow that we had to turn sideways to fit. Not daring to utter a sound, we sped through a courtyard behind a church in the next block, there discovering a path between houses leading up what appeared to be a bluff above the wharf. Fearing even to look behind us, we raced up the steep incline, stopping only when the path ended abruptly, high above the harbor, at a towering wall of lichen-covered stone.

"Lerwick has a castle?" I asked.

"Och, no—the fort is all," she said, her chest still heaving.

"Royal Artillery?"

"Aye. Me Daa told me it was built long ago to ward off the Dutch, but then it was left in ruins until King George rebuilt it and named it for his wife. The main barracks was turned over to the county a few years back for the Sheriff Court and Prison."

"This is . . . *Fort Charlotte?*"

"Aye."

I looked at her, heart racing, remembering John's words in the broch—*They say those that get locked up are never seen again.* "Well, I'll not be lingering, then." I nearly choked on me words. "Come, lass, quickly—let's get on to the shore!"

We crept along in the moonlight, finding another path on the far side of the bluff leading back down to the street. Before us the harbor sparkled in the moonlight, a stiff breeze over the water. Mary pointed to the gray stone buildings, jutting like thick fingers into the rippling waves of Bressay Sound.

"Lodberries," she whispered.

Except for the sound of our steps and the clanging of ships anchored in the harbor, this part of Lerwick was eerily silent. "Are you sure you know where we're going?" I asked when we reached the water.

Mary nodded. Not long after, she stopped at a plain oak door with a heavy iron latch. Above the transom, in gold block letters, were the words WALLACE MARWICK, MERCHANT.

I peered into the window but couldn't make anything out. Then I tried muscling open the latch.

"Shhh!" she whispered and closed her warm hand over mine. "If the warehouseman's here, he'll hear you."

I looked up, startled by her touch, but she quickly pulled her hand away and pointed to a wide ramp of stone that ran along the outside of the lodberry. "Let's get a better look."

We tiptoed out to the end, but the lodberry was deserted. I gazed at the schooners and sloops moored before us, bobbing and creaking in the harbor. "Perhaps your George has the night wrong."

"*My* George?" Mary asked, an eyebrow raised. "And what are you meaning by that?"

"I saw the way you looked at him, Miss. And how he looked at you."

"You think yourself an authority on such things, do you?" she asked, hands to her hips. "A lad from the croft?"

"Not nearly as learned as you Lerwick folk, I suspect."

"Well, I don't see you holding down your Daa's business and protecting your family home from rioting mariners."

"Ah, so you're defending him, then?" I scoffed. "He who's gone to battle with the sheriff by his side?"

Her eyes narrowed as she rounded on me. "You mock him, do you? And what about being grateful! Wasn't it he who told you where you could find your brother?"

"Grateful?" I turned up me head in disgust. "For what? The years of keeping me family half-starved so his Daa can have his bank and his ships, and his fine gabled house? For me wee sisters, waiting at home, no food in their bellies—me kin left with debt they can never repay?"

I stormed back up the ramp to the street.

"I'm sorry," she called, following after me. But I was too angry to face her. "I didn't know."

"Aye. Well, I guess you Lerwick folk *don't* know everything, now, do you?"

For the moment we stood in silence. I had never felt so hopeless or unsure of what to do.

"Come," I said, starting back down the shore. "Let's get you back to Hillhead before I face George's wrath, your Midder sends out the sheriff, or both."

"No!" she said, grabbing me hand and pulling me around. "Wait with me."

I stood for a moment, teeth clenched, but when I finally brought meself to look at her, I was startled to see tears in the corners of her eyes. "Don't be foolish, lass," I said softly. "What if this isn't the night? What if they never come?"

"But they will—they must! And if they do, chances are your brother will be here too." Her voice was strong and unwavering. "Please, Chris. I can't leave until I'm sure. I can't let Uncle go to Lerwick Prison for Mr. Marwick."

The breeze chilled our faces and hands as we crouched across the street from Marwick's lodberry, scanning the dark harbor for signs of the *Ernestine Brennan*. And it was there, in the hours that followed, huddled on the wretchedly cold sand, that I told her about me life in Culswick. About Daa, Gutcher, Aunt Alice, me troublesome sisters, Catherine and Victoria. And about losing dear William and the death of me Midder—

things I'd never spoken of to anyone else before. I told her of Culswick Broch, of its carving of a tree, so strange on the treeless island of Shetland, and of everything that had happened in its crumbled walls on the night of the gale.

"What made him do it?" she asked when I told her of John's letter.

I shrugged, glancing out at the harbor. "For as long as I can remember, he's wanted to break free. To find a better life." I thought of George Marwick and his small, menacing eyes. "I can't say I blame him."

"And you? Did you ever dream of something better?"

I looked away. "Aye. At one time I fancied a life as a blacksmith. Having me own forge, working by the warmth of the fire instead of the cold of the sea. But Daa'd never allow it. And lately, with the times as desperate as they've been, what I've wanted mostly is to fill me belly."

For a while I listened eagerly to her tales of Lerwick and what she knew of Ireland and the family she had never known, and then me eyes grew heavy. It must have been well past midnight when I finally nodded off, only to be jolted awake moments later by her head dropping onto me shoulder. At first afraid to exhale for fear I'd disturb her, I glanced at the delicate contour of her gently closed eyelids, unable to remember a moment when I had been so thrilled and so terrified at the same time. For the next hour, the damp sand pressing uncomfortably into me bones, I sat alert, not daring to move for fear of interrupting the gentle breath at me shoulder.

The wind was picking up and a bank of clouds was moving away from the moon when I thought I saw the faint outline of a ship in the sound. And then, almost immediately, I heard voices coming from the lodberry.

"Mary," I whispered, gently nudging her awake. "I think I see her."

She looked at first as if she didn't know where she was, then shyly pulled away. "I must have dozed off."

I leaned forward, pointing to the silhouette of a packet dropping her sail, and then sprang to me feet. "It's the *Ernestine Brennan*, all right! Do you hear the voices on the lodberry?"

We crept across the street, finding the door now unlatched, and slipped inside. It was a large, nearly empty space. In the moonlight, through the windows facing the water, we could see the shadows of several men standing on the ramp.

"They're waiting to unload," Mary whispered as we watched a yoal loaded with casks row toward the lodberry from the ship. Then, suddenly, from the corner of me eye I saw a small, wiry man spring in front of me and grab Mary from behind.

"Leave her!" I shouted as he wrapped his bulging, tattooed arms tightly around her waist. But as I lunged at him, another pair pulled me back.

"What're you two doin' creepin' round at this time a' night?"

I wrenched me head to see the bearded face of a broad-chested man. He wore a knitted cap pulled down to his bushy eyebrows, his breath hot on me neck.

"I can explain!" Mary cried.

"Hah!" the wiry man exclaimed, slapping his hand over her mouth. "And you'll do just that when we're through with ye!"

Her eyes were wide with fear as I struggled toward her.

"You're making a mistake," I cried. "We mean no harm!"

But before I could say more, the man with the cap slapped a wet, calloused hand over me mouth.

I twisted and squirmed as Mary stamped her boots down on the wiry man's feet and kicked at his shins.

"A fighter, are ye?" he sneered. "We'll see about that when we get these barrels unloaded. For now we need you nice and quiet."

A third man appeared, gagging us with tattered rags that tasted of rotting fish. Then he bound our wrists and ankles before dragging us against the wall behind the door.

"We'll be back for you when we're done," he snarled. The three of them turned to rejoin the other men on the pier.

For what seemed like hours we struggled, rubbing the ropes around our wrists together in hopes of loosening the knots, all the while listening to the grunts and groans as the men silently unloaded the casks of gin rowed in from the *Ernestine Brennan.* Then we heard them haul cask after cask up from a small opening in the floor of the Marwick Lodberry, of what we assumed was Marwick's special cargo bound for Belfast.

Why hadn't I insisted we go back to Hillhead? Perhaps if I had told Reverend Sill all of what had happened that night in the broch, he might have helped. Now there was no going back, no chance of escape.

Then a new voice broke the silence—and the minute Mary heard it, it was as if she had been stung by a swarm of bees. "Where's Mr. Marwick? He was to send instructions." It came from a young man, I surmised, his words clear and direct. As he continued to speak, she somehow propelled herself up and started awkwardly hopping on her bound feet toward the door to the ramp.

The bearded man grunted. "Ain't no one here, sir."

I couldn't get meself up, so I shimmied like a worm in Mary's direction, splinters catching the seat of Charles's fine wool breeks.

"Just some intruders snoopin' round the place before ya arrived," the man continued.

"Intruders?"

"Aye—a lass and lad is all. Tryin' ta pinch from yer master's store. Seen too much of this operation for their own good—I'll get rid of 'em, sir, once you're back aboard."

Just then, Mary lost her balance and crashed loudly against the wall.

"Lor', man—you don't have them secured?" the young man scolded. "Do you have any idea the value of the cargo we're picking up?" He burst through the door, but as he flung himself across the threshold, he tripped over Mary and landed face-first on her chest.

"It canna be!" he cried, staring at her, his face ashen. Then he scrambled to his feet and scooped her bound body high in his arms. "Mary—what are you doing here?"

"Ye know 'er, sir?" the bearded man growled.

"Lor', man! That's me sister!"

The wiry man looked about nervously as Charles Canfield pulled a knife from his belt, cut her gag, and sliced through her ropes.

"I'm here to warn you and Uncle!" she sputtered, spitting the remains of the foul-tasting cloth from her mouth. "But this brute of a man gagged me before I had a chance."

As she quickly explained the troubles with Marwick, the bearded man cut me ropes, thinking, I'm sure, that I, too, might be someone with whom he should take care.

"Lor', lass, we've no time to lose!" Charles said. He took no notice of me as he quickly ushered her out to the small boat loaded with casks waiting at the edge of the ramp. "This is our last load. We'll row you back to the ship to Uncle, while these men make fast work of stashing the gin we're leaving behind."

"But Midder! Oh, Charles—I must confess, she doesn't know I'm here," Mary said as I watched silently in the doorway.

Charles looked at her, aghast, shaking his head. "Well, there's no helping it now. I can't leave you with the streets as you say they are. Uncle will find a way to get you back to shore by morning if we can get safely south of the Customs House."

Only then did he look in me direction.

"Who's that? And—is that me coat he's wearing?"

"I can explain," I said, inching toward them.

"Aye. And you'll do more than that!" Charles said.

"She's come to no harm. I've seen to that."

"No harm? What do you call being bound and gagged? If I hadn't come upon you, there's no tellin' what these men would have done with her!"

"Charles, please," Mary said. And she looked at me. "His name is Christopher Robertson. He's a friend. I asked him to wait with me."

Charles's eyes darted between mine and Mary's. Then he helped her gently into the yoal, and beckoned me to the edge of the ramp.

"When this business is attended to," he said, stepping aboard, bobbing with the ebb and flow of the sea, "I'll be back. And if I find you've been a threat to me sister—"

"Mr. Canfield, sir," a tall, ruddy-faced man sitting at the oars interrupted. "The captain's flashed the signal ten minutes ago."

"Aye, Mr. McNutt," Charles said. And as the yoal moved away from the lodberry, loaded with the last of Marwick's secret cargo, I saw the sails of the *Ernestine Brennan* unfurling in the moonlight in anticipation of a rapid departure. "Remember me words, Robertson. Because I won't forget."

Me throat tightened, a dull ache spreading through me chest as I watched Mary disappear in the night. Behind me, I heard the grunts and groans of the men quickly moving the newly unloaded casks of gin down a trapdoor in the lodberry.

"She's a bonnie lass, Brother," a voice said. "You've done well for yourself this first trip to Lerwick."

John's gaunt face stared back in the moonlight. He was leaning against a cask of gin, his hands resting casually at his hips. In the excitement of the evening I had almost forgotten it was he whom I had been looking for.

For a moment I nearly smiled, basking in the familiar warm features of his face—the immediate comfort of seeing someone from home. And then everything that had happened the night before came rushing back to me. How I waited in the broch for the signal that never came. The faces of me sisters thinking me a thief. The letter.

"The Devil be with ye, John Robertson!" I cried.

"Easy now, lad. Is that any way to greet your own flesh and blood?"

"Flesh and blood, is it? And the letter you left Daa? Was that your way of looking out for your brother?"

"Come, now. How else was I going to buy the time I needed to get to Skeld? Someone had to get those coins out of the Ol' Cod's hands."

"And accuse me a' doing the stealing? What kind of brother does something so dark?"

"Och—I knew a lad as smart as you'd get away in good time. And see—I was right. Here you are, surrounded by casks of Dutch gin and wearing the clothes of a gentleman."

So it was true! As much as I had told meself that there had to be an explanation, that he could never do such a thing—he *had* meant to betray me. I'd been his pawn all along. "Had Daa found me, he'd have beaten me to a pulp and sent me straight to the sheriff. It was pure luck I slipped away when I did."

John's nose twitched, eyes darting from left to right. "And

let's not forget what you did to Mr. Peterson's ewe, lad," he said. "I warned you that night in the broch."

I quickly looked away.

"Cheer up, Chris. We've made it. Finally broken free! I had it worked out all along. Just a few more days and we'll have the cash we need to buy passage to America."

"What? And leave Catherine and Victoria here to starve?" I bellowed, charging at his bony chest. "I've had enough of your schemes, John Robertson! Now hand over that pouch!"

But, as always, he was too quick, grabbing me wrists the moment I got near and slamming me hard against the rough stone wall of the lodberry.

"Keep it down, lads," warned the wiry man who had attacked Mary. Then he shoved John aside and locked his tattooed arms tightly around me neck. "You'll alert the Revenue Men and get us all tossed in Lerwick Prison before we get the Dutch goods below!"

John nodded, his expression cool. "Understood. I'll keep him quiet." But when the man finally released me and moved back to work, a mischievous smile erupted on John's face. Then he nodded to the top of a cask by his side. "Why don't you just take it?"

It was the pouch! Lying in the moonlight. But the moment me fingers touched the soft, worn leather, a powerful blow knocked me to me knees.

"Ain't yers to take," growled the bearded man with the knitted cap. Then he drove his boot into me gut with such force that I wondered if he had split me insides. "This lad's paid for his share fair and square," he said, stuffing the pouch in his breeks. "Marwick's first customer of the evenin'."

"You spent it—*all*?" I gasped, doubled over in pain. "On smuggled gin?"

"Aye—and at the price of my liking," John said with a wry smile. "But don't worry yourself, Brother. Seems Marwick's more desperate for cash than I thought. And this island's so desperate for hooch I already have a customer. You remember Murdoch Bairnstrom—Lord Cummingsburgh's factor? He's already on his way."

Rage quickly replaced the agony in me head and side. In an instant I gathered every bit of strength I had left and hurled me hands to his neck, remembering too late how his strength and agility had always surpassed mine. It took but a single jolt of his knee to me gut and he had me face-first onto the hard, cold ramp. For a moment I saw nothing, the pain too unbearable, blood dripping from me nose. And then, as his tattered rivlins came into focus, I clamped me hands onto his ankles.

Once, twice, I yanked—until he toppled down beside me. Then we rolled—scratching, hitting, and kicking—so close to the edge that I thought we might both fall into the sea. It wasn't until I heard the sound of Charles Canfield's fine woolen jacket rip and felt the piercing force of John's teeth cut into the flesh of me shoulder that I screamed in agony. But when I turned and saw the thick-soled boot at me cheek, it was already too late.

Malcolm MacPherson

Knut Blackbeard grunted. "Them's the brothers I been tellin' you about, Sheriff Nicolson." He raised a lantern over John and me as we lay entangled on the ramp.

And then he pointed a thick, grimy finger at me. "That one's the thief."

I glanced up at the impeccably dressed man standing at his side. He was nearly as tall as Knut but razor thin, with a gold watch, which was attached to a chain across his chest, held tightly in his hand.

"You best be right, Blackbeard," Sheriff Nicolson said. "With all the troubles on the streets tonight, I've more important concerns than complaints from the likes a' you."

As he spoke, he exchanged looks with a balding man carrying a canvas sack.

"Stole William Robertson's pouch, he did!" Knut said. "*And* Pete Peterson's prize ewe. Snuffed her out to cover the crime, but Peterson found out soon enough."

"'Twas me brother who stole that pouch!" I shouted, grabbing at me throbbing shoulder as I tried to sit up. "Ask those men over there. He gave it to them!"

But as I searched around the edge of the lodberry for the wiry brute who had tied Mary and me up, the man in the knitted cap, and the other men who had been moving the gin, they were nowhere to be seen. The door to the lodberry was closed, and not a single cask remained.

"There's no one round but the two of you ruffians," Knut said.

"But they were just here," I blurted, struggling to me feet.

"They?" Sheriff Nicolson raised an eyebrow, then tapped the face of his watch as he looked me up and down. "Was there some activity here at the Marwick Lodberry that I should know about?" he asked.

John flashed me a stern look, and then he quickly turned away.

"Ah . . . ," the sheriff muttered, slowly rubbing his chin. "You lads know something, do you?" He stepped closer, reaching for the lapel of Charles's fine coat, and stroked it with his finger.

"Tell me, son, if you're the crofter Mr. Blackbeard says you are, how is it you're wearing such fine clothes? And—oh my—do I see boots as well?"

"He stole 'em, o' course," Knut said. "A thief, this one." Then he grabbed me fast by the wrists with his grimy, chapped hands. "Go ahead, Sheriff, search him! He has that pouch—that is, unless he spent all his Daa's hard-earned money on those clothes."

"I'm no thief," I yelled as Sheriff Nicolson drove his hands into me pockets. "Me brother John's the one you want!"

"Hah!" Knut laughed, extending his hand to John, who was still lying on the ramp. Then he helped him to his feet. "'Twas John caught him and then went after him when he fled."

"Are you sure about that?" Sheriff Nicolson asked. He seized John's arm and searched his pockets as well. Finding nothing, he motioned to the balding man at his side, who pulled two ropes from his sack. "I want them both. These lads have been up to something, and I intend to find out what."

"Not John." Knut shook his head as the sheriff's assistant tied our wrists together. "You've got the wrong brother."

"Don't be a fool!" the sheriff said. "This is Marwick's personal lodberry. Everyone knows he's desperate for cash. If you ask me, these lads were waiting for a shipment they know is coming in."

"You've no evidence to hold me," John cried.

Me mind raced, thinking of Mary and the *Ernestine Brennan*. Would they have time to flee the harbor before dawn? And what would happen to me family, to so many families, should the shipment be seized and Wallace Marwick go under?

"All right." The words escaping me lips before I knew exactly what I was saying. "You found us out."

I looked at John, me eyes piercing his, his face turning ashen.

"John doesn't want me to tell you this. But you've caught us and there's nothing we can do about it now. You being the sheriff, I figure you'll uncover it soon enough anyway."

"What?" John scoffed. "Tell him, Knut! I have nothing to do with any of this foolishness. Clearly there's no telling what Chris will say to hide the truth."

"Enough!" Sheriff Nicolson said, turning his attention back to me. "Go on, lad."

"It's the *Ernestine Brennan*," I said, thinking quickly as I spoke. "The men who were here tipped us off. She's due in just before dawn. 'Course, it could be tomorrow, or the next day. No one knows for sure. But there's been no sign of her yet. We've been waiting here all night."

"Bah!" Knut said. "He's bluffin'!"

The sheriff turned to Knut. "'Course, *you* have a history with the smuggling yourself, Blackbeard. Though I'd like to think your six months in me prison taught you a lesson or two. For all I know, you were in on it, trying to collect on something yourself."

Knut's eyes narrowed. "Everyone knows you's in Marwick's pockets. I've but one purpose here tonight—to bring back William Robertson's property!"

"Perhaps," Sheriff Nicolson said, exchanging knowing glances with the balding man with the bag. "But we all know those pockets are now empty."

Then he asked the most obvious question of all. The one no one could answer. "Tell me, Knut, what is William Robertson, a penniless crofter-fisherman so buried in debt he can't see clear from his croft to his byre, doing with a pouch of coins?"

Knut twitched uncomfortably as a smile crept from the wicks of Sheriff Nicolson's mouth. Then the sheriff began to laugh. "Relax, Blackbeard! You don't think me so dim as to expect a confession from you out here on the lodberry, now, do you?"

"It's not me you need confessin'!" Knut roared, spit flying from his lips.

"Perhaps. But it will be up to the court to determine which of them is telling the truth, not you. And in the meantime I intend to find out more about what Mr. Marwick has up his sleeve."

Knut began to protest, but Sheriff Nicolson cut him off with the wave of a hand. Then he turned to the balding man and took the ropes bound to John and me. "Run to the Customs House and alert them that the *Ernestine Brennan*'s due. They're to inspect all she has on board the minute she is sighted."

Then the sheriff passed the ropes over to Knut. "Come, Blackbeard. I trust you'll help me get these two troublemakers up the hill. They'll have plenty of time to decide which of them is telling the truth from their new home in Lerwick Prison."

KNUT LED US UP FROM THE SHORE AND THEN
up the steep cobblestone lane to the fort, following closely
on the heels of Sheriff Nicolson. When we lagged behind, he
yanked tightly on the ropes.

"What are you up to?" John whispered.

"Devil be with you, John Robertson!" I muttered, spitting
on his tattered rivlins, the blood from me nose dripping on the
stones before us.

"Enough a' you, thief!" Knut barked, jerking the rope so
cruelly that it cut into me flesh.

For the rest of the walk I remained silent, me body con-
sumed with the dread of what lay ahead. I glanced behind us
as Bressay Sound brightened with the hints of a soon-to-be-
rising sun, smacks and sloops bobbing in the water, hungry
cormorants and gulls circling overhead. But as we entered the
fort through the narrow door in the arched gate, I felt as if we
had entered perpetual darkness.

The barracks on our left was the largest of the four main
buildings. It was an imposing, two-story rectangle of lime-
harled walls and three-paned windows flanking a dark oak
door in the center. Waiting at the door was a line of people,
clothes tattered, their faces pinched with hunger, some peering through the curiously louvered shutters in the first-floor
windows.

"Back—back!" Sheriff Nicolson grumbled as he and Knut
pushed us up the steps. "Court doesn't open till eight o'clock,
you bunch a' ragamuffins!"

Then he snatched our ropes from Knut's hands.

"No farther, Blackbeard," he growled, pulling a long key from his pocket. "You'll be informed if the court needs you to make a statement."

"An' when'll that be? I canna be stayin' round these parts forever!"

"Then my suggestion is you go back to your croft. The sooner Lerwick is rid of the likes of you, the better!" He pushed open the door and ushered us inside, before turning back to face Knut. "I do find it strange that you are eager to return to this building after your residency not so long ago."

Knut spat on the threshold. "Gave William Robertson me word, I did. I'll get that pouch back and this boy locked up for good if it's the last thing I do."

Sheriff Nicolson paused a moment, narrowing his eyes. "Considering what we and Her Majesty's Revenue Men hear of certain shipments coming ashore near Culswick, I'd watch my tongue if I were you."

Then he pulled the door behind him, slamming it in Knut's face.

"Lor'!" I winced, burying me injured nose into the soft sleeve of Charles Canfield's coat. The stench of excrement and urine inside the door was so powerful me eyes began to water.

"Like it, do you?" Sheriff Nicolson asked, flashing a sinister smile. "Well, it only gets worse come summer."

"You've no reason to hold us in this Hell-hole!" John scoffed, searching the cold, damp entryway with disdain.

"Oh, but I do! It's my duty to keep order on this island. Pity you crofters can't seem to stay out of trouble. Smuggling—thievery—just like the rest of those wretched people waiting in line outside for their family members' time in court. As if your kin don't have enough worry in these trying times."

"I'll not be convicted before a trial!" John challenged, his eyes locking with the sheriff's.

"You'll do as I say!" The lean man yanked so harshly on his rope that it cut into John's wrist and John couldn't keep from crying out. "In here I'm the law. And the keeper sees to it anything I say is carried out without question."

Then he turned to the stairs. "Keeper Mann!" A door slammed on the floor above, followed by the sound of footsteps shuffling down the stairs.

Before us I could see a narrow hallway leading to the back of the building, with a stairway to the right. Two adjacent hallways stretched perpendicular to the main hall on either side. I glanced with horror at me boastful, scheming brother cowering powerless at me side. At that moment I felt a sense of revulsion I had never known before.

The keeper was a stout but tilted figure. His left shoulder was pulled higher than his right, as if the neck muscles no longer worked. His nose, nearly purple with its tangle of tiny veins, poked out from above an unruly brown beard, and his lips, ears, and forehead were grotesquely covered with what appeared to be a vast array of warts.

"Lads, meet Hugh Mann," the sheriff announced, handing

him our ropes. "Keeper of Lerwick Prison for so many years I've lost track. Mann, our new guests are from all the way over in Culswick. Brothers, it seems. The wee one is Christopher Robertson. Accused of stealing and then snuffing out Peter Peterson's prize ewe. The other is John. One or both of them stole their Daa's pouch of coins, but we haven't yet the evidence. Picked them up at the Marwick Lodberry trying to get a piece of some smuggled Marwick loot about to come in."

The two men stood side by side, looking us up and down, as if we were goods in a shop window by the shore.

"Pitiful crofters," Keeper Mann scoffed. "Nothin' but skin and bones. Why, the gruel in this place'll probably be a better meal than they had since the corn crop failed last September!"

Sheriff Nicolson nodded satisfactorily, then turned toward the stairs. "I expect you're right about that, Hugh. 'Course, I've seen starving swine turn away from your gruel. Show them to their quarters, but be sure to keep them apart. They're likely to tear each other to shreds before we get our chance to bring them to justice."

I glanced at the peculiar-looking man as the sheriff disappeared up the stairs.

"What you starin' at?" He reached up to a shelf by the door and grabbed what appeared to be two tattered gray garments. Then he ushered us down a long, dark hallway to our left.

"Smugglers, every one!" He pointed to each of the timber doors we passed, all fitted with thick iron locks. "You lazy crofters canna keep your hands off that tobacco and Dutch gin," he chided, banging on the walls at the moans and grumblings from inside. "Cheatin' the Crown when you should be fishin' for the cod and sowin' yer bere!"

John edged closer, as if trying to get near enough to whisper something, but I shoved him away.

"Hey! None a' that!" Keeper Mann shouted, turning to face me as he pulled a twelve-inch knife with an ornately carved scrimshaw handle from a leather pouch on his belt. "Dunna make me use it, lad."

When we came to the last cell in the hall, he pulled a rusted key from his pocket. He turned the lock, and swung open the door to a wee, damp chamber lit only by the faint rays of daylight filtered through the strange, louvered shutters I had noticed from the outside. Then he carelessly sliced the rope from John's wrists and tossed one of the gray smocks at his chest.

"Put it on! I'll be back for your clothes directly." Then he slammed the door and turned the key. "Sheriff says to keep you apart, but at the moment we're full up," he continued. "Lucky for you I've just the roommate."

A cackle burst from the wicks of his wart-encrusted mouth as he inserted the key into the lock of the cell immediately adjacent to John's. "A true criminal, this one, not just one of those smugglin' crofters."

"Sola Gratia," I muttered, burying me nose in me sleeve as the door swung open.

"Ripe smellin', ain't he?" Mann said, jabbing me with a finger as he laughed. "By last count it was Christmas Day we gived ya a bath, isn't that right, Malcolm?"

Sitting on a pallet by the window was a bedraggled man, staring at us through deep-set hazel eyes. His wild crop of hair was as red as me own, sticking out in all directions; an unruly beard, flecked in white, clung in swirls around his mouth and chin. He seemed pale in the muted light, despite the smudges of grime on his cheeks and hands, and his bare feet, which stuck out from under the filthy gray prison uniform, were wide as hooves, and covered by a thick layer of hair.

"Should have a decision from the Crown Council in Edinburgh any day now," the keeper said with a sinister smile. "I'm thinkin' a nice long holiday to Norfolk Island is just about what an incurable thief like yourself deserves. Seven years a' hard labor'll remedy yer ways!"

The man sprang to his feet. "I'll not be goin' to that God-forsaken place!" he cried. "Not away from me wife and bairns!"

"Hah! Shoulda' given that some thought before you stole the valuables from Mr. Arcus."

The man looked toward the shuttered window and spat at the floor.

"Or when you *borrowed* the half peck of oatmeal from Marwick's warehouse two Januarys past. Or, perhaps, when you took William Norton's six geese that Christmas Eve?"

As the keeper continued listing a litany of transgressions, the man stamped his hairy foot in defiance.

"No, I'd say a few months in the hulks down to London

and a trip on a convict ship over the Tasman Sea will do you some good. That is, if you live through it. In the meantime I've brought you a roommate to take your mind off your troubles. Meet Christopher Robertson. Another thief. You two're like two bad cabbages in the same planticrub."

Mann pulled his knife from its case and then tugged hard on the rope around me wrists. "Ready for some cuttin', lad?"

I eyed the blade, trembling.

"Put it down, Mann, ya bloomin' dreep!" the prisoner chided. "He's just a lad." Then he motioned to me. "Don't worry. He canna hurt ya. I don't know what you're in for, but the keeper knows Sheriff Nicolson needs ya alive and unmaimed for yer trial."

Mann laughed as he lowered the knife to me wrists, grazing the skin as he carelessly sliced through the rope. Then he reached his grubby fingers to the ripped shoulder of Charles Canfield's elegant blue coat.

"By the looks of these fancy clothes, I'd say you've committed another crime or two while here in Lerwick, lad. Stolen property, is it? Shame you couldn't take better care of it."

"It's not stolen!" I said, but no sooner had the words come out than Keeper Mann struck me hard across me mouth, the pain reverberating across me cracked nose.

"Shut it!" he bellowed, leaning his face inches from mine. "No haf-krak from Culswick is the rightful owner of clothes the likes o' these!"

"They were lent to me by . . . by . . . ," but before I could finish, his hand came across me face again, this time knocking me to the floor.

"Enough, Mann," the prisoner said, offering a hand to help me up.

"The milk o' human kindness, is it, MacPherson?" Mann laughed. "Comin' straight from a murderer?"

"Bah! Ya know you've no proof!"

"Sure about that, are ya, Malcolm MacPherson?"

"'Twas ten years back you're talkin' of. There's nobody here even remembers the dreep."

"Then you don't deny it?"

"Deny it? Huh! I'll waste no breath on the likes of you."

Keeper Mann laughed as he threw the other smock at me chest. "Get them fancy clothes off before I come back to collect 'em."

Then he pointed to me roommate and gave me a wink.

"Remember what they say—once a murderer, always a murderer. If I were you, lad, I'd sleep with one eye open."

12

Netty's Bundle

Don't blame you if the sight of me makes you tremble," Malcolm MacPherson said as I listened to Mann's key turning the lock behind me. Then the wild-haired man strolled back to his pallet at the other side of the cell. "Even without that dreep of a man fillin' your head with nasty stories, I must be a frightening sight all on me own."

I wrapped me arms tightly to me chest, hugging the wall with me back.

"Cold, isn't it? It's the stone walls that keeps it locked in. Set on a bog, we are. Sunk ten feet since they built the place."

"And the stench?" I managed, through trembling lips. "Me eyes have been tearing ever since I stepped in the doors."

"Och!" Malcolm chuckled. "I've been in so long I hardly notice it no more. Your nose gets used to it after a day or two, Sola Gratia. 'Course, part of it's me. Mann's right about the bathing. They scrubbed me down three months back, and I've been rotting from the outside in ever since."

A rat scurried across the floor. Malcolm gazed at the ceiling and sighed. "Oh, what I'd give for a good soak in a hot tub a' water heated up nice by me Netty round our wee fire . . ."

"What are those?" I asked, pointing to the two grimy bowls sitting under a table in the corner.

"Chamber pots, o' course. Stink something fierce. Only get dumped in the trench at the end of the day."

"The trench?"

"Aye. No privy at Fort Charlotte. Just the ditch off the back side of the barracks. Supposed to drain under us, but it's been choked up for years. Seeps up through the floor when it rains."

I looked about the cell. The walls were of yellowing, cracked plaster. The only daylight came from the window muted by the peculiar louvered blinds jutting from the sill at a forty-five-degree angle to the top of the frame. It was impossible to see out. I gingerly pulled Charles's coat off me shoulder. John's teeth marks were still throbbing deep in me flesh.

"You can keep on your underdraws," he said, wriggling his blackened toes under their thick coat of red hair. "Mine wore out nearly a year ago and I've yearned for them ever since.

You'll be needin' anything you can get under that ratty smock. No heat in the building 'cept for a stove they keep in the hallway for the people waiting to go upstairs to court. At times I think the damp, aching cold will freeze right through me bones."

It was all I could do to pull off those beautiful boots when there was a sudden rap at the window. Malcolm sprang to his feet, and a moment later a small bundle slipped over the top of the wooden shutter onto the floor. He dove for it, eyeing me carefully before squirreling it away in his mattress. Then he rushed back to the window, turning his back to me, and pressed his lips to the wood. "That you, Netty-me-love?"

"Well, who else da ya s'pose be outside your window this time of day, ya old glundie?" a woman's voice chided. "Who else'd be helpin' the likes of you but your good wife, after all you've been up to?"

I looked nervously at the ceiling, trying not to listen.

"Ah, Netty," Malcolm said. "The sound of your sweet voice warms the cockles a' me heart."

"Well, it's your own cockles you'll be warmin' for many years to come if you get the Transportation. And where'll your sweet Netty be then? Still living with me nagging sister, scrapin' and beggin' to keep food in the wee bairns' mouths."

"I know I've been a trial to ya, me bonnie lass. But we've almost all we need. Just one more delivery should do."

"Hmmph." I heard the sound of a boot stamping the ground. "I'm riskin' me neck for you, you Ol' Cod," she chided. "Just make sure your plan works this time, or it'll be the two of us on that boat to Norfolk Island, and no one left to tend the bairns."

"Will ya be back tomorrow, sweet Netty? Same time?"

"Aye. Same time. God willin' and me still breathing the vital air."

And then she was gone.

I pretended to busy meself putting on the smock, not wanting to appear to have overheard. But Malcolm seemed eager to chat.

"Sweetest woman ever lived," he said, sitting back on his pallet. "Two years since I've laid eyes on her, and she tells me she's nothin' but skin and bones. As bonnie as she was plump when we first met, she was. I've been in and out of this place three times since we've been married, but this stay's been the longest by far." He sighed, dropping his head in his hands. "Two years is a long time for a man not to be providin' for his wife and bairns."

I nodded while carefully folding Charles's clothes, stroking the lapel of that glorious blue jacket one last time before placing it on the floor by the door. Then I walked over to the window.

"Mr. MacPherson," I asked, "can *anyone* from the outside send things in through these shutters?"

"Hoot, lad," he said, flashing a smile of jagged yellow and black teeth, "call me Malcolm, will you? And aye—the prison inspector from London, who came last year, was none too pleased with this place for that very reason. We heard he filed a report with the House of Commons, but, lucky for me, nothing's come of it."

"And where is this Norfolk Island Keeper Mann talked about?"

Malcolm rubbed his hands nervously together. "A place no man should ever go."

"I don't know it."

"Well, you know what they mean about the Transportation?"

"Aye. It's when you've done something so bad they ship you clear out to New South Wales."

"Used to be, but they haven't sent many convicts there for a while now. Too many of them liked it, they say, and decided to stay on after they'd served their time. Some even bought land, raised sheep. Sent for their families to join them."

"Me Daa says the land is fine for grazing."

"Och—but the English, they have one thing in mind with the Transportation, of course. And it isn't a future of prosperity. They want us criminals to pay for our crimes—with our very heart and soul. That's why they came up with the idea of sending us to Norfolk Isle instead. The only punishment worse is the hanging, and some say hanging is better. It's in in the middle of the Tasman Sea, where rules of morality and common decency among men don't apply. Hard labor, it is, all in chains. On the sugar plantations and in the mines. The only place in the world, I suspect, where you'd rather be a slave than a convict."

"Why's that?" I asked, eyes widening.

"'Cause a slave—well, they're worth something, so they try to keep 'em alive. Convicts, on the other hand—there'll always be a boatload of replacements coming on the next ship."

"And that's where you're headed? To Norfolk Isle?"

"Och, no! That's just what the sheriff and keeper hope," he said with a shrug of his shoulders. "I *do* have a bit of a history taking things that don't belong to me, however. 'Course I've had every intention of returnin' them—each and every one— but I keep getting thrown back in here before I get a chance. The sheriff, he calls me an 'incurable thief' and a 'menace to the island.' So he's requested permission to send me to Edinburgh to the High Court for a trial so they can give me the Transportation. The ruling is due next week."

"But what if the ruling doesn't go your way?"

"Come, lad," he said with a wave of the hand. "There's always opportunities."

"Opportunities? In this miserable place?"

"'Course!" he said with a wink. "Swarmin' round us—waitin' to be grabbed."

Just then the key rattled and Keeper Mann burst through the door.

"Robertson," he growled. "Get over here, and fast. You have a visitor."

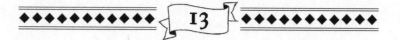

13

The Visitor

Keeper Mann snatched Charles Canfield's clothes from the floor and stuffed them in his bag. Then he picked up Charles's boots.

"I've been needin' some a' these."

"They don't belong to you," I muttered as he grabbed fast to me arm and shoved me into the dimly lit hall.

"You want another smack to the mouth?" he sneered. "Now move along!"

"Who's come to see me?"

"Quit your talking."

"Where are you taking me?"

"The airin' room, of course! Where the law says you good-for-nothin's have to go each day to stretch your limbs and get your exercise grinding grain."

The main door to the barracks was open as we passed, the entryway now lined with the people we had seen waiting outside when we first arrived.

"Court's in session today," Mann muttered. "These bothersome lowlifes will be hangin' round all day waitin' for their turn."

"Ooooo!" A toothless woman cackled, peering at me from under her hap. "Looks like a new one's been caught!"

"One a' the lads the sheriff dragged in this morn," a stooped man in a woolen cap taunted. "All skin and bones, he is!"

"Hey, lad!" another yelled. "You'll be an old, old man when they let you out of here."

"Is it me Daa who's here?" I pleaded with Keeper Mann. Perhaps I could reason with him—explain what had really happened.

"Your Daa?" Mann chuckled, stopping before a well-worn door just opposite the stairs to the second floor. "Not hardly!" And when he flung the door open, the watery, yellowing eyes of Reverend Sill met me like a wall of stone.

The room was bare except for several chairs next to a few tables fitted with small hand mills for grinding bere and oats. I winced at the sudden shock of light from the three tall windows looking out on the back side of the building.

The reverend's bent frame rested over his weathered stauf.

He looked me up and down, slowly shook his head, then turned to the keeper.

"Leave us."

"With this sheep-murderin' thief? Oh, no, Reverend! I'll not be puttin' a fine man such as yourself in danger."

"Young Robertson is a sheep of *my* flock," Reverend Sill said, eyes narrowing. "And it is the Lord's wish that he cleanse his soul before *me*, not the keeper of this filthy establishment. Tell me, does no one in this place have the sense to clean the stench of waste from within these walls? I assure you, even a lowly crofter's byre never smells as foul as this."

"It's the scent of smugglers and thieves your nose is takin' in, Reverend," Mann snapped, spit flying from his mouth. "They bring with them a stench no cow, swine, or sheep could ever make were they stalled up together for all the months of winter."

He leered at me, licking his cracked purple lips.

"Evil, they are—every one. This one, especially, he has the look, he does. I seen it before. I'm not lettin' him from me sight."

Reverend Sill pounded his stauf into the damp stone floor. "Are you telling *me* that the Lord Almighty will not be my protector in the presence of a lad as wee as this? Release him this instant and leave us be, or I'll be speaking with Sheriff Nicolson directly!"

For a moment Mann made a series of grunts and snorts,

before finally dropping his grip. Then he pulled his knife from his belt. "You best not try anythin', Robertson, 'cause I'll be waitin' for you just outside."

When Mann finally closed the door behind him, Reverend Sill pointed a wiry finger at me face. His tone was as icy and dark as the floor, and he stared at me with a piercing intensity from behind long, straggling eyebrows. "I forbade you to leave last night. You disobeyed me."

I glanced, deeply ashamed, at me dirty feet. He had shown me kindness. Tried to keep me from danger. "Aye—I did, sir. But I can explain."

"And you had the audacity to bring Miss Mary Canfield *with* you? A young Christian girl, out in a street of rioting mariners and heathens, with no chaperone and without the knowledge of her midder?"

I looked up, aghast. "Is she safe?"

He paused a moment, stroking his chin. "Aye. Arrived just an hour ago. No thanks to you, I might add. Her brother, Charles, brought her ashore this morning after her Midder and I spent a frantic night searching for her whereabouts."

I closed me eyes. How could I have been so foolish? "It was wrong, sir, to let her come. I should have—"

"Enough!" he said, raising his stauf. "Last evening, before we knew of your unauthorized departure, Mr. Blackbeard and I had a long and very interesting conversation. He suggested you are a lad of deep moral delinquencies. I made the mistake of not believing him."

"He knows only what me Daa told him, and it's not the truth!"

"Not only did he tell me that you had taken your Daa's pouch of coins, he said you had taken the life of Mr. Peterson's prize ewe in an attempt to steal her newly born offspring!"

"No!" I said, shaking me head violently. "It wasn't me intention!"

"Christopher Robertson, have you lied to me?"

"No!"

Me face burned with shame. I dropped to a whisper. "I didn't tell you everything, sir, but I never lied."

"Well, then, lad, the time for an explanation has come. For when the Redeemer asks us to confess our sins, He asks us to speak slowly and distinctly, so as to admit with the utmost honesty what it is we have done."

"It was John who took that pouch," I cried. "As God is me witness! I followed him to Lerwick to get it back!"

"And Mr. Peterson's sheep?"

I could feel the tears creeping from the corners of me eyes to me cheeks. "It all happened so quickly!"

"Bah!" he scoffed. "I'll not stand for this show of emotion!" Then he turned away from me in disgust. "Compose yourself and face your sins."

It was all I could do to keep from shaking as I wiped me eyes on me sleeve. But when he turned back, I was still unprepared for the question.

"Can you deny, Christopher Robertson," he asked, stepping

forward and dropping his face just inches from me as if questioning Satan himself, "that you killed Peter Peterson's ewe?"

I swallowed hard.

"Speak! Or may you be damned to fry with Satan in Hell for the rest of your days!"

"I cannot deny it!" I blurted, casting me eyes to the floor. "But it was me Daa who stole her, not me. She gave birth to twins that night." I hugged me arms around me chest, never finding the courage to raise me eyes. "I begged him, again and again. *Are you sure, Daa? Is this really what you want?* But Mr. Peterson was at the door and Daa—he needed her quiet."

The words spilled out like water from a broken dam, me heart pounding so hard against me chest that I thought it might burst through me ribs.

"*Snuff her out*, Daa said. And, and, and—with me Daa—we all know you can't say no."

When I found the courage to glance up, I saw Reverend Sill strangely hunched over his stauf, as if lost in a trance. And then, suddenly, the door burst open.

"Nicely done, Reverend!" Keeper Mann said, a wide smile beaming from behind his scraggly beard as he slapped the ancient man so hard on the back that the reverend nearly fell over. "You got a confession out a' the sneaky crofter lad, and I am your witness!"

Then he danced a jig around the room, laughing aloud.

"Ho, ho! We'll have a speedy trial with this one now! Two crimes—back-to-back!"

"A confession?" Reverend Sill asked, trying to regain his balance. "I had understood that this was a *private* meeting!"

"Ah, come, now—you know it's your duty as head of the Church to report to the sheriff any cases a' moral misconduct. We can't let privacy get in the way of justice, now, can we?"

Mann leered at me as he grabbed me arm.

"Let's get you back to your cell where you'll be stayin' for a good long time. At least, that is, until they take you away to the hulks to wait for your ship to Norfolk with your roommate, MacPherson!"

I struggled to free meself as he pulled his knife from its sheath. "Heard about them convict ships, have you, lad?" he asked, leaning just inches from me ear. "First they chain you below deck, so you're nice an' comfortable. All goes well for a month or two of the journey—that is, until you get to the tropics. That's when the sun starts beatin' down so strong there's hardly any air below deck. Then, o' course, the fresh water starts to run out. And it's then, they tell me, when it's so beastly hot that the pitch from between the boards on the deck above you starts meltin', hot as fire—drip, drip, drip— onto your skin."

He cackled as he stared at me horror-struck face, then shoved me to the door.

"Please! Reverend Sill!" I cried from the hall. "Don't let him take me!"

But as I searched behind me for the face of the man whose kindness I had betrayed, he was nowhere to be seen.

14

The Rope

Hoot, lad, you look like you've seen better days."
Malcolm looked up from his pallet as I stumbled
back into the cell. "Havin' a visitor can't be that
bad."

"They're sending me!"

"Sending you?"

"With you—to Norfolk Island!"

I ran to the window, grabbing fast to the shutters.

"Oh, Mann's just fillin' you with stories is all. They can't
just send you, lad. First they've gotta give you a trial. And they
need evidence to convict you."

I swallowed hard. "He doesn't need evidence."

"'Course he does!" Malcolm said, letting out a yawn as he stretched his giant arms above his head. "First off, the crime has to be worthy of the punishment. Then they need to try you in the High Court in Edinburgh in order to give you the Transportation."

I turned to face him. "Even when they have a confession?"

Malcolm sat up erect. "You confessed? Lor', lad—no one in his right mind *confesses* when he's committed a crime!"

"Aye," I said, slumping down on me pallet. "Thought I was speaking to Reverend Sill in private. The keeper listened at the door."

Then I found meself telling him about all that had happened the night of the gale, and of me travel to Lerwick, and the night at the Marwick Lodberry.

"Sneaky rat, that Mann," Malcolm muttered, picking a bug from his beard. "But if you can find the pouch John pinched from your Daa—"

"Ah, that's long gone. John spent it on some casks a' smuggled gin, and as long as he's in here too, he can't even claim the goods from the Marwick Lodberry. Even if he could, Marwick's son would take it in payment for me Daa's debts." As I spoke I thought of George Marwick's parting words— *See to it Mary Canfield gets safely home and then bring me those coins. By morning. Or I'll have your family cast from their croft by week's end.*

"And what of the ewe?"

"Doesn't matter. Peterson already knows of the body. Even

though by now Daa's most likely matched the lambs to a ewe of our flock." I stood up suddenly. "Are you sure all that you've heard about Norfolk Island is true?"

"Afraid so, lad. Though your crime hardly seems worthy of the Transportation. But if you must know, most of me information comes from me brother-in-law, Jamie Jameson. He and I shared this very cell at one time or another. An innocent man convicted of murder, servin' on Norfolk as we speak. Netty's and our bairns been livin' with his wife, Patience, while I've been in this place. Been gone a year and the family got a letter. It's the only way Patience knows he's still alive."

I dropped me head in me hands. Suddenly I thought of Catherine and Victoria, of Gutcher and Aunt Alice. Of Mary. Would I never see any of them again?

"Och, Malcolm. Me Daa—he told me to snuff out that ewe. Isn't a lad supposed to do as his Daa says?"

"Aye." He sighed resting his chin in his grubby hand. "It's when you're a lad that you think your Daa has all the answers. Then—poof—you find yourself in a place like this."

"But I'm not yet fourteen! Even if I'm not sent to Norfolk, I can't be locked away. Me family needs me to survive!"

"Dunna give up hope, lad. If there is one thing I've learned from me life of—ah—*transgressions*, it's there's always a way to wriggle out of a tricky situation."

"Wriggle out? This place is made of stone, or haven't ya noticed?" I slammed me hand into the cold outer wall.

"Aye, but as I was saying earlier, there's always opportunities." He reached his arm deep inside his mattress and pulled out the sack from Netty. "Can you keep a secret?"

I shrugged. "Aye. No one but you for me to tell it to."

Then he tossed the sack to me. "Look here at what me good lass's been collecting."

"Bristles?" I asked, peering inside. "And horsehair?"

"Aye. Precious stuff. *Borrowed* from the neighbor's swine and ponies. And I've been putting them to good use, little by little, for nearly a year."

He reached back in the mattress and pulled out what seemed to be an endless skein of tightly twisted fiber. I walked closer and admired the work, knowing that the bristles of the Shetland swine, with its supple, glossy texture, made the strongest, most elastic rope found anywhere. Everyone's choice when fowling from the sea cliffs.

"Was a master rope maker in me younger days," Malcolm explained. "Up north—in Unst—before me troubles began. Me Netty brings by what I need a little at a time, so as not to raise suspicion. Only a bit more and I'll have enough."

"Enough?" I said, pulling at the skein. "Why, it must be thirty feet long!"

"And I only need it half that size. But to make it into a proper rope I have to twist it together, one skein over another."

"When will you be done?"

"Just a bit more to go. Takes two to twist it just right. Mann doesn't know it, but he did me a big favor bringing you here. I hope you'll oblige me when it's time."

"What'll you do with it?"

"Get down from a second-story window, of course!"

"You're planning to escape?"

"Shhh!" Malcolm drew a hairy finger to his lips. "The walls between these cells are nothing but plaster!"

"But how?"

"It's like I've been telling you. Opportunities—they're everywhere! 'Course, you never know when they're comin', so you have to be on your toes. Did you notice, for instance, when you was in the airin' room with the reverend, that there aren't any of these ruddy shutters on those windows?"

"Aye. And I also noticed the keeper has a knife he keeps sharp."

"That he does. And a pistol from time to time. But he's known to get distracted. Every evening, in fact, when he brings us to the trench to empty our chamber pots. We pass the bonnie Miss Pepper doing the washin' across from the airin' room. She's the lass from the village who works nights scrubbing the linen and the underdraws for the officers who occupy the fort. The keeper's got an eye for her, he does, and when he struts his sorry self past her each night, his mind is far, far away from the likes of us and his gleamin' knife."

"But you said the rope had to be long enough for a *second-story* window?"

"Aye," Malcolm whispered. "I aim to be prepared. If my only opportunity is to run up the stairs to make me escape, I'll be ready."

"And if you're caught?"

"Now, don't start thinking about 'if,'" he said, stuffing the cord back in the mattress. "If there's one thing I've learned after being cooped up in here for all these years, it's too much thinking makes you too fearful to act."

"But if they catch you, they'll send you to Norfolk for sure!"

"Lad," Malcolm said, brow furrowed. "It's where I'm headed even if I sit in this stinkin' place on me backside and don't move a lazy finger. Netty and me, we have five bairns to take care of, all with bellies so empty they won't last till summer without me. You heard the keeper—the word from Edinburgh is due any day now. I don't plan to be round to hear it."

A Familiar Tree

Officially lodged a petition 'gainst you, Robertson," the keeper reported, when he returned later with two bowls of gruel. "You're due in court the day after tomorrow."

"You needn't taunt the lad," Malcolm muttered.

"That's enough out of you, MacPherson. Your fate is as dark as his, you lazy dreep of a thief." Then a smile burst across his wart-covered face. "Just heard word that brother-in-law of yours is due back next week."

"Jamie? Back?"

"Aye, six years shy of his seven-year sentence. Any guess as to why?"

Malcolm's face turned ashen.

"Finally agreed to work with us, he did. Seems, after all these years, we're finally gunna learn the truth about who helped him kill Gilbert Bain."

"They'll not get anything out of Jamie, you lying swine!"

A laugh burst from Mann's cracked lips. "From what I hear, they already have!" he said, turning to the door. "Norfolk Island has a way of breakin' a man, you know. Even one as stubborn as Jamie Jameson."

"What was that about?" I asked, shoveling the runny greenish-gray porridge into me mouth.

"Lor', lad, you must be starving to go at it like that," Malcolm said, furiously tugging the skein from his mattress.

"Are you worried about your brother-in-law? What he might say?"

"Who—Jamie? Och, no. Mann's just bluffin'. Trying to get me to talk."

"From the way you described Norfolk, it seems a man might do just about anything to get off the island."

I watched as Malcolm's calloused hands frantically worked the new supply of bristles. "Aye, lad. Like I said, I'm not planning to be round to find out."

"Who was Gilbert Bain?"

"You ask a lot of questions."

"I told you about *me* troubles."

He looked up. "He was a man with a soul as dark as night. Got what he deserved, that one."

"A Lerwick man?"

"Och, no. From Unst—way up north. Where me and Netty lived when we were newly married. Bain was a merchant with a cold heart who took it upon himself to force women to do un-Godly things."

As he spoke I shuddered, then curled up on me mattress of musty straw. It had been a day and a night since I'd slept, and me body suddenly felt heavy and stiff. I reached me hand to the plaster wall that divided me from John—a lump forming in me throat, the stinging shards of betrayal slowly melting into loneliness. As I closed me eyes, listening to the rhythmic sound of Malcolm twisting and braiding his rope, me mind wandered to our Culswick croft—to the click of Aunt Alice's knitting needles, to the sweet smell of warm, burning peat tickling me nose, and to Catherine and Victoria, snuggled together in their box bed. What were they thinking of me, and of Daa's stories of what I had done? And Mary—where was she now? Those eyes—so full of life—the warm cheek that had rested on me shoulder?

I don't know how long I slept, but when I awoke and re-membered where I was, I stiffened, not wanting to move. Me eyes followed a single slant of light creeping through the shut-ters, up the plastered wall, to a spot high and on the right. And then I slowly sat up to get a closer look. At first I wasn't sure of what I was seeing—if, perhaps, I could be dreaming. But as I scrambled to me feet, standing on the pallet to get a better look, there was no doubt.

"I see you've found our work of art," Malcolm muttered.

"Where did it come from?" I cried, me finger gingerly tracing the scratches in the plaster three-quarters of the way up the wall.

"Keep it down!" Malcolm warned. "If you yap too loudly you'll get a bang on the wall from our neighbor Gill Lawrence. Gill is none too fond of noise when he's taking his afternoon nap."

"But I know this!" I said, staring in complete disbelief at the picture of the very same tree carved into the rock in Culswick Broch. Our broch. The tree on the treeless island of Shetland.

"Well, I doubt that, lad," Malcolm mumbled. "Unless, o' course, you've been in this cell in some other life. That, me friend, was scratched there long before you were born."

"But I do!" I said, running the tips of me fingers over the plaster. "There's one just like it carved on a stone in the broch on the west side of the island!"

Malcolm looked up, casually picking at his shaggy red mane.

"Are ya sure?"

"Aye! Only difference is, the one I know is missing some branches down here." I pointed to the lower right-hand corner of the picture.

"Well, well, now—that's a rather interesting piece of information."

"What do you know about it?"

"Oh, just what I've heard. Prison legends, really. Island talk."

"Do you know who carved it?"

He scratched his head. "Done during the war with the Americans. Just after King George rebuilt this fort."

"By a soldier?"

"Och, no—someone much more interesting than that." He walked to the window, tipping a jar of water to his lips. "A spy for the Americans, they say. From New York. Not more than a lad himself when he carved it. His ship was blown off course and wrecked off Bressay Isle way. 1781, I think it was."

I thought back to what John had told me when he first returned from Lerwick. About the buried treasure. "I've heard a similar tale."

"I don't doubt it. Poor lad was on the run for months—it was the talk of the island."

"Did they catch him?"

"'Course! That's why he was here. But this wasn't Lerwick Prison back then—the whole building was the barracks for the Royal Artillery. The American, he was a wily one. They say it took several months to finally bring him in. Shut him in this very cell, for safekeeping, till they got word to send him down to the Tower a' London."

"Are you sure he was a spy?"

"Aye. And a loyal one at that. They say the others who were caught squealed right away. Confessed that they were on their way from Rotterdam, a chest of gold ducats on board. Headed to the West Indies. Too bad for them they were blown off course in a gale."

"What were they after?"

"Well, that's just it," Malcolm said. He wiped his mouth with his sleeve. "Far as I know they never found out. Seems our lad was the only one who had been trusted with the details, and they couldn't get him to talk. They say the English beat him silly while he was here; nearly killed him, in fact. But he kept mum—must have been a brave soul to endure that. Treason being a hanging offense, I don't expect he lasted too long after they sent him to London."

"And what of the ducats? Me brother says they've been searching for them for years."

"Far as I know they've never been found. Although you can bet the people on Bressay Isle keep looking."

For a moment he was silent, and then he turned slowly toward me, eyes wide as saucers.

"Chris Robertson, where exactly is this broch of yours?"

"Miles from Bressay. On the western end of the island."

We could hear Mann's voice bellowing down the hallway: "Chamber pots! Get 'em ready!"

"Tell me, lad," Malcolm continued, his voice barely a whisper. "Is it the kind of place one might hide something of value?"

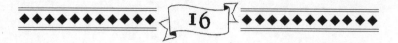

Billy's Bargain

New York City, September 30, 1842

Billy Tweed's "office," as he called it, was a desk on the second floor of the Skaden Brush Works, where he worked as the bookkeeper. Me boardinghouse was but a few blocks south, and when I walked by at dawn on me way to the O'Reilly Forge, I noticed a light in the upstairs window.

"Roberts," Billy said, looking up from a thick volume spread wide on his desk. Then he smiled. "A bit early for an Irish lad to be up."

A bony white cat with gray patches slinked across the towering bins of horsehair and wire to Billy's left, stopping to rub its chin against his shirtsleeve.

"You know why I'm here," I said. His offer to "help" me find Sam Livingston was all I had thought about since the day before—when he had walked out of the O'Reilly Forge with my coin.

"I've something to show you," Billy said, reaching into his desk and pulling out a burgundy colored leather folio. Then he opened it and swiveled it toward me. It was a coin collection, with a variety of pieces inserted in rows of pockets on each side. Under each coin he had scrawled a description. The last coin in the row was mine.

"Belongs to me!" I hissed.

Billy donned a look of surprise. "You mean the coin *I found* on the floor at the O'Reilly Forge? Makes a perfect addition to my collection, wouldn't you say?"

I made a grab for it, but he snapped the binder closed and shoved it back in his desk before I could get it. Then he leaned back in his chair and laughed. "I believe I've stated my terms."

"Aye," I grumbled. "And I've come to meet them. You asked why I was interested in Sam Livingston. He was a friend of me aged grandfather's," I lied. I had conjured me story in haste. Billy Tweed knew nothing of me life, and if I was careful with me words, he never would. "Gave the coin to me grandfather. For safekeeping. On his deathbed, me grandfather asked me to return it."

Billy stared at me, silent as a snake, until I could bear it no longer. "I'm told it's worthless," I blurted. "You canna have a need—"

"Need?" He laughed. "For a coin as rare as this?"

"Rare?"

"Of course! Any memento from our Colonial rebels is a find—everyone knows that. At least those of us who are true Americans," he added with a wink. "And it will only get rarer as time goes on."

"They say you've many talents, Billy Tweed," I said. "A coin expert I hadn't heard."

"Numismatist, they call it, Roberts," he instructed. And then he held up the volume he had been studying when I walked in: *Coins of the Americas, 1600–1825.* "I've been reading up. As of late, I've found it quite profitable to gather more knowledge of the profession."

"Then you've noticed that *me grandfather's* coin is old and worn."

"Oh, yes, and of a most unusual size. A Pine Tree Shilling, as I told you at the forge. Do you know, Robertson, what that is?"

I shrugged me shoulders.

"Says here they were some of the first coins struck by the American Colonists."

"Aye, 1652. Says on the back."

He glanced up. "Studied it, have you?"

I nodded.

"But you might be surprised to learn that what makes this particular coin special is that, although it says 1652, that wasn't the date it was actually struck."

I glanced at him, brow furrowed, as the cat rubbed his delicate pink nose against Billy's cheek.

"It's all in here," Billy said, pointing to the book. The cat started to purr and stretched out on the book's open pages. "Colonists weren't allowed to strike their own coins unless the king said so," he continued, brushing the cat aside, white fur flying about us. Then he held a magnifying glass to the writing before him. "So they found a way round it. They struck coins with the year 1652, because that's after the unlucky King Charles had his head chopped off and no one was sitting on the throne."

I rubbed me eyes, wondering what this had to do with any of us in the year 1842.

"Don't you see, Robertson?" He laughed and hammered his fist on his desk with such force that the cat screeched and leapt from the desk. "They outsmarted the Crown!"

"Aye," I replied, thinking that Wallace Marwick and most everyone in Shetland would highly approve. "An act for which you have great respect, Billy?"

Billy Tweed's eyes twinkled. "But of course!" He chuckled. "Those Colonists remind me of myself!" Then he leaned back in his chair and propped his feet on top of the stack of papers. "Only today it's City Hall we need to outsmart, not the king." He beckoned me closer as if to give me the most private of information. "The only thing Mayor Morris's got going for him is he's a Democrat and not a Whig. Do you know he's set out to *reform* the aldermen?"

"Aldermen?"

"The men the fine citizens of New York elect to run the city. An alderman and assistant alderman from each of the seventeen wards."

I looked at him, puzzled. "And what exactly do they do?"

"Well, pass the laws, for one. And set the taxes. Give out contracts and grants—that sort of thing."

"But isn't reform what Peter O'Reilly and the other workers are always asking for?"

"Of course! Their taxes keep going up! They want to put a stop to what the papers call *rampant peculation.*"

"Peculation?"

Billy tugged on his ear, his eyebrows raised. "The *creative* use of public money, is one way to put it."

"Mayor Morris wants to keep the aldermen from stealing from the people?"

Billy nodded. "From taking bribes for contracts. Special compensation for licenses. Giving themselves and family members *deals* with the city."

I scratched me head. "And who, exactly, *wouldn't* want the mayor to do that?"

He looked up, a sly grin across his face. "Someone who will one day be an alderman. Such as the handsome gentleman sitting before you . . ."

"Ah," I mumbled, everything suddenly clear. "Billy Tweed has ambitions beyond brush making."

"And one needs cash to be elected, of course."

"What does this have to do with me?" Billy stared at me, softly rubbing his angular chin as the wee brass clock on the mantel behind his desk struck 6:00. "I'm due at the forge."

"So you are. And if you're late I'll have that whining Peter O'Reilly coming down here to complain. Lord knows there are hundreds more hungry Irishmen arriving at the docks today to replace you."

"Go on," I muttered, teeth clenched. There I was again. At the mercy of a man more powerful than I. And after all that had happened to me before I arrived in New York, it was a situation I knew all too well. That gnawing, clawing pain in me gut that told me what I was about to be asked to do was going to be wrong. It was going to be dangerous. And it was most certainly going to be against the law.

"I need you to make a delivery. Tonight."

"That's it?" I asked.

"A very special, private delivery. For a friend who's just arrived from the South."

"And then you'll bring me to Sam Livingston?"

"Yes."

I swallowed hard. "All right, then. Where do I go?"

Billy beamed as he always did when he got what he wanted. And then he crossed his arms over his brawny chest. "Magruder's Slaughter House at Henry Street and Market. Eleven o'clock. One of my men will be waiting for you. And be sure you come alone."

"Aye." I turned to the door. "I'll be there."

"And be back here tomorrow," Billy said. "Same time. Then—if you've done the job to my satisfaction—we'll discuss my end of the bargain."

I paused at the top of the stairs, listening to the shuffling sound of the brush workers coming in the door. "And what is it, Billy, that I'm delivering?"

He reached for the magnifying glass and turned back to *Coins of the Americas, 1600–1825.* "Something no one else is desperate enough to move."

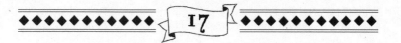

17

Night Delivery

hat I didn't know, of course, was that to Billy Tweed "helping a friend" meant hauling two heavy bags, loaded with goods I was forbidden to see, from the bloodied back entrance of Magruder's Slaughter House to a dock on the East River. It meant delivering them to a man who wouldn't give his name or show his face, and who put a knife to me throat when, in a moment of sheer terror, I forgot the password one of Billy's thugs had given me.

"Birds to Roost," I finally managed, the blade cold at me skin.

"Watch it, kid," the man's gravelly voice scolded through

his hood as he snatched the bags from me and shoved me aside. "Next time I won't be so patient."

"Next time?" I gasped as the hooded figure turned from me to the dock. I wasn't sure what Billy was up to, but I knew it wasn't good. And I also knew, without him ever once having to say it, that if I was caught, or somehow failed in me delivery, I'd never find Sam Livingston. Or would end up facedown in the East River like the other lads who'd crossed him.

The hooded man hesitated, a sinister cackle creeping from his shrouded face. "Don't be a fool, boy. With Billy Tweed, the job is never done."

So when I met Billy at dawn at the door of the Skaden Brush Works, I was quick with me demand.

"You had success, they tell me," he said, leading me past the bins of brass wire and horsehair bristles and blocks of wood waiting for the day's crew of laborers to arrive.

"Kept me word," I replied, rubbing the sleep from me eyes as we climbed the narrow staircase. I hadn't gotten to bed until 2:00 A.M., and was headed for another grueling day at the forge. "Now take me to Sam Livingston."

Billy grimaced as he strolled to his desk and sat down. "You'll be pleased to know I'm working on it."

"*Working* on it?" The blood rushed to me cheeks. "I risked me neck last night and you don't know where Sam Livingston is?"

The white cat with the gray patches meowed and rubbed up against me leg. Then it leapt into the chair next to Billy's desk.

"Now, now," Billy chided, looking at me with a furrowed brow, like a parent twice his age. "I can see you're anxious. Take a seat." He pointed to the chair. "Scat, Nolan! You'll have to find another spot."

"I'm not sitting!" I said.

Nolan glanced at me, sleepily, then tucked his head between his paws and closed his eyes.

"Fine," Billy huffed. "But after all I've done for you since you arrived off that boat from who knows where, I'd think you'd show a bit more respect."

I stared at him, willing meself to stay calm.

"It seems Livingston's more complicated to track down than I'd thought."

"Are you saying you don't actually know him?" I said through gritted teeth.

"Don't put words in my mouth," Billy snapped. "For your information, I've verified that he is indeed alive and kicking. Even you didn't know that for sure, now, did you?"

I rubbed me forehead. From me calculations, the man had to be well over eighty years old. That he might already be dead, after all I'd been through—after all I'd sacrificed—had been gnawing at me for months.

Billy stood and stretched, then paced to the other side of the room. "Problem is, he's moved around quite a bit in the last few years. He's a private man, you see." He paused. "A most private man. And so my sources tell me it will cost you to continue their search."

"*Cost me?*" I asked. "Billy, you know I earn but one dollar a week!"

"'Course I do! Without me you wouldn't have a job."

I looked at me feet.

"But in this case, because of the careful work you did last night, I might be willing to help you secure the extra funds. That is . . . if you're able to help me with another small delivery."

As he dangled the words over me, I thought of the hooded man and his warning.

"My friend from the South—the one I mentioned yesterday . . . It seems he has a few more bags to relocate. And he needs them moved sooner than he expected."

"And if I move them," I muttered, "you'll have the information I'm seeking? Waiting for me here—*by tomorrow morning?*"

"Bright and early." He pounded his fist on the desk as if to reinforce his claim. "And trust me," he added with a wink, "that's saying a lot. I have a Democratic Party gathering tonight at Finney's Saloon with some of the boys from Tammany. After last month's meeting I didn't revive myself before noon, if you know what I mean." Then he stood and leaned toward me. "I like you, Chris Roberts. And for that reason alone I'm willing to sacrifice some shut-eye."

I buried me head in me hands and groaned. Everything inside me told me not to say yes, and yet . . .

"All right," I said. "One more delivery."

And when I looked up, Billy was on his feet, a wily smile painted cross his face.

"Same password?" I asked.

"Same password. Only this time, because of"—he hesitated—"recent complications, you'll be picking up at the Dudley Glue Factory on Twenty-Third Street and Third Avenue."

"Twenty-Third Street!" I'd been as far north as Fourteenth Street, but never to Twenty-Third. In fact, until that moment, I hadn't realized the streets went that high.

It was when I was halfway up Broad Way to the forge that I heard the lad who sold the morning paper calling at the corner. "*New York Sun*! Hot off the press!" he shouted. "Georgia's new Dahlonega Mint robbed! Nationwide search begins!"

"Where's Georgia?" I asked.

The lad wiped his runny nose with his ragged sleeve and laughed. "Don't know nothin', do you?"

"Just tell me," I demanded, grabbing his arm. I had already had a dose of Billy, and wasn't about to be insulted by a newspaper boy two times smaller than meself. "Where is it?"

"In the South, you idiot," he scoffed, yanking himself free. "Everyone knows that, don't they? 'Cept you immigrants!"

I had only one penny in me pocket, but I used it to buy a copy. And when I read the headline, I knew what it was I would be delivering.

18

A Murderer
Shetland, March 23, 1842

Quit your drittlin','" Mann barked at the door. He stood, brandishing a rusted flintlock pistol. "I've got better things to do than wait around for lazy smugglers."

Taking care not to spill the nearly overflowing chamber pots, we ambled down the hall, stopping to collect the other prisoners at each of the cells.

First John, then Gill Lawrence, the grumpy man Malcolm had warned me about waking, then Buck Sinclair, Rufus Wrightson, and Ivan Inge. Each of their faces was dirtier than the next, with sunken eyes and skin long deprived of the sun.

"Chris," John whispered, managing to draw close, "are they treating you right?"

I shrugged, torn between the urge to cuff him and an almost desperate yearning to tell him about the carving of the tree.

"Mann tells me the trial is the day after tomorrow, but without the evidence they don't have much to go by."

"No evidence?" I asked. "And what do you call a dead ewe and that letter you left for Daa?"

He looked away quickly. "I *told* you I was gunna tell Daa the truth when I paid him back. I just needed time to do it right."

Was it possible, I wondered—could he somehow think his actions just? "And offer your wee brother as a sacrifice? How do I know you woulda ever come back?"

"I gave you me word is how!" he said, eyebrows raised. "Haven't I always looked after you? Are you *questioning* your own brother's word?"

"That's enough chatter out of you Robertsons!" Keeper Mann snarled, hustling us along. But as we neared the washroom, he gradually slowed his pace and peered inside. "Well, good evenin' to ya, Miss Pepper."

"Good evenin', Keeper Mann." A thin woman the age of Aunt Alice looked up from a tub of hot, soapy water.

"*Opportunities*," Malcolm whispered, brushing by me with a wink and a nudge.

By the time we reached the end of the hall, Mann caught back up with us and unlocked the door. When he flung it open, me knees nearly buckled at the smell.

"Solus Christus!" John gasped. "Is it ever cleaned out?"

Before us, extending along the back side of the entire building, was the trench.

"Only when we get hardworkin' crofters like you to do it." Keeper Mann cackled. "You lads are accustomed to shovelin' the sludge from your byre to your fields. Perhaps you can show us how it's done!"

"And may the Devil take you straight to Hell," John muttered under his breath, his eyes flashing angrily.

"Oh, this is nothin'," Mann added. "Just wait till summer. That's when you'll know you're a long way from home."

As we dumped our pots, I noticed Rufus Wrightson lean over to John and whisper into his ear.

"All right, then, that's enough fresh air for the evenin'." Keeper Mann motioned us back and swung closed the door. But as we made our way down the hall, John brushed up beside me.

"I'll get us out of this," he whispered. "I have a plan."

"No more of your plans, Brother," I scoffed. "I'm safer on me own."

"Trust me," he said, grasping urgently to me arm. "I have it all worked out." Then he darted his eyes at Malcolm. "Listen, Chris, you're in danger. Rufus just told me your cellmate's a murderer. Killed a man from Unst—they say they have the evidence to prove it."

"Malcolm? Bah! He's harmless," I muttered. "And last I heard, they dunna allow murder weapons in the cells."

"Aye," John said, eyebrows raised. "From what I hear, MacPherson uses a rope."

JOHN'S WORDS ECHOED INSIDE ME, AND THIS time, when I listened to the sound of Mann's key locking me back in that cell with Malcolm MacPherson, I couldn't stop trembling.

"It's a miracle a' sorts, I reckon," Malcolm said, yanking the cord from his mattress.

I jumped back toward the door. "How do you mean?"

"That you knew of the carving in the broch and then ended up in the same cell as the carver. Why, you should slap a muckle smoorikin on your thieving brother for the trouble he's caused. If it weren't for his haf-krakked, double-crossing scheme to do you in, you'd never a' found it."

"Not much good it'll do me being locked in this place," I said, suddenly realizing the size of his thick, muscular arms.

"What're ya looking so pale-faced about? It's nearly complete!"

Me body froze as he slowly coiled the cord between his hands.

"If, by some miracle, we got away with that rope of yours," I managed, "and by another miracle we got ourselves out of Lerwick without being caught, we'd be convicts on the run. Prison breakers at that! What good would that do us or our families?"

"With a trunk full of ducats? Are you daft?" Malcolm

scoffed. "Why, one could buy his way off the island forever—his entire family included!"

"So you reckon—"

"Well, of course I do! It all makes perfect sense. The spy had to be hiding up in that broch of yours—no one else would've carved that tree."

"But what if—"

"He was bored and simply liked to carve? Hah! That tree's an American symbol, and he left it for a reason. He wanted to come back for what he left, but he also knew the chances were good he'd never get to. So he left a clue so someone else could, just in case."

"But it's been more than sixty years," I argued, allowing meself to forget for a moment that I might soon be me cellmate's next victim. "Do you actually think there's a chance a trunk load of ducats has been hidden in the broch all this time?"

"I canna say for sure," he answered, inching ever closer. "Does anyone else know of the carving?"

"Och, no. You need to know where to look. It's only John and me ever goes there."

"All these years I've looked at that strange tree and wondered what it meant." Malcolm chuckled, the coil taut between his hands.

"John has a plan," I blurted, me breath quickening. "To get me out. Maybe he could help you too!"

"Hah!" Malcolm scoffed, a wild glint in his eye. "I saw him

trying to get to you out there in the hall. Don't tell me you want to count on him after what he's done! I know it's tempting, him being your big brother and all. But just because you love someone don't mean you can trust 'em."

"Love?" I said, spitting at the floor. "You can't have love for someone who betrays you."

Malcolm whistled, so close I felt his stale breath brush across me face.

"'Course you can. We humans can't help it. Just look at me Netty—after all I've done, she still comes round faithfully with everything I ask. Love in family's a powerful thing—you just can't let it mess with *opportunities!*"

I looked quickly about the room, finding nowhere to move, Malcolm's hulking body towering over me.

"John—he's cleverer than most." I felt sweat forming on me brow. "Perhaps we should hear him out."

"Hmmph! Seems all that knowledge hasn't gotten him too far. He's in Lerwick Prison, isn't he? And he's gotten you stuck in here with a dangerous man like me." He grimaced. "What's bothering you, lad? You're jittery all of a sudden."

I swallowed hard, eyes fixed on the cord, Malcolm's hand raised just inches from me neck.

"Just relax. Won't take but a minute if you don't put up a struggle. The bristles cut at your flesh a bit at first—but before you know it, the worst part's over and you don't feel a thing."

"Is—is—is that what you said to Gilbert Bain?" I blurted, me back pressed so tightly into the door I thought me spine would crack. "Did you strangle him, Malcolm? Did you use a rope?"

As me words spilled out, his mouth dropped open. And then he slowly stepped back. "Lor', lad! Were you thinking I was about to do you in?"

I held me breath, staring at his hands.

And then Malcolm suddenly burst into laughter. "I was handing you the skein is all—so we can twist it into the rope. Remember what I told you? Takes two to do the job!"

"John said . . . ," I started, not daring to exhale. "I asked you a question!"

And as I spoke, his expression turned to ice. "What happened in Unst is between me and the Almighty."

"You're wanting me trust, when you can't tell me the truth?"

"And you, Chris Robertson, is there nothing you've ever kept to yourself?"

As he uncoiled the cord from his hands, I thought of Mary and what I hadn't said about what I did to Pete Peterson's ewe.

"Och, lad, you have every right not to take me at me word," me bedraggled cellmate continued, his voice beginning to soften. Then he threw the unfinished rope at me feet. "You've known me but a few hours. To expect that would be asking more than I deserve. 'Twas fate brought you here—I know it. And whether it's with me or with your double-crossing brother that you bust out of this place, you owe it to that American spy to find what he meant you to find."

I stared at the cord, throat tight, not knowing what to believe.

"You've an entire life ahead of you," Malcolm continued. "Do you want to help your family or spend the next few years locked up in here?"

I pictured Catherine and Victoria, waking hungry, as pudgy George Marwick's threat of eviction loomed over them.

"All right." I swallowed hard. Then I reached down and grabbed the cord with both hands. "Show me how it's done."

19

Unexpected Help

oot, lad! Will ya sit?" Malcolm chided. "Much
more of that pacing and you'll get me nerves up."

"Sorry," I said. But I couldn't keep me mind
from spinning. I had hardly slept, and the trial
was set for ten o'clock the next morning. "Explain to me again where the stairs are?"

Malcolm rolled his eyes. "Partway down the hall on the
right, just opposite the entrance to the washing room and
airin' room—you've passed them three times now."

"And you're quite certain Keeper Mann will stop?"

"Always does. Trust me, there's nothin'll keep that dreep
from looking in on Priscilla Pepper. She's as bonnie a lass as

his ugly face ever gets the chance to see. Even has one or two teeth left!"

"You're sure she'll be there?"

"Hasn't missed an evening since last Christmas."

We had already completed the rope, me standing at one end of the cell and Malcolm at the other, turning the pig bristle and horsehair skein in opposite directions until it was taut, and then folding it back on itself, causing it to twist naturally together into one two-ply cord. Malcolm had wrapped the finished piece around his waist, carefully hiding it under his tattered, gray smock.

All that was left was to wait.

But when the keeper unlocked the door for the evening trip to the trench, the whiskey on his breath was our first clue that something wasn't right. His nose was purple, eyes like slits, and as he barged in, pistol raised above his head, he did so with such force that the door slammed back against the wall and dented the plaster.

We were nearly down the hall when Gill Lawrence leaned his head to Malcolm's.

"Look sharp," I overheard him whisper. "Word has it the keeper's had a bit too much a' the hooch. Got a bee in his bonnet 'cause the rumor is the laundress is bein' replaced."

Gill was still speaking when Mann's pistol came driving into his back.

"Any more outta you, Lawrence, and that chamber pot'll be overflowin' before I let you out again!"

I tried to get Malcolm's attention. There were no more chances—me trial was the next day!

Suddenly John butted between us. Then, just as we neared the washroom, he caught me eye and winked. It was at that moment that he kicked out his foot, and before I could register what he had done, the already unsteady keeper flew face-first onto the cold stone floor.

"Over here!" John shouted, waving his hand to the others as he burst through the door into the airing room, where I had met with Reverend Sill. "Let's stretch our limbs a bit, lads!"

"Hey!" Keeper Mann bellowed, flailing on the floor. "Get back here, ya good-for-nothin', haf-krakked crofters!"

But as I and the other men dropped our chamber pots and started after John, a hand tugged firmly at me arm. "*Opportunities*," Malcolm whispered.

The next thing I knew, we were flying up the rickety set of stairs to the second floor.

"In here!" he said, grabbing the latch of the first door we came to on the right at the top of the stairs.

But it held fast.

I darted to the door on the opposite side of the hall. "How about this one?" I was about to grab the latch, when Malcolm jerked me arm back so hard that he nearly pulled it out of its joint.

"That's the sheriff's chambers!" he whispered, a finger to his lips.

We raced down the hall, hearing voices shouting below

us. But when I reached for the next door on the left, he again pulled me away.

"Courtroom. Windows open to the side—they'll see us climb out!"

That left only one more door, at the end of the hall on the right. Together we charged toward it—but its latch, too, held fast.

"We're trapped!" I cried, me heart pounding so hard inside me ribs I thought they might break.

"Not yet we're not," he said, throwing his massive frame at the rough, splintered boards. "Keeper Mann's quarters."

In an instant we burst into a sparsely furnished room, an unmade iron bed by the window. Outside, a thick fog had taken over Lerwick. Malcolm flung up the sash, then lifted his smock so I could unravel the rope from his waist. We had just finished tying it to the bedpost when we heard footsteps clambering up the stairs.

"Down you go!" he shouted.

"It's your rope!"

"Don't be daft—you're the only one knows the way to the broch!"

"What about Netty and your bairns?"

But before I could finish, he grabbed me by the waist and hoisted me over the sill. "I'm right behind ya, lad!"

Me feet had just touched the ground at the edge of the trench when there was a loud crash from above.

"MacPherson! You're a goner!" Keeper Mann's voice bellowed. And then there was the ear-piercing blast of his pistol and the smell of gunpowder.

"Prisoner escape! Prisoner escape!" a voice cried. "Secure the gates! Fire the cannons!"

Malcolm had been shot at close range. Even if he was still alive, I knew he wasn't coming down that rope.

Not daring to look back, I leapt over the trench. Then I felt me way through the blanket of fog along the fort wall, slipping under the archway of the west entrance behind the barracks, shouts and a parade of heavy footsteps thundering behind me. When I disappeared down the high-walled lane, I could hear the cannons boom three times from the garrison wall. All of buildings had been alerted to me escape.

It was dusk, but you'd never know it, the fog clinging to buildings in every direction. If only I hadn't been wearing the prison smock, I thought, there might be a chance to slip out of the city unnoticed. And then I remembered me clothes behind the hedge at Canfield House.

For nearly an hour I searched frantically for landmarks that would lead me to Hillhead—ducking in and out of alleys, anything that seemed familiar. Sounds carried around me, confused by the misty air—every lane looking like the last. If only I had paid more attention when I had been with Mary. I turned left and then right, nearly finding meself back at Fort Charlotte twice before finally hovering in an alley behind a shop to collect me thoughts. The one thing I knew for certain was that I had no idea where I was.

And then I heard a voice from but ten feet away.

"Saw a lad just a minute ago, Sheriff Nicolson," a wee, bent woman said, standing in a doorway a hundred yards away from me. She motioned to the familiar angular outline of a man inspecting his pocket watch, then turned and pointed in me direction. It was at that moment there was a cry from down the lane and the sound of gunfire. And as the faint outline of Sheriff Nicolson darted away, I sprinted up the nearest alley, sparing not even a second to look behind me.

Hair matted and body trembling, I stumbled one way and another, hoping for something—anything—that I recognized. Then I saw it: the grand stairs leading to Canfield House.

In minutes I was in the back behind the hedge, stripping off the prison smock and pulling me old shirt, gansey, breeks, and rivlins from behind a rock in the wall. They had never looked so good!

"Chris?"

I must have jumped five feet in the air as Mary's face appeared through the branches. "Lor', lass!" I said, hugging me worn garments tightly to me chest. "You nearly frightened me to death!"

But before she could say another word, we heard more shouts from the street, and she ducked behind the hedge next to me. For a moment we cowered, too frightened to breathe, as the fog turned into drizzle. Then, finally, the voices passed.

"Midder and I heard the cannons, and the calls about the prison break. I hoped it was you!" she whispered.

"How did you know I'd come here?"

"I remembered the clothes. Thought there was a chance you'd be back for them."

"Aye. Your Midder was cheering they'd catch me, no doubt, after all the trouble I've caused."

"Well, I admit I didn't tell her why I was stepping out," she said, a smile creeping from her lips. And then she noticed the wound on me bare shoulder. And me newly bent nose.

"Lor', Chris. What did they do to you in there?"

"I must be a sight," I said, eyeing me shoulder. "Was John did that. Found him in the Marwick Lodberry, just after you left with your brother."

"And what of the pouch—did he have it?"

I sighed. "Already spent. It's a long tale. Perhaps one day I'll have time to tell it."

"And Sheriff Nicolson? They say it was he who brought you in."

"He and Knut found us. Right there on the dock. Your uncle was lucky to get away when he did."

"We made it south of the harbor without even a chase. After I explained all that had happened, me uncle and Charles couldn't believe they had slipped away so easily."

"Aye. Well, before Sheriff Nicolson took John and me to Fort Charlotte, I happened to mention we were expecting a shipment from the *Ernestine Brennan* at the Marwick Lodberry. The Revenue Men are still waiting there for your uncle, I expect."

"You threw them off?"

I smiled quickly, happy to have done at least one good deed: "Figured I didn't need any more reasons for your brother not to approve of me. He already has quite a list."

Her cheeks colored as she glanced away. "We came ashore before dawn at the Sands of Sound, just south of here. When Charles brought me home, Reverend Sill told us about you being taken to the prison. He was fuming when he left to see you, but quite distraught when he returned."

"Hah! The old goat nearly managed to get me the Transportation!"

"Och, Chris, you can't mean it!"

"Aye. Well, they'll have to catch me first."

She gingerly touched me shoulder. "I should get this cleaned and bandaged."

"No," I said, pulling her hand down, but somehow finding the courage to keep it in mine. "I don't have time."

I glanced at her face, but in the end it was Mary who took a step closer, wrapping her arms tightly around me back, me spine tingling at her touch.

"Oh Lor', Mary, I can't let you go," I said, surprised by her wet cheek on me shoulder.

"You have no choice!" she whispered, burying her face in me chest. "The whole island's looking for you."

"Then I'll come back—just as soon as I can!" I awkwardly touched the edge of her hap, me fingers at her hair as the drizzle continued.

"No, Chris, you can't," she said softly. "You've caused more trouble than anyone is likely to forget—even if you wait years to return."

"I have a plan, Mary. I just have to get to the broch."

"In Culswick? The one you told me about with the carving of the tree?"

"Aye."

"But why? It's near your croft! Surely your Daa will find you."

"There's something hidden there. At least I think there is. And it's me only chance to . . ." I stopped short, glancing at her hand, now wet with rain but still in mine.

"What?"

"Get free of Shetland."

As I spoke I could feel her tremble.

"Come with me," I said, pushing her back gently, touching her warm cheeks with me hands. "Will you, Mary?"

"Yes—no! Lor', Chris, we're far too young for that." Then she reached for me shirt and helped me pull it on. "And I can't leave Midder by herself."

"Then one day," I pleaded. "When we've grown? I'll send word when I know I'm safe."

"Do you ever look at the stars?" she whispered, grabbing me hand once again and pointing to the sky. "That is, on the rare occasion we Shetlanders can see them."

I followed her gaze to the murky gray above us.

"My favorite constellation is Orion. Do you know it?"

I nodded, imagining the warrior's arms and legs sprawled above us, the three diagonal stars of his belt. "Aye, I do," I said. "But it's not the stars I'm thinking of right now."

"When me Daa would leave us," she continued, "Charles and me, for a trip or journey of some sort, he'd point to Orion. Just before he left. And he'd tell us that when we missed him we were to look for the warrior, high in the sky. And that would be our connection, no matter how far apart we were. Because he'd be looking too."

"Our connection?" I asked. And then I suddenly knew she was saying good-bye. "Please, Mary! Don't tell me I'll never see you again!"

"Chris," she said, her voice trembling. Then she pointed to a cloth sack tucked behind the branches. "I gathered what food I could without Midder seeing, after we first heard the cannons. It should feed you for a day or so, at least." Then she reached into her pocket and slipped a cool, round object into the palm of me hand. "Since you'll not have me to show you the way, you'll be needing this."

It was a compass. Silver with a heavy glass face and the initials "C.C.C." engraved on the cover.

I looked at it, stunned. "Are you sure?"

She nodded, pressing it into me hand. "You know how to use it?"

"Aye." I looked up and smiled at her, suddenly shivering in the growing wind. "You of all people know I'm quick to get lost."

She laughed as I slipped it into me pocket. "Well, I must say I was stunned you found your way this far."

I touched me fingers lightly to her cheek. Then, suddenly, there was shouting in the distance.

"Go!" she said, pushing the sack into me chest and pulling me through the hedge.

"Which way?" I asked.

"Down Hillhead till it ends. Then you'll turn left until the second lane, where you'll take a right. That will take you to the road out of Lerwick. Can you remember that, Chris? Can you?"

I nodded, glancing nervously up and down Hillhead.

"If you're quick about it you'll be west of the Hill of Dale by sunrise."

I turned to look at her one last time before releasing her hand. "I won't forget you, Mary Canfield," I whispered. "Ever." Then I sprinted into the night.

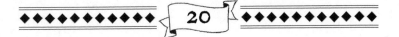

20

On the Run

I was thankful for the cover of darkness as I darted through the wet, frigid air. In time the grand houses of Lerwick were behind me. And when the sun rose, I curled up behind a shrub on the Hill of Dale, high above the path Reverend Sill and I had taken, and slept. It was when I awoke at sundown that I heard voices, and from me perch I saw a group of men gathered on the path below. Among them, unmistakable, even from a distance, was Sheriff Nicolson.

"Knut Blackbeard says he's headed to America," I heard one of the men say. "If that's true, he'll linger round Lerwick. That is, if he wants to hitch a ride."

"Nah," Sheriff Nicolson scoffed. "Too scared, that one. Headed straight for home, he is. I'd put money on it."

"To Culswick?"

"Aye."

"Then west it is. We'll spend the night at the Sinclair croft outside of Tingwall. Then set out again at first light."

I didn't linger to hear more. With the help of Mary's compass, I stumbled through the moonlight as best I could, staying off the path until I was several miles north of Tingwall. Only then did I cut west in the direction of Culswick, knowing that, with no lantern to guide me and with the need to stay well off the path, the journey would take much longer than it had when I had traveled with Reverend Sill. Even without his heavy kishie on me shoulders, the rugged hills of heather and peat seemed endless.

As I trudged along, I tried to make sense of all that had happened. Why Malcolm had foolishly sent me ahead of him. Why John, of all people, had made it possible for me to escape. In the end John had protected me, just as he promised. And in doing so sacrificed the freedom he wanted more than anything else.

By the close of the second day I finished the last of the bread and cheese Mary had packed, and by the third was so ravenous I began to feel dizzy and weak. In desperation I scavenged the soft moss on the edge of a burn, as me Midder had taught me to do in the worst of times. But with no way to cook it, the bitter greens churned miserably in me belly and me pace slowed considerably. I knew it was only a matter of time before Sheriff Nicolson and his men caught up with me.

It wasn't until nearly dusk on the third day that the familiar thatched roof of Knut's croft came into view. Not long afterward I made out the dim outline of me own croft house in Culswick, smoke from the fire wafting from the roof. Oh, how I longed to cross that familiar threshold! To swallow but a mouthful of Aunt Alice's broth or a piece of dried cod! But I forced meself to think of those hidden ducats. How I might use them to help save me family. To save meself. How I might use them to buy John's freedom.

As always in Shetland, the wind pulled hard across the heather and through me gansey and shirt. I waited again for dark, shivering in the shelter of an ancient byre, long since abandoned and roofless, as clouds whipped across the dim light of the moon. It being lambing season, the wee baaing sounds reverberated from all directions of the scattald. Had Daa, I wondered, had success attaching the Peterson lambs to one of our ewes as he had many times before?

The climb to Culswick Broch, which had always seemed effortless, took everything I had. When I finally dropped to me hands and knees and crawled under the lintel stone above the entrance and into its circular inner wall, I lay still for a moment, head throbbing, too weak to pull meself up.

As if in a daze, I thought of Malcolm. Gone forever—his wife and children left with no one to care for them. And of

Catherine and Victoria—soon to be cast from the croft by the likes of George Marwick because I hadn't retrieved the coins. And then a bank of clouds drifted over the moon, leaving me in darkness.

I staggered to me feet and felt across the wall for the chiseled outline of the tree. Just seven nights before, John had been there—in that very spot—in the wilds of the March gale, the promise of the new life he had dreamed of alive in his eyes.

When I felt the carving, I searched around frantically with me fingers for an opening in the wall where the ducats might be. I threw me body against the surrounding stones, then tried grasping the carving itself—left side, right, top, and bottom—but it was so perfectly wedged into the stones surrounding it that me fingernails couldn't find any leverage.

It was when the clouds finally parted from the moon that I noticed a cluster of smaller rocks driven between two larger stones to the left of the carving. I clawed at one, driving me jagged fingernails around it until it eventually pulled free. Then the stone beside it came loose, and another, until I was able to work me fingers behind one of the two larger stones and swivel it out just enough for me hand to find its way inside. What for all those years I had presumed was one four-foot-wide circular wall was actually two walls—with an open chamber between!

Removing more of the small stones, I swiveled the large one farther still, until I could reach me entire arm—up to the shoulder—into the cold, damp space between. Feeling around wildly—high and low, back and forth, I suddenly brushed something soft, just beyond me grasp. Then I frantically clawed away more stones, widening the opening even more until, bent at the hip, I stretched me shoulders and chest inside.

It was just as I clamped both hands to the object that I felt a sharp pull at me breeks. The next thing I knew I was flying backward, landing on me back, a heavy, weathered satchel pressed into me belly.

"Guess we always knew that carving was special," John said, looking down at me, his wide smile beaming in the moonlight.

"Solus Christus, Brother!" I cheered. I had never been so happy to see anyone in me life.

"Told you I'd get us out of there. All you and Mal needed was a chance to get upstairs."

"But . . . but . . . Keeper Mann had his pistol!" I said, slowly sitting up.

"Soon as he noticed you and Malcolm were missing, the fool flew up those stairs like a rat to cheese. Forgot all about me and the other men, so we just opened the back door and jumped the blasted trench."

"*All* of you?"

"Aye." He reached out a hand and pulled me to me feet. "Gill, Buck, Rufus, Ivan—overall, I'd say it was a poor evening for Keeper Mann."

"Shouldn't have doubted you," I said, brushing off the sleeve of me gansey. "Lor', John. Can you forgive me?"

"You have MacPherson to blame for that. The murdering liar. Fillin' your head with stories."

"How did you know where to find me?"

"Caught sight of you on the outskirts of Lerwick three nights ago. Been following you ever since. Knew if we traveled alone, Sheriff Nicolson and his men would have a harder time catching up with us. They're searching. Saw them only a few miles behind us earlier today."

"Where can we go?"

"Oh, I have an idea or two," he said. His eyes were wild like on the night he stole the pouch. "Now let's see those ducats."

"Wait—how did you know?"

"Och—there's not much you miss through the thin plastered walls of Lerwick Prison." But as he spoke, his voice turned strangely cold. "You and ol' Malcolm ought to be more careful next time when you talk of finding treasure."

Suddenly Midder's warning of so many years ago came back to me: *Christopher, take care with your brother John. For I fear there are times when his honor is not as it should be.*

"Hand it over," John said, reaching out as I pulled the sack tightly to me chest. Then he lunged for me as I took a diving leap into the opening of the broch wall, scrambling frantically through the wet scree, digging in with me elbows, wrenching meself forward.

"Think you can best me, Brother?" He grabbed fast to me ankles and pulled me back inside. Then he flipped me over and drove his rivlin-clad foot into the center of me gut. "You never have!"

I screamed in agony, recoiling around the satchel. And then, to me horror, watched as he stood above me, one of the stones I had loosened from the wall gripped tightly in his hand.

"Lor', John," I gasped. *"You'd stone your own brother?"*

"Damn you, Chris Robertson. No one escapes Marwick and our life of misery without a sacrifice. *No one!* That's why we grovel here, generation after generation, clawing the barren land for food, fishing empty seas!"

For a moment he hesitated, and though the light was dim, I thought I saw tears on his hollow cheeks. "Hand over the ducats!" he commanded, voice trembling. "Don't make me do this!"

"Put it down!" a voice shouted from the darkness. A lantern appeared over the top of the wall, illuminating the barrel of a pistol and the familiar weathered face of Reverend Sill.

"Surprised to see a man of the cloth with a weapon as fine as this?" His knurled finger rested steadily at the trigger. "Accurate. Very accurate. Given to me by me Daa when I was just a lad. And though the Lord has blessed me with a voice and guides me to use words, there *has* been the rare occasion that a wayward sheep has needed more than words to chase him home from Satan."

I glanced at John, the rock still defiantly poised above me. Then I saw his eyes dart to the opening under the lintel stone I had just tried crawling out of.

"A man never lost much till he lost his soul!" Reverend Sill bellowed, pulling back the pistol's hammer. "Although it would be a great blessing to the Godly people of Shetland to be rid of you forever, John Robertson!"

"Wait! Don't shoot!" I screamed, scrambling to me feet as John finally lowered the rock. In the dim light I could make out me once strong, bold brother's hands trembling at his side.

"Don't trouble yourself, lad," Reverend Sill said. "I shan't break the Lord's commandments for the likes of him. That is, unless he gives me a reason. Although I haven't had the pleasure of firing this pistol in some time. Tell me, John Robertson, what do you suppose is in the satchel Christopher clutches to his chest?"

"I have me theories," John said, swallowing hard. "And I expect they are the same as yours."

"Go on."

"Gold ducats. Dutch, perhaps. Or at least that's how the story goes. But the American spy was supposed to have buried them on Bressay Isle, not in Culswick Broch. So I suppose it's possible there is nothing in it at all."

"Ah. You know the legend," Reverend Sill said.

"Aye." John scowled, jaw clenched. "Thought it but an island yarn till I overheard me brother and MacPherson chatting about the carving in their cell. It didn't take much to put the pieces together."

"Then let's find out what's here, shall we?" I said, tugging at the brass buckle that secured the outer flap. "Once and for all."

"Leave it, lad!" Reverend Sill commanded, still pointing his pistol at John. "Your brother doesn't deserve the pleasure of finding out what's inside."

"Don't I?" John said, eyes flashing. "Chris and I found the carving. We've been coming here since we were bairns."

"You, John Robertson, are a lad of deep moral delinquencies. This very night I will be relieving this island of your presence for a very long time."

"Hah—you can't force me from the island."

"Can't I? As we speak, anchored just off nearby Skeld Voe, my dear friend Captain Leisk awaits in his whaler. Word has it he is in need of another sturdy Shetlander to complete his crew. He leaves for the Davis Strait at dawn."

John's eyes narrowed, fists clenched at his sides. "You'll not force me to sea!"

And at that moment, it seemed, everything happened at once. John sprang like a rabbit into the shadows of the partially collapsed back wall of the broch, Reverend Sill's pistol exploded, and the dusty odor of gunpowder spilled into the night. What followed was a great commotion of grunts and thuds—until a massive silhouette, holding John firmly by the wrists, bounded into the light.

Knut Blackbeard had found us already! I was so terrified me feet wouldn't move! And then, when the figure slowly edged into the light, yanking John ahead of him, I could hardly contain meself.

"Phew, Reverend! You nearly blew me head off when I scrambled over the wall to stop him."

"Malcolm!" I cried.

He appeared more bedraggled than ever, hair a-fly, and a

bloodstain on the shoulder of his tattered prison smock. "Turns out the keeper was so full of the hooch, he only managed to graze me shoulder. When I finally slipped down the rope, you was runnin' so fast I just couldn't catch you."

Malcolm looked about the inside of the broch. "You mean to tell me that this jumble a' stones is what all the fuss is about?"

I pointed to the carving of the tree. "Look familiar?"

He ran the fingers of his right hand over the etched stone while gripping John tightly with his left. "Your brother said you was the smart one," he said to John. "So what were you doing tryin' to climb that wall when the reverend had a pistol to your back?"

John spat. "I'll not go to sea!"

"Aha!" Reverend Sill said, shaking his head. "He—like the dogs of Satan's tribe—fears the danger of the sea more than the wrath of the Almighty! Oh, you'll go to sea, John Robertson. And Mr. MacPherson here, in repentance for his *many* past transgressions, will volunteer to escort you personally to Captain Leisk's ship."

John struggled wildly in Malcolm's grip.

"How did you find me?" I asked Reverend Sill.

He smiled. "Let's just say your brother's pride betrayed him."

"Pride?"

"Aye. But there'll be time for explaining later." He tossed a rope over to Malcolm, who quickly bound John's wrists.

"I'll not go down like our brother William!" John cried, pulling this way and that as Malcolm muscled him up and over the crumbled wall of the broch. "Not in the dark waters of the north!"

"Aye," Reverend Sill said. "With the Devil blowing wind through his teeth, you may one day try to return. But remember, lad—Sheriff Nicolson, Keeper Mann, and their crew will be waiting." He primed the pistol, pouring in another measure of powder and shoving a ball down the barrel. Then he turned to Malcolm. "No time for delay, Mr. MacPherson. You, too, are a wanted man. If you're to get off this island undetected, you'll need the cover of darkness to do it."

"Och, aye, Reverend," Malcolm said. "You're not sendin' me away without first seein' what's in the sack, are you?"

"Have I not been clear about your mission?"

"Aye, ya have, sir. But just a wee peek? I never touched a ducat—"

"Lor', man, have you no shame? After the sins you have committed? Thefts of your neighbor's goods—leaving your wife and bairns with no father or means for sustenance. As I told you back in Lerwick, the time has come for penance, not treasure!"

Malcolm listened and dropped his head. "I stand by me word, Reverend. I shan't let you down."

"I would expect no less."

"But please—before I go—that wee matter we discussed . . ."

"Aye, man. On that you can lay your mind to rest."

"Thank you! Thank you! It's everything to me!"

I reached across the wall and grabbed his thick, calloused hand.

"Made it, didn't we?" he said, a smile bursting from his bearded face. "Just like I told ya we would!"

"'Twas your rope that did it. We have Netty to thank for that."

"Aye, we do, lad."

"Hah!" John blurted, spitting at the ground. "'Twas me got you bumblers out! And you're not rid a' me yet!"

"Enough out a' you!" Malcolm said, pulling tight on the rope as he shoved John ahead. "We've got a ship waitin'."

"Hunt you down, I will!" John shouted, turning back to me as Malcolm dragged him into the night. "Till I get what's rightfully mine."

Coins

Mr. MacPherson and I weren't sure we'd find you here," Reverend Sill said. "Although, with the Almighty watching over us, I knew there was a chance." He placed a loaf of bread and wedge of cheese on the wall between us. "Now take some nourishment."

I stuffed the bread greedily into me mouth, a thousand questions swirling in me head. "But—why?" I asked, between mouthfuls.

He grimaced. "Keeper Mann's trickery was the Devil's work. When I heard the cannons blast and news of your escape, I knew it to be the work of the Almighty making amends for what had happened."

"And you thought to come *here*?"

"No. Certainly not. On the night of your escape I searched the streets of Lerwick, hoping to find you before Sheriff Nicolson and his men. It was Mr. MacPherson I discovered instead. Poor soul—huddled in an alley off Quendale Lane."

"He told you about the carving in the broch. And the spy."

"Aye. The only problem was he knew not the name of the broch. Nor could he tell me precisely where it resided. There being who knows how many brochs across the island, this proved quite a dilemma."

"Mary told you."

"Aye."

"But what of John?"

"Ah—well, as it turns out, I wasn't the first to find Mr. MacPherson that night. He hadn't but cleared Fort Charlotte's walls when he ran smack into your brother. And it was at this meeting that John boasted of knowing your plan to find the treasure hidden at the broch."

"He helped us escape," I said. "Why didn't he just make a break for it himself and head to the broch alone?"

"I have wondered that myself." Reverend Sill shook his head. "Was it that he felt a tinge of remorse for what he had done? Or that he needed the distraction of your escape to accomplish his own? I suspect it might have been a little of both."

"I wanted to tell you everything," I blurted. "But if you

knew the truth, you'd have had no choice but to take me to the sheriff. And then I wouldn't have had the chance to get Daa's pouch back from John." I looked down, picturing the bearded man with the knitted cap at the lodberry stuffing the pouch in his pocket. "'Course, I never did get it back. But I had to try."

Reverend Sill gazed into the dark of the scattald. "That night, in the croft, you killed the Peterson ewe not because you wanted to but because you couldn't cross your Daa." He looked back at me, eyes glassy, and continued. "When you finally confessed the truth, it jarred a memory. One I've kept buried deep. I, too, had a Daa, you see. And a fierce one at that. He was a powerful man in the Church—led the parish of Lerwick for more than thirty years. While I was a lad we had a servant boy, Jan Josephson, who was about my age. We were like brothers. I was the reverend's son and wasn't allowed to play with the other lads of the parish because they were considered wild and un-Godly. Jan was my only friend."

I tried to picture Reverend Sill as a lad, but it hardly seemed possible.

"Then, one day, Jan was caught stealing a loaf of bread from the baker, and Daa decided it was time I showed him his place. Told me, 'Son, you're to whip that boy, no less than twenty-five times, to be sure he has learned his lesson. For he has sinned, and we alone, as his masters, can show him the true way to redemption.' To this day I can still feel that whip in my hand." He stretched his knurled fingers before him. "And hear the sound of Jan's screams. Begging me to stop, pleading, as blood streamed down his back. But I didn't. I couldn't. For there, by my side, stood Daa—arrow-straight, in his black hat and cape—his steel-gray eyes willing me on with nary a word."

He paused for a moment, his Adam's apple bobbing in his wrinkled, leathery throat. "It's a powerful force a Daa has over his son. A powerful force."

I looked away, me arms hugged tightly to me chest. "And when that force is dark?"

Reverend Sill cocked his head. "The strong grow to defy it—the weak to give in."

"And the weak?" I asked, glancing down. "Do they ever get a second chance?"

He nodded slowly. "Aye, lad. I searched for you that night because I believe they do."

"How did you and Malcolm get all the way to this side of the island?"

"Hoot!" he said, grasping the stones on the crumbled wall in front of him. "We sailed, of course!"

I raised me eyebrows. "Didn't you tell me, sir, on our walk from Skeld, that you would never again—"

"Aye, but this was a bit of an exception," he interrupted. Then cleared his throat. "After Mary explained how you had thrown Sheriff Nicolson off the *Ernestine Brennan*'s trail, George Marwick himself made the arrangements. The wind being perfect, Captain Canfield had us to Skeld Voe by day's end."

"And the pistol?"

"Never go anywhere without it. Why, it was you who carried it all the way from Skeld."

"So that's what was in the kishie." I laughed. "And here I thought I was carrying a load of stones!"

THE SACK FROM INSIDE THE BROCH WALL WAS coated with a lichen-colored mold that came off easily on me fingertips as I unfastened the buckle securing the outer flap. Inside, me fingers touched what seemed to be a jumble of odd-shaped objects—and then, suddenly, something flat and round.

It was cold to the touch and sparkled in the lantern light. "It's a coin," I cried, laying it on the wall. "But is it a ducat?"

Reverend Sill grabbed the coin in his crooked fingers and held it to the light. It was beautifully struck: a knight on the front, sword over his shoulder, and a bundle of arrows clutched in his hand. "Aye," he said, his wrinkled face stretched into a satisfied smile. "From 1780. Shetland hasn't seen the likes of these in many, many years."

He held it out to me. "See these words on the outer edge? Latin, it is. PAR.CRES.HOL.CONCORDIA.RES. 'Through concord wee things grow—Holland.' In other words, 'Union is strength.'"

I pulled out more and stacked them neatly together. And then a hammer and chisel. "Tools he used to make the carving in the stone?"

"Go on, lad!" Reverend Sill said, brushing them aside. "We haven't much time. Pull out the rest of the coins so we can make a full count."

I glanced at the stack before me. "Five in all, I'd say."

"Can't be. There are many more than that."

I felt around inside the sack again. "Only this," I said, pulling out one remaining coin and placing it on the wall. It was nearly three times the size of the ducats but surprisingly lighter and struck with the word MASATHVSETS. I held it to the light. In the center was the exact replica of the tree chiseled into the broch and scratched into the wall in Lerwick Prison! On the back, the year 1652. "The tree on the treeless island of Shetland!"

"Bah!" Reverend Sill said. He grabbed it from me, and gave it a sniff. "Silver is all. An American piece. Worthless!" Then he hurled it into the dark reaches of the broch. "There must be other sacks! Crawl back in the wall, lad, and have a good look around."

He handed me the lantern. I scrambled into the slippery, moss-coated space I had already uncovered, groveling on me hands and knees.

"Nothing," I called.

"Nonsense! Look again!"

I crawled out. "What makes you so sure?"

"Hoot, lad! It was the talk of the island at the time. The captain of the ship, a Dutchman, was caught but a day after the wreck. It was he who confessed that they set sail from Rotterdam with a trunk filled with ducats. When the English officers returned to Bressay Isle where the ship had come aground, the trunk was empty!"

I thought of Bressay Isle, across the sound from Lerwick Harbor, clear on the other side of Shetland from where we stood. "But that's many days' journey from here," I said, brushing the dirt and lichen from me breeks.

"Aye, by land."

"And the American—he was on the run for months?"

Reverend Sill nodded, looking longingly at the five gold coins neatly stacked on the wall.

I rubbed me chin. "I've been on the run meself these last three days. I couldn't have made it with a sack loaded with ducats."

At first Reverend Sill said nothing, and then he erupted into a low, guttural moan, clapping his hand to his brow. "Of course! How could I have been such a fool?"

I nodded to the five coins. "But he did bring these."

"Aye, lad. More gold than any man in this parish has seen in a lifetime."

I looked at him, puzzled. The old man turned to the scattald below us. "A dream is all," he muttered, his voice steeped in anguish. "Satan luring me, senseless, with treasure. I thought—had we found the missing ducats—the people of the parish would finally have the capital to end, for good, this ruthless oppression."

"To free us from *Marwick*?" I asked.

"Aye, lad." He dropped his head in his hands. "To start our own fishery—set our own prices. I was foolish to hope . . ."

For a moment I didn't understand. And then I thought of

why John yearned to leave for America. To live in a place free of the hand of Marwick. If we were able to start our own fishery, that place would be here in Shetland!

"Forgive me." His voice quavered. And then he cleared his throat. "It will not surprise you, lad, that Sheriff Nicolson has offered a reward for your capture. And should you be discovered, with a charge of prison-breaking added to your list of offenses, I have no doubt it will be the Transportation you will face."

"How is it, sir," I asked softly, "that a lad can make but one bad turn—just one—and by doing so leave the rest of his life in shambles?"

"Life," he sighed, "is but a trail of decisions. When you're a lad you do as you're told. It's only when you're a man that you choose for yourself between dark and light."

He pulled a rolled piece of parchment from his pocket. "Captain Canfield will be waiting for you tomorrow night."

"I don't understand."

"It's all here," he said, handing it over the wall. "Now, tell me, lad, have you considered what you will be doing with your good fortune?"

I shrugged, suddenly unable to look at him for fear me eyes would start to tear. "Malcolm's wife." I bit me lip to keep me composure. "She and her bairns have no one to provide for them. Netty is her name. She lives in Lerwick with a Mrs. Jameson, I think he said."

The reverend glanced at me soberly. "Aye. Mr. MacPherson

has spoken to me of his concern for her well-being, and I have promised to look in on her and their offspring. Shall I take her a ducat, then?"

I nodded as he placed one in his pocket. Then I turned, fist clenched in the direction of our croft. "And one to Mr. Peterson. I—our family—owe him that."

I thought about Catherine and Victoria. Of Gutcher and Aunt Alice, and our dwindling supplies. Of how Daa had for years hoarded that pouch of coins as we struggled to survive. "George Marwick was *kind* enough to tell me we'd be evicted by week's end if he didn't get the contents of Daa's pouch to cover our debts," I continued, grasping another ducat and handing it across the stones. "Will this cover it?"

"Yes. I should think so," the old man said, hesitating a moment before placing the coins in his pocket. Then he stared at the two remaining ducats on the wall. "Your heart is generous, Christopher Robertson. But remember—you, too, face hard times. Perhaps harder than those you leave behind."

I glanced at the coins and tried to smile. "Imagine. A crofter with coins. It's more than I've ever dreamed of."

"Aye, lad. A gift unimaginable in our lifetime. Enough to start a life anew. Use them with discretion. In times such as these, a crofter with even one coin will raise suspicion."

"'Course," I scoffed, stuffing them into me pocket, remembering what Keeper Mann had said about me in Charles Canfield's clothing. "They'll think me a thief. And what of the ducats I've placed in your care? Will they not raise suspicion?"

"Not if I credit the generosity of a lord of my acquaintance from Inverness," he said with a wink. "Your new life will be well away from Shetland. There'll be no way to trace their origin."

And then, suddenly, I understood. "I can't go, Reverend, if it means not coming back!"

"Don't be daft, lad! Young George Marwick went to great lengths to make these arrangements. If you stay, you'll find yourself back at Fort Charlotte by week's end."

"But once you pay Mr. Peterson and Marwick the rent for the Robertson croft, there'll be nothing to hold against me!"

The old man scoffed. "Charges were pressed, and you confessed to the crime. And never underestimate the power of humiliation to fuel the quest for revenge. You and your brother, along with Mr. MacPherson, aided the escape of four other men from Lerwick Prison, and in doing so challenged the Crown's authority in the islands. You can't think that the sheriff and his court will ever look upon you favorably, can you?"

Me throat tightened, the dull ache of dread building in me gut. I thought of Catherine and Victoria without John and me to help with the chores. And of traveling to a land I'd hardly imagined. But most of all, I thought of Mary Canfield.

"This is me home," I pleaded. "Please . . . there must be another way!"

Reverend Sill stared at me a moment and then glanced in the direction of the sea. "Perhaps there is something. Unlikely, but a dim hope nevertheless."

"What? Anything!"

"Should you find the American . . ."

"Surely he's not alive," I said. "He was captured more than sixty years ago."

"Perhaps. Sam Livingston was his name. We were once acquainted."

"You've met?"

"Aye. I was but a young lad at the time, with only a flicker of ambition of ever reaching the pulpit. When word about the American and the missing ducats spread across the island, there wasn't a man, woman, or bairn in Shetland who wasn't searching for him—the Crown, you see, having offered a grand reward for his capture. He was from New York—one of those rebellious American colonies, completely disloyal to our king. And he championed the cause of the Colonists—one at the time I not only abhorred but considered aligned with Satan himself." He hesitated for a moment, then looked down. "Alas, my hatred blinded me to his immense bravery before it was too late."

"They took him to the Tower of London. Hung him for treason."

The old man winced. "That was what we expected. Nevertheless, I've not met anyone who could confirm it. They say only one American has ever been held at the Tower, and it wasn't Livingston."

But no sooner had the words left his lips than he pulled his hand quickly back and waved it before him. "Bah! It's no use.

Had he survived the ordeal, he would have returned for the ducats long ago."

"And if he didn't come back for them?"

The old man sighed. "Then, I suspect, should he live, Sam Livingston is back in New York. And the coins are in a deep pit of earth on Bressay."

"And you think, should I find this American, he would tell me where they are buried?" I asked, me heart pounding in me chest.

"To this I have no answer," he said. "It is something, I am afraid, you must seek and discover for yourself."

"But surely, finding the gold won't make Sheriff Nicolson forget me."

"Oh, but it might. For is it not Satan's treasure that lures the Lord's people from reason?"

He stared at me for a moment, then reached slowly into his kishie and placed another large hunk of bread and wedge of cheese on the wall. "Alas, I've lingered too long."

"You believe there's a chance?" I asked, me eyes finding his, searching for even a glimmer of encouragement. "That he still lives?"

"Chance?" Reverend Sill coughed, gripping his stauf tightly. "Over Divine Providence we have no power."

"I'll find him!"

Reverend Sill steadied himself on his stauf and slowly started down the hill. "Godspeed, lad," he called over his shoulder. "May we one day meet again."

"Wait!" I cried, scrambling to the top of the crumbled wall, the dim glimmer of his lantern disappearing in the night. "How did you know him, this Sam Livingston?"

"Och, lad," the old man's voice trailed in the darkness, "it was I who turned him in."

22

Good-bye

I crouched inside Culswick Broch, the sun peeking over the horizon, and slowly unfurled the rolled parchment in me lap. Me hands trembled as I touched the stiff, cream-colored paper. The elegant black letters penned precisely and deliberately, as if written with the steadiest of hands.

March 24, 1842

Dear C,

I write in haste, as the reverend tells me your life is in danger. You are to wait at the inlet near the cave by the Cliffs of Culswick.

Look for two lights from the sea. This will be your sign that a boat is coming to take you to the packet we both have awaited once before.

When you lose your way, as I have every reason to believe you will, use my compass. And when you do, I hope you will think of me. But wherever you go, you must remember to never speak of Shetland. Uncle says there are people with connections to this island in every port.

Although our meeting was ever so brief, it is one I will never forget.

Yours most sincerely,

M.

I read it over and over, tracing her letters with me finger across the surface of the paper. She had been careful with her words, no doubt fearing the letter might be intercepted. But her generous heart shone through nonetheless.

From me perch in the broch I spent the day secretly watching the goings-on in the life of which I was suddenly and strangely no longer a part. Daa turning the soil of the arable land. Aunt Alice laying the wash on the rocks behind the croft house. Poor Gutcher, a kishie burdening his decrepit back, slowly trudging across the scattald with a load of the peat. And then there was Catherine, her frail body struggling to haul kishies of sludge from the byre to where we would soon plant. Something John and I were meant to do.

Only wee Victoria was oddly nowhere to be seen.

It was a long day, the longest I can remember, until something shiny caught me eye. Against the wall at the far end of the broch was the large American coin Reverend Sill had cast away. It was nearly two hundred years old—the date 1652 struck on the back side! For hours I turned it over in me palm, the tarnished silver dull and worn. Was it the unusually grand size or the image of the tree that seemed to link the past to the present? One thing was certain: It had been important enough to Sam Livingston to hide it.

The wind was picking up at dusk when I slipped in the back door of our byre. It was the time me sisters milked the cows, and Catherine gasped when she saw me.

"You shouldn't be here! The sheriff and his men just left!"

I nodded, me finger to me lips. "Where's Vic?"

"Oh, Chris, she's been tossing and turning for two days now. Aunt Alice just canna cool her down."

The fever! I pictured her nearly emaciated body and pale face. "She needs care!"

"Aye. But mostly bread and broth, only we've no way to pay for it. Daa's beside himself with worry."

"Daa?" Did he suddenly care that his own hoarding of those coins had kept her too long from a proper meal? That if the fever didn't break soon she'd have no strength left to fight?

Without a thought, I plunged me fingers into me pocket. "Take these and bury them," I whispered, pressing the remaining two ducats into her tiny palm. "And if the fever's not passed by morning, dig them up and bring them to Reverend Sill. He will get you what you need." I had meant to give her one of the ducats and keep the other for me journey, but suddenly me own needs seemed pointless.

She stared wide-eyed and nodded.

"And you mustn't tell a soul other than the reverend that you have them," I cautioned. "No one! Especially Daa. For if they see them, they will come after you for stealing."

"Did *you* steal them, Chris?"

"Och, no! They were left many years before by someone who meant for me to find them."

"I don't understand."

"And I don't have time to explain."

"You're leaving again," she said, looking away.

I felt a lump in me throat as I turned to her. "Aye. There's no helping it, Cath."

"And John?"

"You'll not see him again. Not for a very long time. He left for sea just yesterday."

"But how will we get along? There'll be no one to help Daa with bringing in the cod!"

"There'll be no fishing for anyone this year, I'm afraid," I said. "Hard times are coming—worse than you've ever seen before. But Daa will have what he needs to cover the rent. Reverend Sill is seeing to it."

"The reverend is helping Daa?"

"Aye," I said, swallowing hard. "If there's one thing I've learned since I left here the other night, it's that most things aren't what you might suspect." I touched me right hand lightly to me heart as I had when last I'd seen her on that storming night eight days before. "It may be a long time before I see you again, Cath. But while I'm gone, I'll keep you with me."

And then I knelt down and hugged me wee sister, wanting never to let her go.

THE STIFF WEST WIND WAS RAW UNDER THE blanket of moonlight, and I was shivering when I finally saw the two flashes on the horizon. I had made up me mind—I wasn't leaving the island. Not with wee Victoria fighting for her life. And yet George Marwick had made arrangements for me escape, and put the *Ernestine Brennan* at considerable risk to pick me up. As I huddled in the shrubs at the rocky shore, at the very spot Daa and the other men of the parish had so many times before waited for boatloads of smuggled gin and tobacco, I wrestled with what message I could possibly send to convey me deep regrets for not coming aboard.

It wasn't long before I heard the slapping sound of oars on water and then saw the shadow of a yoal approaching the shore. "Over here!" I called, bounding toward the water. But as I sprinted through the darkness, a powerful arm grabbed me from behind. And then I gasped as a snarled beard brushed me neck.

"Hah!" Knut Blackbeard grunted. He held a thick bat in his hand. "You wee rat of a lad! Cuttin' into yer Daa's business, eh? Even after you robbed him blind of his life's earnin's?"

I struggled to free meself from his arm at me throat. "Lor',

Knut," I managed. "Do you think I'm here to meet a drop of goods?"

"Aye, you are! Just as you tried at the Marwick Lodberry the other night!" he growled, dragging me back from the water. "Me sources tell me you went and squandered every last one of your Daa's coins on barrels of gin you've already lost!"

"That's a lie," I cried, struggling to escape his grip.

"You know those two flashes was meant for us. We've spied the *Ernestine Brennan* lurkin' about these shores for two days now. As long as there's gin to come ashore at Culswick, it's your Daa and me's who's in charge."

And as he spoke, I eyed a familiar figure hobbling toward us, lantern in hand. "Daa!" I shouted, wrestling to free meself from Knut's grip. "Help me!"

"Caught him trying to meet the shipment!" Knut muttered, tightening his hold as Daa grabbed fast to me shoulders.

"First me pouch and now me livelihood!" Daa growled, eyes piercing mine. "Thought by now Sheriff Nicolson'd have you penned up for good."

"'Twas John who took the pouch!" I cried. "I never lie to you, Daa. You know that!"

He scowled. "Loyalty. That's all I've asked. Put cod on the table. Kept you in rivlins. To think I've raised a thief!"

"And what do you call taking the Peterson ewe?" I asked, the palm of me right hand twitching.

He laughed, a maniacal grin pulling across his bearded face. "Survival, it is. That's what it's always been on this Godforsaken island! Marwick's stacked the deck against us. What you dunna have, you take, 'cause you'll never get it any other way."

"But you had coins, Daa! We're *starving* and you had coins!"

"Aye!" he said, his voice turning icy cold. "*And I had plans for those coins.*"

I looked at him, suddenly so overcome by years of unspoken rage I couldn't hold back. "Plans?" I screamed. "While we went to bed hungry? While wee Victoria grew so weak she canna fight a fever?"

He released his grip as I spoke, his face losing all expression as Knut hung on. But before Daa could reply, we were startled by a loud crack.

Knut's arm dropped suddenly and then he stumbled forward. There was another crack, louder than the first, and I watched in amazement as the hulking, bearded giant collapsed face-first into the sand. Standing above him was Malcolm—a piece of driftwood raised high above his head.

"Come on, lad!" Malcolm shouted, yanking me down the beach to the faint outline of the yoal from the *Ernestine Brennan.* "It's our ride to the ship!"

"Malcolm!" I cried. "But . . . but I can't go! Me sister—*she has the fever!*"

"Well, you'll not be curing her from behind the bars of Lerwick Prison, I can tell you that much," his wonderfully familiar voice roared. Then he leapt aboard the yoal and took a seat at the oars in front of a young lad in a red cap. "Push us off, Chris! We've no time to lose!"

"Oh no, you don't," Daa bellowed, hobbling after us. "That's me son!"

And the moment I heard the rage in his voice, I knew Malcolm was right. But by the time I grasped the gunwales and started pushing the boat from the shore, Daa's arms locked around me waist. Then I heard the words that hit me like shards of ice to me heart.

"Those coins were for our stones," he hissed, lips hot at me ear. "For a monument, tall and important, chiseled with the Robertson name. Like the one Marwick'll have, and the other thievin' merchants who've clawed their way to greatness on the back of the crofter!"

I wrenched me neck around, at first not believing what I was hearing.

"Not just the unmarked mounds of the other crofter graves like your Midder's and William's," he continued, dragging me inland. "A Robertson plot—all on its own—away from the grounds of the Godforsaken Kirk!"

"You were hoarding those coins . . . *for our gravestones?*" I gasped.

"Aye, I was," he growled. He threw his right arm around me neck. "Marwick sees to it we Robertsons are nothin' from the day we're born till we breathe our last. *But I'll be damned if we'll be nothin' when we're dead!*"

"Enough!" Malcolm cried suddenly from behind us, an oar from the yoal raised above his head. Then he drove it like a javelin into the small of Daa's back, and yanked me to his side. "Run, lad, run!"

We raced back to the water. Then Malcolm leapt aboard, as I drove me rivlins into the rocky beach and launched us from the shore.

"Get up, Knut, ya big glundie!" Daa commanded, scrambling to his knees in the icy surf. "He's getting away!"

Knut staggered to his feet, shaking the sand from his beard, still dazed from Malcolm's blows. "Curse you, William! Ya know I canna swim!"

As I flung meself over the gunwales, Malcolm met me with his familiar crooked smile. He settled into the seat in front of what I could now see was a lad not much older than meself. Then he grabbed fast to a set of oars.

"You haven't seen the last of me, you good-for-nothin' son!" Daa bellowed from the shore, fist in the air. "I'll get you if I have to hunt you down all the way to Greenland!"

"Row faster, Malcolm!" I cried.

"Oh, I think we've got 'em licked," he said. "They won't be forgettin' them blows I gave them anytime soon!"

I stared at me wayward friend in the gray-blue light of the moon. "Thought you were headed to the Davis Strait with John."

"Didn't they tell you? The lass, Mary, arranged for me to join you on your trip. Convinced the Marwick lad that some-

one with me *experience* might come in handy. I'd been waitin'
for you."

"But what of Netty and your bairns?"

"Aye. Well, the way I see it, a wee foray into the high seas
beats Norfolk Isle by a long shot. And as soon as I get meself
established, I'll send for them." Then he threw back his shoulders, a black-toothed grin stretching from cheek to cheek. "It's
like I told you, lad—never stop lookin' for opportunities!"

I shook me head and smiled at this most unlikely of com-
panions. Then I turned back to the fading outlines of Knut
Blackbeard and Daa cursing from the shore of the island I
might never see again. I thought of wee Victoria, weak with
fever. Catherine, Gutcher, and Aunt Alice. Me Midder's and
William's unmarked graves. But mostly I thought of Daa—
craving a name in the hereafter over food for our survival. Not
right in the head he was. John had known it all along.

Before long the clouds drifted from the moon, and the faint
silhouette of the *Ernestine Brennan* appeared amid whitecaps
on glistening black water. Deep in me pocket the American
coin and Mary's letter and compass felt warm at me fingertips.
They were more than I had ever had, and all I had left.

23

The Flight of the Ernestine Brennan

North Sea, March 29, 1842

ook sharp! She's startin' to tear!" First Mate
Magnus McNutt bellowed from across the deck.
I winced at the sound of ripping cloth as the pony
snatched a mouthful of hay from me arms with
her sharp yellow teeth. The southwesterly gale
that had propelled the *Ernestine Brennan* forward since dawn
had torn clear through a broadseam on the mainsail.

The wind was perfect. McNutt knew it, and we were mov-
ing like the Devil. Deliver the ponies to the east coast of
England and then on to Belfast with the rest. All by April 30.
Those were Captain Canfield's orders, and it was already the

twenty-ninth of March. It took everything Helmsman Compie Twills had just to hold the wheel steady.

"All hands, all hands!" McNutt commanded.

There were thirty-two ponies on deck, picked up the night before Malcolm and I came aboard. All Shetlands. Each more frantic than the next—snorting and whinnying, their shaggy manes drenched with sea spray—bound for collieries in England, where they would work in the pits. Me job was to feed the troublesome beasts, and the sweet smell of their damp, matted fur was everywhere in the frigid March air.

I tried to make me way across the deck, but a particularly ornery stallion stood in the way. And when the packet gave a heel suddenly to port, I found meself pinned between the gunwale and his steaming chestnut withers.

"You there," McNutt bellowed again from across the deck, looking at me and pointing to the sail. We could all hear the raw, tearing sound of the seam—even through the deafening howl of the wind. "Get yourself out from behind that pony and find me Martin!"

"Back!" I shouted at the animal. "Don't ya know I'm the one who feeds ya?"

The hull was now nearly level with the water, with me head, pinned behind the pony, just above the bulwarks. A wave crashed over the deck, matting the desperate animal's coat flat to his skin. He whinnied and tossed his head from side to side.

McNutt scowled and grabbed the arm of the young seaman

in the red knitted cap who had helped row Malcolm and me the night before. "Jimmy—*you* find me Martin, or we'll still be waiting for Robertson come Christmas. And tell the man to bring his needle. If we don't patch that tear now, this wind'll rip her to shreds!"

I gasped. The weight of the beast was flattening me chest, and the back of me head was numb from the icy cold spray. Only twelve hours before I had been standing in Shetland, desperate not to be returned to the damp, foul-smelling cell in Lerwick Prison. Now, it seemed, aboard Wallace Marwick's favorite ship, I would be lucky to make it another day.

I scanned the deck as the roar of the wind ratcheted up, drowning out me cries for help. McNutt stood there, his hands on his hips, scowling up at the sail as the other seamen tried to maneuver the rigging as best they could through the maze of ponies.

As luck would have it, it was Angus Moncrieff of all people, me brother's brute of a friend from Culswick, who took notice of me predicament. Surely, I thought, despite all that had happened, he would take pity on me—put the past aside.

I waved frantically as his stocky body drew closer. Me spine was now driven so deep into the gunwale that I thought it might snap. But Angus stopped short, just inches from me outstretched hand. Then he rubbed his chapped knuckles lightly between his lips and running nose.

"Angus!" I pleaded with the little breath I had left. "Pull him off me!"

A smile cracked from the wicks of his mouth. And then he wrapped his arms across his bulging chest. "Got yourself out a' Lerwick Prison," he mused. "Seems a lad so clever would have no problem with a wee pony such as this."

He stared straight into me eyes. Hard and deep. "Tell me— how do you think your brother is faring on that whaler?"

I held his stare until he spat at me feet. And then he turned away, maneuvering himself around the ponies to the other side of the deck, where McNutt and the other seamen were pointing to the sail.

"Ill-tempered dreep!" I wanted to shout, but me chest was so compressed the words were nearly inaudible.

It was seeing Angus that had surprised me most when Malcolm and I had climbed aboard the *Ernestine Brennan.*

"Where's John?" he had demanded, the dim light of a lantern flashing in me face. I remember staring at his wide, pimpled forehead and thick smudge of eyebrows, unable to fathom how he had come to be on Wallace Marwick's ship.

I shook me head. "Gone where he deserves."

"And where might that be?"

"Davis Strait. On a whaler with Captain Leisk."

Angus furrowed his dense brow, leaning into me. "Don't believe ya! John feared the sea. He'd never a' joined up on a whaler—even if his life depended on it."

"Right you are, lad," Malcolm replied. "He was kickin' and screamin' all the way out to the ship. I had the pleasure a' rowing him there meself."

"Forced him, did ya?" Angus barked, jutting his face inches from Malcolm's shaggy red beard.

"Hah! Not me. I'd a' thumped him a blow to the head meself while we were still on the Mainland. 'Twas your Reverend Sill made the arrangement." Then Malcolm placed a hand on Angus's shoulder. "You're a God-fearing lad, now, aren't ya? You can thank the reverend yerself when you're next at the Kirk."

"Why, that's kidnappin', it is!" Angus sneered, swiping Malcolm's hand away.

"Aye." Malcolm laughed. "You could think of it that way. Me, I thought it was kind a' the reverend not to take him directly back to Sheriff Nicolson. I'm sure the sheriff would a' been pleased to get back the person responsible for freeing himself and six other convicts."

Angus glared at Malcolm, then at me. "You'll be payin' for this, you will. I'll see to it."

And now, wedged behind the solid body of that stallion, I guess I was.

I moaned as the pony whinnied and shifted his weight against me ribs. If the ship didn't right herself quickly I would be crushed. Then, just when I thought things couldn't be more desperate, we crested a towering wave so enormous that another pony roped nearby lost its balance and fell against him.

"Arrgh!" I grunted, feeling me ribs cracking, the air nearly cut off.

The way I saw it at that moment, I had two choices—muscle meself up on the gunwale and risk falling overboard or wriggle down under the beast's belly to the deck and risk crushing me face in the process. One way or the other I needed to breathe. Glancing out at the biting black sea behind me, I chose the latter.

With every ounce of strength I could muster, I wriggled me underfed body down until me nose was buried in the steaming wet fur of the pony's withers. Then I kicked frantically at the back of his knees—anything to get him to shift just enough for me to slip through. His ears flattened in disgust, but I didn't give up. That is, until he careened his neck toward me and sunk his sharp yellowed teeth into me ear.

Ya evil beast! I thought, blood running down me neck, me mouth too full of fur to mutter a sound. But just then a wave washed over the side of the packet, making his coat smooth and slippery. So I closed me eyes, me newly bitten ear scraping raw against the splintered gunwale, let the weight of me wet body slip underneath his matted belly, and crawled to freedom on me hands and knees across the muck-littered deck.

"Lor', Robertson! What are ya doin' grovelin' down there?" McNutt cursed as the scuffed boots of a red-nosed Abner Martin stumbled past me. "Don't know how you were granted passage on this ship, but until the captain tells me to cast ya over the side, you'll come when I call."

I staggered to me feet and glanced about, head dizzy, ribs throbbing, blood trickling from me ear. When me eyes found Angus holding fast to one of the ropes across the deck, I flashed a triumphant smile. Then I turned to Martin, who was hoisting himself up on the boom. He struggled to steady himself, needle and waxed thread trembling in his hand. The tear in the seam had already grown another foot.

"Wind's too strong, sir!" Martin shouted. "Take down the sail and I'll do a proper job."

"Fool!" McNutt growled. "Wind's perfect—she's runnin' eight knots! If we're to deliver the ponies before we head to Ireland, I'm not slowing down to change the sail."

"But surely the captain dunna want us to risk losin' the sail in the process," the red-capped Jimmy reasoned, his calloused hands gripping a line.

McNutt spat. "Aye—on another trip, perhaps. But you know as well as I that if we dunna get these beasts to the east coast a' England before the Crown catches up to us, inspects our cargo, and takes the *Ernestine Brennan* as her own, we'll lose more than a sail."

"Aye, and me pay!" Angus muttered. "They say Marwick hadna' paid any man since January. How are we to know we'll get our wages when we make the delivery?"

McNutt turned on him, eyes flashing. "Moncrieff, I had me doubts 'bout where your loyalty lies when we took you on. Don't prove me right before we get two days into the trip."

Angus stared back defiantly.

"You'll get yer pay. But only when it's due. Captain Canfield's the most loyal master in the entire Marwick fleet. And with Mr. Marwick, the rewards for loyalty are always met."

I watched as Martin tried desperately, again and again, to

stab the needle into the frozen sailcloth. His hands trembled while the wind tormented the fibers of the growing tear.

"Been drinkin'," I heard someone mutter as I brushed off me shirt and breeks. It was Mary's brother, Charles. He stared at Martin, then shook his head as he strode to McNutt's side. "He'll poke himself in the eye and jeopardize the rest of the ship in the process."

"Get a hold a' yerself, Martin," McNutt shouted.

"Malcolm can fix it," I said.

McNutt turned in a flash, eyes narrowed. "Robertson, did you just address me without me permission?"

I dropped me head, cheeks hot.

"You mean MacPherson?" Charles demanded.

"Aye." I looked up cautiously, remembering our last meeting at the Marwick Lodberry.

"He's a rope maker, is he not? Seen him below deck repairing lines."

"And a master at that," I stammered. "At rope making and mending things."

"Aye—and takin' what dunna belong to him," McNutt quipped. "Wonder how much practice he's had all the years he's spent rottin' in his cell in Lerwick Prison? They say no one's been caught with the fast fingers more times than he."

I watched sweat drip from Martin's brow as he pathetically tried to pull the torn pieces of sailcloth together. And then, suddenly, there was a shout from the stern.

"Revenue cruiser—one o'clock—port side!"

McNutt pressed the glass to his eye. "I knew the Crown'd spot us eventually, but not this soon. All right, Robertson. Get MacPherson—and fast! Even a thief would be an improvement over what we have here, and I have no intention of slowing down."

24

Roker

Everyone on board knew that the stakes for the *Ernestine Brennan*'s success couldn't be higher. Hundreds of families dependent on one callous man for their livelihood—and though many would revel should Marwick go under, there wasn't anyone on board whose family wouldn't be perilously affected by his financial demise.

The choice was as it had been for the crofter-fisherman for generations—save the brutal merchant who keeps you in poverty, or starve.

Mary had been right. With the Crown looking to seize

Marwick's entire fleet to cover his mounting debt, the *Ernestine Brennan* was doomed. That is, unless the cargo she carried could be unloaded first and the payment collected. The Shetland ponies snorting before us were both small enough to maneuver in a mine shaft and sturdy enough to haul more coal than a beast twice their size. And with the new Mines Act just approved by Parliament keeping children under ten from laboring underground, the ponies were now more valuable to the English colliers than ever before.

But word on board was that Marwick needed more than a sale of ponies to stay ahead of his creditors. Much more. Which is why the duty-free delivery of the three hundred casks of extremely rare French brandy stashed below deck, rumored to once have been part of Napoleon's private collection, also had to find a customer. And fast. You could say the successful voyage of the *Ernestine Brennan* was, in fact, Wallace Marwick's last chance. His last, very desperate chance.

After so many years locked in Lerwick Prison, Malcolm seemed to revel in the relentless blow of fresh sea air. Even McNutt appeared impressed at the speed with which he deftly stitched the fabric this way and that, his tangled mat of red hair flying as the ship pitched up and over the waves.

By noon Marwick's spry packet had outrun Her Majesty's cruiser, and by sundown we were already nearing the Orkney Islands.

I had never slept at sea, and me nights below deck were misery: swaying this way and that, me cracked ribs throbbing against the moldy canvas hammock, me stomach heaving. Oh, how I longed for our croft house and me sturdy box bed. Hour after hour I raced above deck, propelling meself over the gunwale and retching in the darkness.

On the third morning I staggered up the ladder, hair crisp with sea salt, and pitched what little hay we had left to the ponies. Like me, they were restless and frightened, whinnying desperately and pawing their hooves in the butter-yellow light on the deck.

"Where are we, sir?" I asked Compie Twills. He was standing at the binnacle, the sextant and charts before him.

"North Sea," he said, eyes a-twinkle.

"You mock me, Mr. Twills," I said, blushing at me ignorance.

"See that, over there?" he said, pointing off the port side. I could just make out a dark line above the water. "Mainland Scotland that is."

"So soon?"

"Aye. Thought for sure we'd been blown off course in the night when I couldn't get a sighting, but, by God, we've come over a hundred miles! Been out on the sea all me life, and not but a few other times have gone so fast. The captain'll be pleased about that, I suspect."

"Aye. And he is, Mr. Twills."

I was startled to see Captain Canfield standing behind me. His Irish brogue mixed with shortened quips of Shetland speech gave a peculiar, commanding rhythm to his words.

Compie nodded and then quickly glanced at his charts. "McNutt—he's making good work of this wind."

"We got lucky," Captain Canfield said. "Canna last long, but we'll take what we can get."

Since coming aboard, I had only observed the captain from afar. He was a proud, square-shouldered man with a long face, his nose and cheeks red and crusty from years of sun and wind.

"Robertson, is it?" he asked. "Do you know you're standing next to one of the most gifted helmsmen on the North Sea?"

I shook me head. "I've little knowledge of the sea, sir. Mr. McNutt will tell you it's all I can do to keep from falling overboard."

"Your Daa, he is a crofter-fisherman, no?"

"Aye." I nodded. "And me Gutcher as well. Should I be home, this would be me first year to join in taking of the cod."

Captain Canfield studied me, his eyes taking in me frayed gansey and breeks. "My niece tells me that you read."

"Aye," I answered. I was surprised by the comment, me face coloring as he spoke. "Me Midder was an educated woman. And me Daa reads as well. Me brothers and I attend school when we can manage it."

"Then I'll need your help tomorrow night."

"Help, sir?"

"Aye. When we near land."

"Sunderland, is it? Near the mines?" I asked, having heard of shipments of coal coming from that part of England. "Is that where we are to land?"

The captain paused and drew his fingers down his closely cut orange-and-gray whiskers. "Not quite. A beach just to the north. Where there'll be no need to register with a Customs House. Roker, it's called. Mr. Twills here knows it well."

Compie raised his eyebrows.

"Am I to help unload the ponies?" I asked, touching me hand to me tender ribs.

"No. The other men will see to that. Something far more important. I'll be sending you ahead to deliver a message. One that must be relayed accurately to a Mr. Plimpton. Do you think you can do that, lad?"

Compie looked over, aghast. "Plimpton, sir? The lad?"

"Aye, Mr. Twills," Captain Canfield answered, but he looked straight at me.

I swallowed hard, glancing at Compie and then back at the captain. "That's it, then? Bring a message to this Mr. Plimpton?"

"My niece tells me you are trustworthy. And yet one has to wonder. You were, after all, in Lerwick Prison, were you not?"

"I was," I said, quickly looking down.

"Then, perhaps, by doing what I have asked, you can prove to me that my niece is not misguided in her thoughts. As you know, she has done much to arrange for your safety."

Me breath quickened as he spoke, but as I looked up there seemed a slight glint in his eye. "I will na' let you down, sir," I said. And oh, how I meant it.

"SO WHAT YA SUPPOSE HE'S AFTER?" MALCOLM asked later that day when we found ourselves shoveling the ponies' muck from the deck. With eleven men and thirty-two ponies on board, it was the first time we had managed to have private words since leaving Shetland.

"Best I can figure, it's Plimpton buying the ponies. To sell to some colliery."

Malcolm shuddered. "Ooooo, it's an evil fate—a pony sent to the coal mine. They say once they lower 'em down in the pits, they don't see the light a' day for the rest of their pitiful lives."

"Must come up to feed." I reached me hand to stroke the shaggy-haired animal munching straw beside me.

"Nah. Do it all belowground, I'm told. And when the coal dust gets to their eyes and starts to fester, they sew 'em shut."

"Sew their eyes?" Me stomach turned as I studied the animal's dark pupils and silky, long lashes. I hadn't forgotten that stallion's teeth on me ear, but I couldn't wish a fate such as that on any living creature.

Malcolm nodded, grimly. "The captain's in charge of the sale. He's Marwick's man. It's on his shoulders that the money is collected and accounted for."

"Doesn't explain why he asked if I could read and write," I murmured. As I bent over to pitch a shovelful overboard, a pair of large rivlins came into focus.

"What's this I hear about you goin' ashore at Roker?" Angus Moncrieff asked.

I glanced up at his sneering face. "Dunna remember talkin' to you."

"The captain's wrong in the head to send you ashore. Told him, I did, that he'd be lucky to have you return. That you'll take the payment for the ponies and flee your merry way into England!"

I had to admit, the thought had crossed me mind. England, after all, was the last place anyone knew Sam Livingston had gone. If he had returned to America, it would be from those shores he would have sailed.

"Keep to your own affairs, Moncrieff," Malcolm snapped. "Or pick up a shovel. There's plenty a' piles a muck from these ponies to be cleaned off deck."

"Hah! I didn't sign on to this ill-fated ship to shovel. Gave that up when I left the croft. The way I see it, the only good in bringing you two convicts aboard is to clear the stinkin' piles o' manure from the deck so the rest of us seamen can handle the real work."

"Shut it, Moncrieff," McNutt barked, seeing us from across the deck. "Get back to tarring those ropes or I'll have you join them!"

But as Angus stomped off, Malcolm dropped his head to me ear. "He's got a point, ya know. It'll be dark when you get ashore. If you run for it, no one's gunna go after ye. Canfield'll be too wrapped up in deliverin' the ponies to take the time."

I looked to me left and right. "Don't be a haf-krak, Malcolm! I'm not leavin' without you."

"Well, you're never gunna find Livingston or his gold cooped up here on Marwick's ship. After we get rid of the ponies, we're on our way to Belfast!"

AT SUNSET ON NIGHT SIX OF OUR JOURNEY, Roker beach was already in sight. Compie saw to it that the *Ernestine Brennan* drifted cautiously inland, just close enough for her to be seen from the steep cliffs above the beach. He nodded to Captain Canfield when he was sure of his spot, and McNutt dropped anchor. But it wasn't until well past midnight when a blue light flashed twice from the shore, and McNutt responded with the flash of a lantern from the bow.

"Are you ready, lad?" Captain Canfield asked as red-capped Jimmy and two other seamen lowered the yoal into the water off the starboard side.

I nodded, still unsure of what I was to do once ashore.

"There may be others," he cautioned, "but you must only speak to Plimpton. He will ask why I have not come personally. You're to let him wonder." Then he handed me a roll of parchment tied with string, and beckoned Compie and McNutt to our side.

"These are the terms of sale. Mr. Marwick will accept nothing less. Get Mr. Plimpton's signature and return it to me with the security money. Only then will I start rowing the ponies ashore."

"And if he doesn't pay?" I asked.

Compie glanced at McNutt.

"He will," Captain Canfield said. "With the mining reforms, Mansfield Colliery and others like it are desperate for ponies. Not to mention the price is such that he will make a tidy profit. What Plimpton doesn't know is I haven't the time to sail farther south to garner a better price."

I started down the ladder to the boat and then stopped. "I mean no disrespect, sir," I whispered, "but why me? Surely Charles or one of the other men would be more . . . convincing."

"Aye, sir." McNutt snorted. "I canna see how a lad his size will have much effect on Plimpton."

"Precisely," Captain Canfield replied. "My orders are to get two hundred fifty pounds for the lot. Not a copper less. Should I go personally to negotiate the deal on a mere load of ponies, or send you or Charles in my place—it will be immediately apparent to a shark such as Plimpton the true desperation of our situation."

He gazed out into the dark night, the stars twinkling above, and sighed. "With any luck, no word of Mr. Marwick's troubles has yet reached these shores."

"But if the lad fails," McNutt started. "Surely we canna take the chance—"

"Which is why I am sending Mr. MacPherson as well," Captain Canfield said.

Me heart skipped a beat as Malcolm's formidable frame appeared in the darkness before me.

McNutt grimaced. "A lad and a thief?"

Captain Canfield grinned, slapping McNutt on the back as

I continued down the ladder. "The way I see it, two ginger-haired escapees from Lerwick Prison are just what we need to get the job done."

But as Malcolm started down, I saw the captain grab his shoulder. "We've no room for mistakes, MacPherson," he said, his hushed tone harsh and direct. "Do I make myself clear?"

"Aye," Malcolm said, dropping into the seat in front of me and reaching for the oars.

"Be quick about it, then," McNutt called down to us. "It'll take eight trips in that yoal to get these ponies ashore. We've three hours at the most."

MALCOLM AND I CUT THE OARS THROUGH THE choppy black sea, following the waves in to shore. When I felt the boat scrape bottom, I jumped into the icy water and hauled us onto the sand.

"Now's our chance!" Malcolm said, springing over the gunwale and grabbing fast to me arm. "Run for it! To the top of the bluff!"

But it was as if me feet were frozen in the sand.

"Come on!" he whispered, whipping around to face me. "Opportunities, lad, opportunities! We've gotta take 'em when they come our way!"

I yanked me arm free and looked away. "Gave the captain me word."

"Ya canna be serious!" Malcolm scoffed. "The man works

for Marwick. He's the reason all a' Shetland's on the brink a' starvation! Dunna tell me you're lookin' out for *him*!"

"If Marwick goes, so goes the rest of the island. Me family and yours included."

"Aye! And if he stays in business, his stranglehold will never end!"

I turned back in the direction of the ship, afraid to meet his eyes. "I know that, Malcolm," I whispered. "Even so, I canna run."

"Aye, the good captain, he took us on. But come, lad—it's not as if we owe him our lives. And who knows what kinda man this Plimpton is?"

I looked at me friend, the words spilling out before I knew what I was saying. "He asked if he could trust me, Malcolm. I gave him me word."

"Your word?" Malcolm rolled his eyes and moaned into the breeze. "Look here, Chris Robertson, do ya want to find Sam Livingston and that gold or not?"

"'Course I do! But, but—"

"Then dunna be daft, lad! Don't you see fate is helpin' us once again? We just got a free ride to England! Could be in Liverpool in just a few days' time, catching a ship to America. We may never get a chance like this again!"

I kicked the sand, shifting from one foot to the next. "He's Mary's uncle, Mal. She told him I could be trusted."

For a moment Malcolm stared, mouth open, the waves

crashing behind him. And then the flesh of his cheeks began to quiver in the moonlight.

"So that's it, is it? It's Miss Mary you canna let down, not the captain? Lor', lad—ya didn't tell me you were in love with her!"

"It's not that, it's, it's . . ." I looked away, thankful for the cover of darkness, me cheeks growing hot.

"Here we are, halfway to finding out about a stash of gold ducats," Malcolm blurted, "and you want to prove yourself *trustworthy*?"

He threw back his head, a deep-throated chuckle bursting into the night. "All right, then, lad. I canna believe I'm agreein' to this, but have it your way. Just keep in mind that if I get me throat slit by Mr. Plimpton, it's on your shoulders."

The clouds drifted across the moon as we scanned the shoreline, the crisp March wind stinging our cheeks. Just then I heard a rustling to me left and a figure sprang from the darkness. The next thing I knew, Malcolm lay face-first in the sand at me feet, a dark figure on his back. And before I had even a chance to cry out, the cool edge of a blade was at me throat.

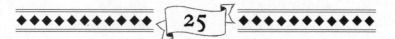

Mr. Plimpton

ho are you?" a foul-breathed voice whispered in me ear. From the corner of my eye I could see two scrawny figures flip Malcolm over, with three other dark figures surrounding us.

"We're here for Plimpton," Malcolm managed, spitting sand from his mouth.

"Plimpton's not here," sneered the man with his knife to me throat.

"Take us to him, then," I said. "We've got somethin' we think he wants."

"I don't know you," the man replied, pressing the blade into me skin. His ragged sleeve smelled of decaying fish.

"Captain Canfield sent us," I said, me heart pounding in me chest. "With a message."

"Oh, did he now?" one of the men said with a chuckle. "And what would that message be?"

"Me orders are to speak only to Mr. Plimpton," I answered, trying desperately to keep me voice from trembling.

"And what if I say that's not possible?"

"Then we leave," Malcolm barked. "There's plenty down this coast in need a' the captain's cargo."

The men were silent for a moment or two.

"If we're not back in ten minutes' time," Malcolm continued, "Captain's orders are to leave us."

"He'll leave his own men, will he?"

"Aye, he will. He has business elsewhere."

A long-faced figure emerged from behind the others. He had dark greasy hair hanging like sheets about his eyes, and a small lad cowered at his side. I suspected he was no older than me sister Victoria. "What is it ya have that'll take so long to unload?" the man asked.

"As I said, me orders are to speak only with Mr. Plimpton," I quavered, the blade still at me throat.

"I'm Plimpton," the greasy-haired man said, his upturned lip showing a twist of yellowed teeth. He grabbed cruelly to the boy's struggling arm, and then he shoved the lad in front of him.

"It's ponies we have," Malcolm cursed. "Shetlands. Now call off your brutes and Chris here'll hand over the terms. Unless, o' course, you are na' in need a' the business."

Plimpton laughed, his hands folded at his chest. "More honest prospects down the coast, has he? Such as John Miller in Morpeth? Or perhaps he's happier with *honest* Stan Waterhouse in Durham? Aye—all savory characters—each one. Waitin' dutifully for the fine captain?"

"Perhaps," Malcolm said as he staggered to his feet. "That's the captain's business, now, isn't it?"

Plimpton stared for a moment. Then, with a wave of his hand, the man behind me lowered the blade from me throat. "Let's see what you has to offer."

I glanced quickly at Malcolm as I pulled the parchment from me pocket. But when I handed it to Plimpton, he shoved it back violently and spat on the ground.

"Captain says you're to sign it if he's to unload the goods," I said. I reached down and grabbed it back, me heart beating wildly.

Malcolm elbowed me. "Think he's needin' ya to read it to him." And I finally understood why I'd been sent.

One of the men pulled up the metal plate covering the light from his lantern as I unrolled the parchment. And then I cleared me throat. "Thirty-two Shetland ponies. Sturdy and in good health. Price: two hundred fifty pounds," I read. "One hundred pounds security to start unloading. Yours sincerely, Captain James Canfield IV."

Plimpton laughed and spat on the beach, and as he did I saw the small child slowly slip behind him.

"Sign here and pay the security money and we'll start bringing them ashore," I said, pushing the document toward him.

Plimpton licked his cracked lips, the white of his eye darting in the moonlight. Then he suddenly noticed the child and his hand shot out like a cannon, grabbing him by the scruff of the collar. "You'll stand by me side and learn or I'll give ya a beatin' worse than yesterday," he commanded, darting his eyes from me as he hauled the child back before us. "I'll give ya five pounds each pony and be done with it."

"That's only one hundred sixty, total," I said.

"Not a chance," Malcolm scoffed. "These are purebred Shetland stallions. Your collier friends are na' gunna find nothin' finer for that price, and you know it."

Plimpton glared, while the lad seemed to sink into the body of his oversized coat. "One eighty-five for the lot, then. And that's me final offer."

Malcolm stared for a few moments and then gave me a nod. "Come, lad. Back to the ship."

"But, Malcolm," I whispered as we started, "we need to sell 'em!"

"Shut it and walk," Malcolm muttered. But it wasn't until I started pushing the yoal back into the water that Plimpton's lad ran up and grabbed the back of me gansey.

"Me dad," he stuttered. "He—he—he . . . You've gotta come back!"

When we returned to the group, Plimpton snatched the parchment from me hand. Then he pulled a knife from his belt and deftly slit the tip of his thumb and pressed it firmly to the parchment. "Don't worry," he laughed as I looked on in horror. "The captain'll know it's from me." As he spoke, he reached into the dark leather sack slung over his shoulder, counted out a stack of bills, and slapped them on me palm.

"Had to be trustworthy," Malcolm muttered as we rowed back to the ship. But he didn't say anything more.

When we delivered the parchment and security money to the captain, McNutt ordered the crew to begin lowering the first of the ponies, bucking and kicking, by rope, down into the yoal. Only four ponies fit in each load, and it was all Jimmy could do to keep the boat from capsizing as he and Angus rowed to shore.

"Well done," Charles said as we watched the spectacle before us. "Me uncle took a big risk sending you and Malcolm down there alone. Frankly, I half expected you would run."

I shrugged, relieved to be safely back on board.

"Yes," Captain Canfield said, approaching from behind. "One can never be sure things will go as planned with a man like Plimpton. Makes his livelihood from double-crossing both us *and* the Crown, and making sure his goods come in at the best price possible. The trick now will be for you and Mr. MacPherson to collect the remaining one hundred fifty pounds."

I turned to him, aghast. "You're sending us back?"

"Aye, Robertson. A deal is only a deal when both parties

have met their obligations." Then he pulled Malcolm aside and whispered something I couldn't make out.

Sweat formed on me brow as Malcolm and I watched Angus and Jimmy row back and forth to the beach, McNutt all the while fretting over the time. "Go—move!" he bellowed each time they returned and four more struggling ponies were lowered from deck.

When the final four ponies were secured, Jimmy came back aboard and Malcolm and I were sent down the ladder to join Angus.

With the three of us plus the ponies, the boat moved precariously through the chop of the sea. The nervous beasts, feet hobbled with rope, snorted and struggled to get their hooves up on the gunwales. We nearly capsized three times before we finally reached shore. And as I looked at the pitiful, trembling beasts, I thought of their cruel and heartless fate.

"Angus, drop anchor and wait here," Malcolm ordered.

"I'll not take orders from you!"

"Captain says we're not to unload the last of the ornery beasts until we have the rest of the money," Malcolm said. "'Course, if you'd like me and Chris to stay aboard and you collect from Plimpton, just say so."

Angus glared at him. "Be quick about it, then. I'll not hold the panicking ponies for long in these waves."

As we waded ashore we could see the men waiting, the other ponies now unhobbled and corralled together nearby.

"One hundred fifty pounds," I said meekly, finding Plimpton

among his men. But as I spoke I noticed a strange flicker of light from the top of the cliff beyond the beach.

Plimpton leaned into me face, spit flying as he spoke, while the four men with him closed around. "I canna read, lad, but I've *always* been able ta count. The captain promised thirty-two ponies. Only twenty-eight have come ashore."

"Hand over the rest of the money, and you'll get the lot," Malcolm barked, eyeing the leather satchel over Plimpton's shoulder.

As he spoke, I gave his ankle a swift kick, raising me head to the cliffs. "You got company up there, Plimpton?" Malcolm asked, stepping back toward the boat. "'Cause if ya do, this deal is over!"

Suddenly one of the men also noticed the light. "Revenue Men!" he cried. "They've seen us!" And then the one light was joined by another two, then three. And as the sound of a gun blasted in the distance, the ponies reared and bolted free across the sand.

"The ponies! Get the ponies!" Plimpton commanded, shoving his son ahead of him, men scattering in all directions.

"Not without our full payment," I screamed, grabbing but just missing the satchel from Plimpton's shoulder as he slipped into the dark.

"Oh no, ya don't," Malcolm cursed, tackling him to the sand.

"Stop—smugglers—in the name of Her Majesty!" a voice shouted from the cliff. And then another shot boomed into the sand before us.

As Malcolm and Plimpton rolled this way and that, I noticed a glint. Plimpton's knife had come loose from his belt. But as I sprang to grab it, Plimpton's hand got there first.

"He has a knife!" I yelled as Plimpton, lip bloodied, inched the blade toward Malcolm's powerful arms. "No!" I shouted, grabbing his greasy hand just as a bullet from the approaching officers grazed past me. Then I forced the knife to drop into the sand.

"The satchel, Chris," Malcolm screamed, holding Plimpton down. "Grab it!" His massive arms pummeled the smuggler as the lights of the Revenue Men closed in on us. Then Malcolm rolled him over and I ripped the satchel from his shoulder.

"Run!" Malcolm shouted, walloping Plimpton in the gut as another bullet sped past us. And the next thing I knew we were waist deep in water and throwing ourselves into the yoal.

"Row like the Devil, Angus!" Malcolm shouted as I struggled to pull up the anchor.

"We're not goin' anywhere with these stallions on board!" he cursed. "Load's too great!"

"Well, let 'em go, you haf-krakked idiot," Malcolm shouted. "With any luck they'll find the others and run to freedom."

Angus and I quickly unhobbled the ponies, the boat nearly capsizing as the terrified animals—snorting and kicking—scrambled awkwardly over the gunwale and into the waist-deep water. As we rowed furiously to the ship we watched them swim ashore, whinnying wildly to the other ponies on the run, and finally galloping free along the beach in the moonlight.

"Beasts'll lead them officers straight to Plimpton's men," Malcolm said. "Couldn't happen to a nicer lot."

I grinned, tossing him the satchel as he settled into the bow. When we reached the *Ernestine Brennan*, McNutt was already unfurling her sails.

"Move, move!" McNutt ordered as we climbed up the ladder, gunfire still roaring from shore.

"Ah, young Robertson," the captain said. Charles was waiting eagerly at his side as we climbed aboard. "Am I to assume you've had a successful night of it?"

"If you mean with delivering the ponies, sir, I guess you could say we were successful."

Charles cleared his throat. "And the additional one hundred fifty pounds?"

"We collected, all right," Malcolm said, pulling himself over the gunwale and onto the deck. "And damned near died in the process." Then he pulled Plimpton's satchel from his shoulder and presented it to the captain.

"Is it all there?" the captain asked, eyebrow raised.

"No idea. Not much time for countin' with bullets flyin' over your head. Whatever's in here, it's all Plimpton had."

Captain Canfield glanced quickly from Malcolm to me. "I half expected the two of you would run."

"Aye. Well, that might a' been the smarter thing for us to do," Malcolm quipped. "Seein' how you sent us to a killer without any warnin'."

"Had I warned you of the danger, would you have gone?"

Malcolm shrugged. "Not likely. But Christopher here, now, that's another story. Seems he was on a mission to prove himself *trustworthy*. I assume he was successful in his attempt."

I scowled at Malcolm as the captain and Charles looked on.

"Aye. I believe he was," the captain said, a hint of a smile creeping from his lips.

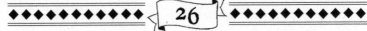

26

Gold Half Eagles

New York City, October 1, 1842

A s it turned out, Plimpton's satchel carried much more than anyone had imagined, and the captain was most pleased. In thanks for our work, he set us ashore just to the north near Blyth, and as I watched the *Ernestine Brennan* disappear into the dawn's pea-green light, I knew me last tie to Shetland was gone.

Only Malcolm seemed sure of where to go next.

"It's off to Liverpool," he proclaimed. "Shouldn't take but a few days. Then we'll book passage on the next ship to America."

"So far from home," I sighed, heart heavy.

"Aye, lad. But if we linger in England, Nicolson'll catch up with us for sure."

"And if we get all the way to America and don't find Sam Livingston?"

"Hoot, lad! New York is where the work is! Think of it—we could change our names, start anew! Earn an honest wage to send back to our families—or better yet, bring them to us!"

"Hah," I scoffed. "We've nary a copper between us for a loaf of bread, much less passage to America."

He chuckled as he turned to face me. "Tell me, lad, who was it carried old Plimpton's sack of money back from shore?"

I stared at him, aghast.

"Come now—dunna look so shocked. You know as well as I Marwick didn't deserve it all. 'Twas us risked our necks to get it." Then he reached into his pocket and pulled out a wad of banknotes. "By the looks of it, I swiped enough to get us where we need to go."

It was the second week of May when we arrived in New York Harbor, and that morning the fog was so dense I couldn't see ten feet ahead of me. Which was why, I suppose, most of just getting there still seems like a dream. We had used nearly all the Plimpton money to buy food and our passage, and by the time we staggered off the ship, we were as bedraggled, confused, and hungry as the other passengers from Ireland and England who shuffled to our left and right.

"Need a place to stay, boy?" a one-eyed man shouted as we passed. A bright orange scarf was tied tightly around his neck.

I could smell the whiskey on his breath as he grabbed fast to me arm. "I'll set ya up!"

"Leave him be, Dickie," a stern voice chided above the throngs of bread sellers, flower cart vendors, con artists, and thieves waiting to take advantage of the new arrivals. "Wait'll he has a job before you try to pick his pocket."

It was Billy Tweed—a warmer smile we'd never seen— looking dapper and smart in his dark woolen suit and neatly combed hair. "Stick with me." He winked. "There're plenty the likes of him here in New York who'll steal the shirt right off your back."

By week's end, of course, we were indebted to Billy for our jobs and lodgings. And five months later I was on me way to the Dudley Glue Factory to pick up goods no one else was desperate enough to deliver.

WHEN I LEFT THE FORGE THE NIGHT OF THE delivery, I waited at the Rope Walk off Mulberry Street for Malcolm to get off work. The building was nearly a quarter mile long, and, thanks to Billy, Malcolm spent his days with the other men, hemp coiled around their waists, walking backward through the stifling, dust-filled air, spinning lines 120 fathoms long.

"Don't do it," Malcolm snorted when I showed him the paper. By now the headline of every paper in the city screamed the news: "Theft of Dahlonega Mint Gold Half Eagles Traced to New York. Watchmen on Alert!"

"We've been here for months now, Mal," I said. "Do you want me to find Sam Livingston or not?"

"Aye, I do," he said. "Got as much stake in this as you do. It's Tweed I don't trust. Who's to say, even if you're successful with the haf-krakked delivery, dodging every Watchman in the city who'll be running after you, that he'll keep his word?"

"What choice do I have? If Sam Livingston's alive, I have to take the chance."

"If he's alive, why hasn't anyone else heard of him?"

I looked away. It was growing dark and I was hungry. If I was going to hike all the way to Twenty-Third Street in the wee hours of the night, I needed coffee and bread.

"Want company?" Malcolm asked.

"No!" I said. "Billy was clear. I'm to go alone."

"And if you're caught?"

"Wasn't it you who told me back in Lerwick Prison that too much thinking makes you too fearful to act?"

Malcolm grimaced. "Aye, it was. But I got a bad feelin' about this." Then he grasped me shoulder. "Take it from a thief with experience who's made a bad choice or two in his life. This one's high stakes, Chris. And Billy Tweed knows it better than anyone."

I shrugged. "As Billy always says, when the city sleeps, the Watchmen do, too."

"Hah! And do you think they'll snooze with the chance at grabbing a few bags of gold Half Eagles? Hoot—they're five dollars apiece!"

"Maybe I'm wrong. We don't know for sure that's what's in the sacks."

"Don't we?" Malcolm asked, raising his brows. "The Dahlonega Mint—they tell me that's in the state of Georgia. In the part of America they call *the South*. Didn't you say Billy's friend was from *the South*?"

"Billy tells a good tale, but he can't be much older than John. Have you asked yourself, Mal, how a lad so young could have gotten hold of those stolen coins?"

Malcolm raised his brows. *"Gotten hold of* and *deliverin'* are two different things. The *southern friend* pays Billy a handsome sum to move the goods to the river, where they can be slipped out of New York to who knows where. Then Billy washes his hands clean of the whole thing and pockets the money for his campaign for alderman."

"You mean for *me* to move the goods to the river."

"Aye. And remember this: If you're caught, there'll be no tracing the gold back to Billy. Just your word against his. And take a guess whether they'd believe you over the likes of Billy Tweed when they discover you're the same lad who's wanted for stealin' back in Shetland?"

I reached into me pocket and felt the cool of Mary's compass at me fingertips. And then I thought, as I had so many times since leaving Shetland, what it would be like to never see her again. Or Catherine or Victoria.

"What of Netty and your bairns, left hungry without you?" I asked.

Malcolm glanced away.

"Aye," I said. "Well, then, it's a chance I'm willing to take."

AND THINGS MIGHT HAVE BEEN FINE IF THE scar-faced man at the Dudley Glue Factory had given me two bags instead of three.

"I canna carry three!" I said in a hushed voice, stumbling over a mound of foul-smelling animal carcasses waiting to become the next batch of glue.

"Them's me orders," he grumbled.

"But it's only me!"

"That's your worry, lad," he sneered, slowly backing into the dark. "Me part of the job ends here."

This time, as I staggered forward, there was no doubt it was coins that I was carrying: the dead weight within me arms, the slight jingle in the canvas bags. The same sound, perhaps, that Sam Livingston had heard so long ago in Shetland when he pulled the ducats from his ship and buried them who knows where.

Lerwick and its winding streets were one thing, but New York, at least five times its size, was quite another. To deliver to a pier near the Dry Docks at the east end of Tenth Street was me order, and I had Mary's compass. East—the river would always be east, I told meself, picturing in me mind the route I would take. Twenty-Third Street to First Avenue, then south on First to Tenth Street. From Tenth it would be only five blocks east to the river! That was simple enough. Until I spotted a Watchman only a block from the glue factory, his leather helmet just visible in the distant glimmer of a streetlamp.

I darted into an alley before he saw me, me arms already aching from the weight of the bags, slipping through the shadows to the next block south before turning east again. But I made it only two more blocks before another Watchman appeared. Gasping for breath, I dropped the bags in the shadows to massage me aching forearms. Malcolm was right, the Watchmen were everywhere, and with every change of direction I thought of the hooded man, waiting, and what he would do if I was late.

An hour passed and I'd only made it as far as Fourteenth Street. Me back was wet with sweat and me forearms so stretched I feared they would snap in two. That's when the tall figure started moving toward me, and with every ounce of strength I had left I hefted the bags to me chest and raced ahead. It was when I tripped on a loose cobblestone and the bags flew from me hands that I realized me only chance was to leave them. And when the hand clamped to me ankle before I could get up, I knew it was over.

"Where you think you're goin'?" a voice whispered. "I'm willin' to heft two of these, but I'm not about to heft all three."

"Malcolm!" I said. "Do you always just appear out of nowhere?"

"Been followin' you all night," he said. "Nearly thumped the guy when he gave you three bags. You looked so pathetic I couldn't take it anymore. Now, quick, grab one up and move!"

Together we made our way south and east, maneuvering

the blocks, one at a time, each of us signaling the other when the coast was clear.

When we finally were a block from the river, he handed his two bags back to me. "I'll be waitin'," he said, motioning me on ahead.

But when I got to the pier where Billy's man had told me to go, it was deserted. Until, out of the shadows, a thick arm grabbed me around the neck from behind.

"Birds to Roost," I gasped.

"You didn't come alone," the voice sneered. The same voice from the night before.

"I *am* alone," I said, dropping the bags at me feet, me entire body trembling.

"Liar!" The hooded man's arm tightened around me neck as he spoke. "I seen you four blocks back with another."

"They gave me three bags!" I gasped, as his grip grew tighter. "I—couldn't—carry—them—meself."

"Bah!" he said. "You've been warned!"

"Do you want 'em, or not?" I choked. "Or should I yell to the Watchman round the corner?"

Just then there was a cry from down the street and the flash of a lantern as a Watchman's leather hat came into view. "You there! Stop!"

In an instant the hooded man let me go and gathered the three bags under his cloak.

Whether he made it to the boat I'll never know, because I didn't stop running until I was back on Pearl Street.

27

Opportunities

I'm cursed," I said, slumping down on the stoop across from Finney's Saloon. I couldn't be farther from Shetland. It was 2:00 A.M. Drunken, ragged men staggered about the manure-littered street. Rats picked through piles of garbage, and the clanging sounds of an untuned piano blared through the windows. Inside, Billy Tweed and his Tammany friends were still "meeting" in full force.

"Bah," Malcolm scoffed. "Made the delivery, didn't you?"

"Aye. But even if the coins slipped out of the city, Billy'll know I didn't keep me word. As me man in the hood so kindly put it, the job for Billy is never done."

Malcolm slumped down beside me. "If he's not going to

deliver his end of the bargain, there's nothing stoppin' us from takin' what's due."

"From *Billy*? In case you haven't noticed, he owns us, Mal. Just like Marwick."

Malcolm shook his head. "No. Not just like Marwick. Billy sees we get paid, don't he? Cash for our wages every week?"

"Aye."

"This is America, Chris. Not Shetland. Don't you think it's time we learn from Billy and take what's rightfully ours?"

It only took Malcolm seconds to pick the lock on the back door, and as we climbed the stairs to the second floor of the Skaden Brush Works, me heart was beating so loudly I thought they could surely hear it in the streets below. *Click, click, click* went the brass clock on the mantel behind Billy's desk, and the minute Malcolm lit the lamp, there was a loud thump at me feet and I nearly screamed.

"Do you want all of Finney's Saloon to know what we're up to?" Malcolm chided. It was Nolan, the white cat with gray patches. "He's only a kitty. Knocked a book down when he jumped from the shelf is all."

Nolan purred, jumping up on Billy's desk looking for a scratch as we rifled through the stacks of receipts and journal entries. "Nothin'," Malcolm muttered.

We had already been there too long—I could feel it. And from the shouts and laughter from the street below, I could tell that the saloon crowd was starting for home. "Let's get out of here, Mal," I said. "Before someone notices the light!"

It was at that moment that I glimpsed a thick volume at me feet that Nolan must have knocked from the shelf.

"*Longworth's American Almanac: New-York Register and City Directory, 1841,*" I read. Then I reached down and pulled it into the light. "This must list everyone in the city. That dreep Billy had it all along!"

I pushed Nolan aside, dropped the registry on the desk, and whipped it open. *Livingston, Ansel, Livingston, Carroll,* I read frantically, tracing me finger down the page.

"Heard somethin' fall out a' that when you picked it up," Malcolm said, dropping to his knees and scrounging around the floor near me feet.

"Here it is!" I cried. "Livingston, S! He lives on 278 Greenwich Street!"

But Malcolm was too busy unlocking the desk to look up.

"Snuff out the lamp and let's get out of here!" I whispered. "We have everything we need!"

"Not everything," he said, a wide smile stretching across his lips as he tossed me the key to Billy's desk drawer. "Must have been hidden in that registry." Then he pulled out the folio of coins. I grabbed Sam Livingston's Pine Tree Shilling from under Nolan's white paw, and Malcolm grabbed the newly placed Dahlonega Gold Half Eagle from the pocket beside it.

WE KNEW WE HADN'T MUCH TIME—AN HOUR or two at most—before Billy discovered what we'd been up to and sent his thugs to find us. And so we raced across town and waited on the stoop of 278 Greenwich Street until the sun came up and it seemed a respectful enough time to knock.

It was a stately brick home, with ten-foot-high windows and rosebushes adorning either side of the front stoop. A sharp contrast to the sagging boardinghouses to its right and left, and the paint-chipped saloon across the street.

"Looks like the neighborhood's gotten a bit rough since Livingston's day," Malcolm muttered. Then he slapped me on the shoulder. "Good luck, lad. I'll keep watch from the street."

The pointy-chinned butler who came to the door looked me up and down.

"Mr. Livingston?" I asked. "Is he at home?"

"At home?" the man asked. He drew his few remaining strands of hair across his scalp and set his shoulders back in disgust. "Certainly not!" And then he stepped back and started to close the door.

"Wait!" I said, grabbing to the gleaming brass knob with all me might. "Then can you tell me where I can find him, sir? Please! I've not much time to spare!"

"No time indeed!" the man scoffed, rolling his eyes to the back of his head. "As Mr. Livingston is no longer living, I can assure you anything you need to discuss with him will most certainly have to wait."

"He's—he's . . . *dead?*" I asked, all air suddenly escaping me body.

The man cocked his head. "I should say so. Now, if you'll excuse me—"

"Edgar," a faint voice called from within. "Is there something wrong?"

"Nothing to concern yourself with, Madam," he said as a wee, wrinkled lady with a tightly stacked bun shuffled behind him. She was dressed in a faded lavender gown, and was so bent over that her back was nearly parallel to the floor.

"Did I hear someone ask for Mr. Livingston?" Her lively, somehow familiar green eyes flashed through the crack in the door. Confident and direct.

"Yes. A bit of a ragamuffin, I'm afraid. No need to alarm you. I'll see to it he's sent away."

"Oh," she said, peering at me. "He's just a boy, Edgar. Ask him his name."

"Christopher Robertson, ma'am," I said, too stunned by what I had just learned to remember that in New York I was Chris Roberts. "I was just leaving."

"But you asked for my husband, did you not?" she inquired as I started down the steps.

"Aye. I did." I hung me head. "I'm sorry for your loss."

"You know of him?" she pressed, as Edgar slowly pulled the door back open.

"Aye. From me homeland. In Shetland," I said. "Stories is all. He was quite famous there."

She looked at me, her familiar eyes crinkling at me words. "Was he?" she asked. "Then will you do an ancient lady the honor of coming inside and telling me what you know?"

As pointy-chinned Edgar poured tea and passed a plate of

scones, Mrs. Livingston told me the story of how, as the war began, she and Sam had wanted to marry. Her father was of the powerful Beekman family and didn't approve of the match. "The Livingstons, of course, are a prominent New York family, too," she added. "But my Sam was from a distant branch. A family of stonecutters—a working-class line that my father found completely unsuitable."

She slowly sipped her tea, then set down the cup and dabbed her mouth with a delicate lace napkin. "But we were madly in love, you see, and being apart simply wouldn't do. And that's when Sam came up with a plan."

"You couldn't just . . . marry?" I asked.

"Oh no! It would have been a scandal!" she laughed. "What Sam needed was stature, and so he went to his cousin Robert Livingston. They struck a deal. Robert—the Chancellor, everyone called him—was the first chancellor of New York and a most respected gentleman. But what made him especially interesting was his service in the Second Continental Congress." She looked at me, raising an eyebrow and dropping her voice. "It was rumored that he was a member of an important committee having to do with the war. The *Secret* Committee, they called it."

"He was a spy?"

"No. Not quite." She laughed, her eyes smiling as she spoke. "But Cousin Robert and the others on the committee were said to be in charge of getting secret cargoes of gunpowder delivered from the West Indies to General Washington's army. And heaven knows, Washington was in desperate need at the time."

"So it was Robert who sent your Sam on his mission?"

"Yes. With the agreement that, if he were successful picking up payment in Rotterdam and getting it to the West Indies to purchase what was needed, Robert would set Sam up in the law."

"And you could marry."

"Yes," she said, blushing as she spoke. Then she lowered her voice once again. "But what Cousin Robert and my family didn't know was that we married in secret before he left."

Edgar cleared his throat. "Another scone, Madam?"

"No, no." She smiled. "I'm quite sated."

"So it must have been when he was on his way to the West Indies that he wrecked in Shetland," I said. I told her what I knew of his time at the Culswick Broch and in Lerwick Prison. Everything except the part about the ducats. "People in me homeland guess he died in the Tower of London. But no one knows for sure."

"Hung for treason?" she shuddered. "Oh, thank heavens, no! Although that might have been better than the hours of torture he endured at the hands of the British while they tried to get the information out of him about who had financed his trip." As she spoke, her eyes wandered to a portrait on the wall of a fair-haired man. He wore a handsome navy blue uniform with sparkling gold buttons and bright crimson lapels.

"That's him?"

"My Sam," she said. "He never did wear the uniform, but

when we commissioned Mr. Copley to paint his portrait years after his death, the family thought it a fitting wardrobe."

From the canvas, Sam Livingston glanced ahead, a wry smile on his lips, his right hand extended before him.

I swallowed hard. "If you don't mind me asking, how did he die?"

"It was Mr. Henry Laurens who managed to get him out of the Tower. Perhaps you've heard of him—the minister to the Netherlands who was captured at sea while bringing dispatches from Congress to Amsterdam? They say Laurens is the only American to have been imprisoned in the Tower of London, but it isn't true. While he was there he befriended my Sam, and, although there is no official record of the act, when they exchanged Laurens for General Cornwallis, Sam was part of the bargain. New Year's Eve 1781, to be exact."

Mrs. Livingston labored to her feet and shuffled closer to the portrait. "When the letter arrived saying he was free, it was the happiest day of my life!"

"Mrs. Livingston," I said, walking to her side. "While he was in Shetland . . . your husband left some things behind."

She glanced back at me, her eyes direct and steady. Eyes that reminded me of ones I'd seen somewhere before. "Things?"

"Aye. A leather sack. Left in the broch near me home. Where he had been hiding. It had some stonecutting tools. And something else." I reached into me pocket and held out the shilling. "Does this look familiar?"

Her eyes widened, and she grabbed it with trembling fingers. Then she looked at me quizzically. "Do you know what this is?"

"A Pine Tree Shilling, I've been told."

She stared at me a moment, her eyes studying mine, as if she was about to say something privately, but then Edgar moved in closer.

"More tea, Madam?" he asked.

She shook her head and turned back to the portrait. "It was considered a token of good luck. Probably given to him by Cousin Robert. As you can see, my Sam's holding just such a coin in the painting." Me eyes widened as she spoke, as I hadn't noticed it before. In the painted hand of Sam Livingston, extended before him, lay the coin.

"They were all about the symbol of the white pine," Mrs. Livingston explained, as if lost in a dream. "And all that it represented to the Revolution. General Washington even had it on his flag."

"And the coin?" I asked, clearing me throat. "Did your husband ever mention it? Or"—I hesitated—"perhaps anything else he might have left behind in Shetland?"

But it was as if she didn't hear me words. And when she turned back to me, tears were streaked down the deep crevasses of her withered cheeks. "So ill was he from the journey home—we had very little time," she murmured. Then she stopped to pull a yellowed handkerchief from her pockets and touched it to her eyes. "The consumption, you see—he picked it up in prison. And while at sea, on his return home, it festered mercilessly in his lungs. It was but five days after he came back to me that he took his last breath."

I looked at her, aghast. Sam Livingston's secrets, whatever they were, had died with him!

"Forgive me, child," she sniffled. "Even after all these years my heart breaks when I think of it."

"There, there, now, Mrs. Livingston," Edgar said, guiding her back to her seat. "Come, boy. I'll see you out."

As the door to 278 Greenwich Street creaked shut behind me, I stood for a moment, unable yet to fully comprehend what I had just learned. Until the door creaked open once again.

"Mrs. Livingston wants you to have this," Edgar said, handing me the shilling.

I looked up, all hope of ever returning to Shetland drained from me heart. "No," I said, pushing it back. "I've no need for it now."

"Ah, but she asked that you take it, boy," Edgar said, pressing it back into me hand. "And she asked me to tell you—how did she put it? Ah, yes! To put the secrets that it holds to good use." I looked at him, bewildered, as Edgar shrugged. "After all these years, I know better than to deny Mrs. Livingston her wishes." Then he slowly closed the door.

"Well?" Malcolm asked, reappearing from down the street and taking a seat on the steps.

"He was dead all along!" I managed, through clenched teeth. "All this time—wasted—searching for a man who's been dead for sixty years!"

Malcolm stared, motionless, but it was as if every bit of anger inside me suddenly exploded. The feel of the Peterson ewe's breath at me hand, John's letter to Daa, George Marwick and his threats, Keeper Mann, Knut Blackbeard, Mr. Plimpton, Billy Tweed, Daa's cursed pouch of hoarded coins—no matter how I tried to right a wrong, another sprang up in its place!

"Curse Sam Livingston!" I shouted. "And everything he stood for! And curse his blasted ducats!" Then I stormed down the steps to Greenwich Street and hurled the Pine Tree Shilling onto the cobblestones before me so hard that it broke in two.

"Now what'd ya go and do that for?" Malcolm said, stooping down to pick it up.

And that's when we discovered that Sam Livingston's coin wasn't a coin after all. It was a case disguised as a coin, held together with a spring that burst open when it hit the stone.

And something was inside.

I gingerly tugged at a thin, yellowed scrap of parchment pressed into one of the halves and unfolded its brittle edges. It was a sketch—a crude one at best—of what appeared to be an island. And on a small rock formation just above the northern shoreline was a very large X.

"Bressay Island?" I whispered, almost afraid to say the words. And then Malcolm let out a wild hoot.

Over his shoulder I noticed Mrs. Livingston watching me through the window. She smiled, knowingly, as our eyes met.

Then she nodded deeply as she held out her hand before her as Sam Livingston did in his portrait.

"The secret of the coin," I breathed. "She knew!" And then it finally came to me what it was about Mrs. Livingston that seemed so familiar. Her eyes were like Mary's eyes—with all the warmth and confidence that had dazzled me the first day we met.

"Like I always say," Malcolm cried, slapping his arm across me shoulders. "Opportunities, lad, opportunities!"

And suddenly, at that moment, amid the drunken shouts from the saloon across the street, piles of filth at our feet, and the rush of carriages passing us by, the chaos of New York faded before me. Suddenly, at that moment, everything seemed possible.

Glossary

bairn—child

ben—back room of croft house where the family sleeps

bere—a variety of barley

breeks—trousers

broch—round, drystone, Iron Age fortress found in Scotland

burn—river or stream

byre—building attached to croft house where cows are stabled

caaing whales—pilot whales, known to follow one leader

croft—a tenant farm

crofter—a tenant farmer

Daa—father

dreep—jerk

drittling—dawdling

faa—afterbirth

flan—squall or sudden gust of wind

fourareen—four-oared fishing boat

fowling—the dangerous activity of collecting eggs from cliff-nesting seafowl

gansey—sweater

General Assembly—Surpreme Court of the Church of
  Scotland

gold ducats—gold coins commonly used in trade, sometimes
  known as Trade Ducats

guano—seafowl refuse used as fertilizer

Gutcher—grandfather

haf-krak—person of little intelligence

half-deckers—fishing boats unique to Shetland, with
  partially sheltered decks

hap—shawl

Kirk—general term for the Church of Scotland (Presbyterian)

kishie—woven reed basket carried on back, commonly used
  to haul peat and other goods

kist—wooden chest

lime-harled—masonry walls sealed with a weatherproof
  coating of lime plaster and pebbles

linksten—rock weight used to hold down roof thatch

lodberry—warehouse/dock built out over the water

lug mark—unique cut in sheep's ear identifying owner

lüm—shiny slick of oil on water

Martinmas—November 11; one of the four Scottish "term
  days" when rents were due

Midder—mother

midder wit—mother's intuition

muckle—big

patronymics—old Scandinavian practice of passing down a
  father's given name to his offspring as a surname

peat—partially decayed organic matter, often cut into bricks, dried, and burned for fuel

peerie—little

planticrub—a stone enclosure offering protection from the wind for growing cabbages

quartering—system in Shetland overseen by the Kirk of rotating paupers from croft to croft for food and shelter

Revenue Men—officers of the Queen entrusted with the collection of import duties; a smuggler's worst enemy

rivlins—traditional sealskin shoes laced below the ankle

scattald—land held in common for grazing

Sheriff Court—local court of law

sixareen—six-oared fishing boat

smoorikin—kiss

Society in Scotland for Propagating Christian Knowledge—religious organization founded in eighteenth century with mission to bring "virtuous" education to "uncivilized" areas of Scotland

Sola Fide—Latin: "by faith alone"

Sola Gratia—Latin: "by grace alone"

Soli Deo Gloria—Latin: "glory to God alone"

Solus Christus—Latin: "through Christ alone"

stap—stew of white fish and livers

stauf—staff or walking stick

Tammany—short for Tammany Hall, New York City's powerful Democratic Party organization

the Transportation—sentence of imprisonment outside the
United Kingdom in places such as Australia, Tasmania,
and Norfolk Island

truck system—oppressive economic system in which
workers are paid in goods rather than cash

tuskhar—tool used for cutting peat

voe—narrow sea inlet

wadmal—homespun woven cloth often used to pay rent

Watchmen—men hired prior to the 1845 establishment of
the New York Police Department to wander the streets at
night and keep watch for fires and crime

wee—small

Whitsunday—May 15; one of the four Scottish "term days,"
when rents were due

yoal—wooden boat used in the Shetland Islands

Appendix

Where are the Shetland Islands?

The Shetland Islands, also called just Shetland, are an archipelago of nearly three hundred islands, including a large main one where this story takes place, in the northernmost reaches of Great Britain. Originally colonized by the Vikings in the ninth century, they became part of Scotland in 1469 when the cashless King Christian I of Denmark and Norway pawned the Orkney and Shetland Islands for his thirteen-year-old daughter Margaret's dowry when she married King James III of Scotland. Before that time the inhabitants spoke Norn, a language derived from Old Norse and spoken by Shetland's early Scandinavian settlers. It wasn't until the 1700s that Scots English became the common language of the people.

Why is Shetland treeless?

No one knows for sure, but roots and branches of hazel and birch have long been uncovered under deep layers of peat, giving credence to the notion that the islands were at one time a much different place. When Daa and Gutcher set out during the gale at the beginning of the book, they are scavenging for anything of value that might have washed up on shore. Because wood was not available, islanders would use driftwood for things such as tools and, as was the case with Christopher's croft, doors and rafters to hold up the thatched roof. Shipwrecks were especially prized not just for the cargo but also for the wood and other supplies that could be salvaged.

What are brochs?

If you travel to Shetland you can see the ruins of more than one hundred round, drystone fortresses scattered along the coast. Sadly, their builders left few clues behind about how and why they were made, although some attribute their construction to the Iron Age people known as the Picts. Culswick Broch is a real place. It is made of stunning, pinkish-red stone and has an unusual, triangular lintel stone over its only entrance. It sits near spectacular sea cliffs on a hill not far from where my crofter-fishermen ancestors were born, and where I imagined the Robertson croft to be. There are historical descriptions from the late 1700s noting that it stood thirty feet tall. Although Culswick Broch is now partially collapsed, much of its once ten-foot-wide, double-walled perimeter still stands. The Shetland island of Mousa has a broch that is still intact, its towering structure more than forty feet high. The intricate drystone construction is truly an engineering marvel, and I have had the pleasure of climbing to the top on the perfectly designed staircase that winds within its double-walled perimeter.

Were the merchants that terrible?

At the time of the story, many communities in Britain were operated under what is called a "truck system," in which the working class (crofter-fishermen) received payment in goods from a merchant's store and/or credit toward their rent rather than cash. Although there didn't appear to be written contracts between the merchant-landowners and their crofter tenants, it was widely understood that the fish caught by the crofters would be sold to and cured by the merchant-landowner at the price that he set. If a tenant went elsewhere for a better price, he risked eviction from his home. It was an oppressive arrangement that went on for generations and kept crofters forever in debt to the merchant or landlord. In the late 1800s, Parliament passed a series of legislative reforms known as the Truck Acts, which prohibited such arrangements, and the crofters of Shetland were finally able to gain access to cash.

Was Wallace Marwick a real person?

No. But his character was greatly influenced by stories of the powerful merchants William Hay and Charles Ogilvy, who employed much of the island population in the early 1800s. They owned Shetland's only bank, had a substantial import-export trade and fish-curing stations, and were also shipbuilders employing carpenters, coopers, sailmakers, and chandlers. In 1842, after several years of depleted fishing and crop failures due to what people say was a climatic cooling on the European side of the Atlantic Ocean and other weather-related disasters,

Hay and Ogilvy went into bankruptcy, forcing the sale of their fleet, a liquidation of the bank, and massive job loss across much of the main island. The results were devastating to the Shetland economy and had lasting effects.

Did islanders really steal eggs from puffins?

Yes. Gathering eggs from cliff-dwelling seafowl, referred to as *fowling*, was an important food source for the often starving islanders. I decided to include the scene of John and Chris and the puffins after reading a 1777 account of a young Shetland boy slipping to his death while fowling on the southern tip of the island.

Was there smuggling in Shetland?

Yes. It was a hot spot for ships coming across the North Sea from large ports such as Rotterdam and Bergen. At the time of the novel, as at many other times in history, the British government relied on high duties on imported goods to cover its large war debt. Because of Shetland's many narrow harbors (voes) and caves, it was a natural place to run goods ashore "duty free" without being seen by the Crown's Revenue Men. Crofters were known to be hired by merchants like my fictional Wallace Marwick to haul casks of gin ashore on their backs to earn extra income for their families. A large, powerful man like Knut Blackbeard would be called to stand watch. As is the case in the story, many of the smugglers incarcerated in Lerwick Prison were considered heroes rather than criminals by their fellow islanders for attempting to outsmart the Crown.

Was Norfolk Island real?

Yes. It was a British penal colony in the Tasman Sea. Norfolk had a reputation for extreme brutality that has been compared to that of the Japanese prisoner-of-war camps of World War II. Prisoners were kept in leg irons and were flogged and beaten as they worked the fields. They often died before completing their sentences. As Malcolm mentions in the story, one might prefer to die rather than experience such a place.

What about the pig bristle rope?

The Shetland swine, known as a grice, had long, stiff bristles along its back and tail that were highly valued in rope making. Prized for strength and flexibility, it was the source of one of the strongest cordages available at that time and was quite laborious to make—the kind of cordage one would rely on for highly risky activities such as fowling. Sadly, the grice is now extinct, although a model was recently re-created and is on display at the Shetland Museum in Lerwick.

What did it mean to be "in quartering"?

What scared Chris more than almost anything was that his family could be cast from their croft for not paying their rent and added to the parish's list of paupers. If a family was left destitute, as was common when fathers were lost at sea, it was placed "in quartering," or passed from croft to croft among the parish, working for shelter and a meager share of food.

Why were the roads so difficult to travel?

At the time of the story, Shetland's spongy, peat-riddled land-scape made travel by land very difficult. Most people traveled by boat if they could. It wasn't until the late 1840s that proper roads began to be constructed.

Patronymics

Sometime around the period of my story, Shetlanders began to drop the old Scandinavian tradition, known as patro-nymics, of passing a father's first name to his children. For example, if your name was Mary and your father was Anders, your name would be Mary Andersdaughter. If your name was Michael and your father was John, your name was Michael Johnson. When Daa, William Robertson, decided to keep the Robertson name for his children instead of Williamson, he made his family line much easier to track for generations to come. Patronymics is still in use in Iceland, making even the simple task of finding someone by their name in the phone book a true adventure!

Was starvation common?

Hunger was a way of life for my Shetland ancestors, and I hoped to convey that in this story. The harsh island weather made crop failures common, and the fishing, due to tempera-ture fluctuations in the North Atlantic, often failed for several years in a row. When you read firsthand accounts of people cooking moss to fill their stomachs, and of cows so weak from lack of fodder that they have to be lifted by ropes, you find yourself incredibly appreciative of what you have.

Gravestones

The idea for Daa wanting a gravestone for his family came to me while I was doing my own family research. When I learned that my ancestors lived in Culswick, I tried to find their graves—wanting desperately to see, chiseled in stone, the names and dates that connected them to me. Sadly, I discovered, most crofter-fishermen and their families didn't have gravestones. Not only did they struggle to survive, they were too poor to honor their dead with even the simplest, lasting indication that they once had lived.

Shetland ponies

As a child I had a Shetland pony named Beau, who was opinionated, spiteful, and incredibly cute. He had a good life on our farm in northern New Hampshire—but, sadly, the ponies of Shetland at the time of my story weren't so fortunate. When Parliament passed the Mines Act of 1842, prohibiting women and children ten and younger from working underground, the collieries of England used tens of thousands of Shetland ponies to take their place. These ponies were not well treated. They were taken underground into the coal pits at a young age and never brought back up into the light of day for the rest of their long (sometimes thirty-year) lives. And, as Malcolm explains in the story, the poor creatures' eyes were sometimes purposefully destroyed and eyelids sewn shut to prevent infections from coal dust.

Was Henry Laurens a real person?

Yes. He was an American merchant and a president of the Second Continental Congress. During the American Revolution he was minister to the Netherlands and captured at sea by the British while carrying a draft of a Dutch-American treaty. After seeing the draft treaty, Britain declared war on the Netherlands. Laurens was charged with treason and imprisoned in the Tower of London, the only known American to have been held there. On December 31, 1781, he was released in exchange for Lord Cornwallis, a leading British general.

Was Billy Tweed a real person?

Yes. The Billy Tweed in my story eventually grew to become the notorious William M. Tweed—New York political boss and longtime leader of Tammany Hall, New York City's Democratic Party political "machine" of that time. Tammany Hall was the master of coercing political support from newly arrived, downtrodden immigrants like Chris and Malcolm in return for finding them jobs and lodgings. William Tweed was elected alderman in 1851 and to the U.S. House of Representatives in 1852. At the time of Tweed's conviction on corruption charges in 1877, it is estimated that he had stolen between 25 million and 45 million dollars in taxpayers' money from the citizens of New York City.

Are the other characters in the story real people?

My great-great-grandfather Robert Christie inspired much of the story. He grew up in a croft house in Culswick, Shetland, immigrated to New York, became a blacksmith, and relied on the bosses of Tammany Hall for his job. Christopher Robertson (I had fun playing with the name) and all the other characters are from my imagination. I used the name Reverend Sill as a nod to the Reverend Frederick Herbert Sill, founder of Kent School, where I learned to write, but the character was inspired by the fire-and-brimstone Presbyterian minister the Reverend John Mill (1712–1805), whose detailed diary is an amazing eyewitness account of life in Shetland. Robert Livingston, the cousin of my fictional character Sam Livingston, was a real person. He was the first Chancellor of New York, a member of the "Secret Committee" of the Second Continental Congress, and member of the "Committee of Five" that drafted the Declaration of Independence. He came from a large family, so I thought it plausible that he would have a cousin like Sam. Oh, and there is a real Nolan the cat, who loves to walk across my keyboard and printed manuscripts as I write, tufts of white and gray hair flying in all directions.

Was there such a thing as a Pine Tree Shilling?

Yes. It was one of the original coins struck in the American colonies. The white pine was an important symbol of the American Revolution, and George Washington used it in his design of the well-known "An Appeal to Heaven" flag. Revolutionary spies were known to carry documents hidden in cases made to pass for coins.

Was there a Dahlonega Mint?

Yes, from 1838 to 1861. It was in Dahlonega, Georgia, and was chartered to provide a place for miners of the "Georgia Gold Rush" to take their bounty. Gold Half Eagles had a five-dollar face value and were the first coins produced at Dahlonega.

Bibliography and Suggested Reading

Arcus, Robert. "James Arcus—Convict—Australian Bound."
Coontin Kin, Shetland Family History Society. Vol. 73.
Yule 2009, pp. 24–27.

Bryden, the Reverend John, and the Reverend Thomas
Barclay. *The Statistical Account of Scotland by the Ministers
of the Respected Parishes, under the Superintendence of a
Committee of the Society for the Benefit of the Sons and
Daughters of the Clergy.* Vol. 15. Edinburgh and London:
William Blackwood and Sons, 1845.

Burrows, Edwin G. and Wallace, Mike. *Gotham: A History
of New York City to 1898.* New York: Oxford University
Press, 2000.

Canter, Kate. "An Involuntary Migration from Shetland."
Coontin Kin, Shetland Family History Society. Vol. 73. Yule
2009, pp. 3–8.

Christie-Johnston, A. & E. *Shetland Words: A Dictionary of
Shetland Dialect.* Lerwick: Shetland Times, 2010.

Cowie, Robert. *Shetland: Descriptive and Historical; and Topographical Description of That County.* Aberdeen, 1879.

Gear, Sheila. *Foula: Island West of the Sun.* London: Robert Hale, 1983.

Goudie, Gilbert. *The Celtic and Scandinavian Antiquities of Shetland.* Edinburgh and London: William Blackwood and Sons, 1904.

Goudie, Gilbert, ed. *The Diary of the Reverend John Mill, Minister of the Parishes of Dunrossness, Sandwick and Cunningsburgh in Shetland (Scotland), 1740–1803, with Selections from Local Records and Original Documents Relating to the District.* Bowie, Md.: Heritage Books, 2004.

Graham, John J. *"A Vehement Thirst After Knowledge": Four Centuries of Education in Shetland.* Lerwick: Shetland Times, 1998.

Hibbert, Samuel. *A Description of the Shetland Islands: Comprising an Account of the Geology, Scenery, Antiquities, and Superstitions.* Edinburgh, 1822.

Irvine, James W. *Lerwick: The Birth and Growth of an Island Town.* Lerwick Community Council, 1985.

Johnson, James W. "Roond Aboot Skelda Voe 1869." *Skeld Festival of the Seas, 15th–17th June 2007.* 2007.

Lerwick Jail Records, 1837–78.

McCullough, J. R., Esq. *A Descriptive and Statistical Account of the British Empire: Its Extent, Physical Capacities, Population, Industry, and Civil and Religious Institutions.* rev. 4th ed. Vol. 2. London: Longman, Brown, Green and Longmans, 1854.

Nicolson, James R. *Hay & Company: Merchants in Shetland.* Lerwick: Hay & Company, 1982.

O'Brien, D. *Parliamentary Papers, House of Commons, Third Report of the Inspectors of Prisons of Great Britain.* August 16, 1847.

Platt, Richard. *Smuggling in the British Isles: A History.* Stroud, Gloucestershire: Tempus Publishing, 2007.

Shetland Museum and Archives. http://www.shetland-museum.org.uk/.

Shetland words and language: http://www.shetlanddialect .org.uk/.

Simpson, Charlie. *Shetland Heritage of Sail.* Lerwick: Shetland Times, 2011.

Sinclair, Douglas M. *A Glimpse of Lerwick's Waterfront History.* Millgaet Media, 2010.

Smith, Hance D. *Shetland Life and Trade, 1550–1914.* Edinburgh: John Donald Publishers, 1984.

Spann, Edward K. *The New Metropolis: New York City, 1840–1857.* New York: Columbia University Press, 1981.

Tait, Ian. *Rural Life in Shetland & Guidebook to the Croft House Museum.* Lerwick: Shetland Museum, 2000.

Tudor, John R. *The Orkneys and Shetland: Their Past and Present State.* London: Edward Stanford, 1883.

Acknowledgments

Years ago I found a shoe box in the back of my father's closet filled with cassette recordings made by my grandfather George Robert Christie. He was eighty-four when he made them, and if he hadn't thought the stories important enough to pass down, nearly all of what we know about our family would have been lost forever. When I heard him say that his grandfather Robert Christie "lived in a place where they had little ponies with long hair," I had to know more. I will be forever thankful to him for this exceptional gift.

Writing a novel is, at first, a solitary experience, and then it requires the kindness of good friends and generosity of the learned to bring it to fruition. Carolyn and Rob Miller were fantastic supporters, detailed readers, and cheerleaders from beginning to end. I had many early readers who were both gentle with the delicate ego of a first-time author and generous with their advice: Rebecca Briccetti, Beatrice Burack, Bob Cole, Sarah Crow, Leigh Maynard, and Ellen Goldsberry— thank you! Hopkinton Mother-Daughter Book Club members Danielle and Katelyn Meserve, Emily and Lisa Metzger, Lillie and Alicia Presti, Maddy and Betsey Rhynhart, and Maura and

Susan Zankel shared important feedback as did Nick Miller. Public historian Kathleen Hulser made sure I had my New York facts straight, and Larsen Burack worked hard to keep me humble. Thanks also to Susan LeFevre and Janet Wilkinson for a home away from home and to Krysia Burnham for opening a door.

And I'll be forever indebted to the many people of the Shetland Islands who helped along the way: Merryn Henderson (who referred me to the invaluable *Diary of the Reverend John Mill*) and Elizabeth Angus of the Shetland Family History Society; Bertie Grey (who showed me the remains of the Christie family croft!); historian Douglas Sinclair for information on Fort Charlotte, lodberries, and the early Lerwick waterfront; Laureen Johnson at shetlanddialect.org.uk for verifying some word choices; Angus Johnson of the Shetland Museum & Archives for his help identifying ships; and Dr. Ian Tait, Curator of the Shetland Museum & Archives, whose fantastic book, *Rural Life in Shetland* (Shetland Museum, 2000), and knowledge of how rope was made from the bristles of the now extinct Shetland grice, helped me to understand many details of the period.

My amazing agent, Charlotte Sheedy, believed in this novel from the beginning, and the wonderful Maggie Lehrman saw its potential, and then gently and graciously helped me make it so much better. Howard Reeves, Maria Middleton, Jim Armstrong, Jason Wells, Orlando DosReis, and the rest of the Abrams team brought it to life. Thank you all.

But my biggest thanks goes to my husband, Tom, who read draft after draft—red pen at the ready—more times than anyone, followed me to Shetland and back, and never let me quit. Muckle smoorikins!

About the Author

When **Emilie Christie Burack** learned that her ancestors had come from the islands "where they had little ponies with long hair," she had to know more. She has traveled to the Shetland Islands and researched its history. She now resides in New Hampshire. This is her first book.